PENGUIN BOOKS

CHEERFUL WEATHER FOR THE WEDDING
and AN INTEGRATED MAN

Julia Strachey was born in India in 1901, the daughter of a civil servant who administered the railways – later a cryptographer in two wars – and a member of the noted intellectual family (whose members included Lytton Strachey, James Strachey and Dorothy Bussy, the author of *Olivia*). Brought up in England by successive foster-parents, in particular Mrs Bertrand Russell, she was educated at Bedales, the subject of one of her stories, and at the Slade and Bedford College. She worked as a mannequin for Poiret, a photographer, a shop-assistant, and a publisher.

A long series of her short stories has appeared in various periodicals since 1930. *Cheerful Weather for the Wedding* was her first novel and appeared in 1932; her second, originally entitled *An Integrated Man*, was published as *The Man on the Pier* in 1951. She has been married to the sculptor Stephen Tomlin, and to the painter Lawrence Gowing, and now lives in London.

TWO SHORT NOVELS BY
JULIA STRACHEY

Cheerful Weather for
the Wedding
and
An Integrated Man

PENGUIN BOOKS

Penguin Books Ltd, Harmondsworth, Middlesex, England
Penguin Books, 625 Madison Avenue, New York, New York 10022, U.S.A.
Penguin Books Australia Ltd, Ringwood, Victoria, Australia
Penguin Books Canada Ltd, 2801 John Street, Markham, Ontario, Canada L3R 1B4
Penguin Books (N.Z.) Ltd, 182–190 Wairau Road, Auckland 10, New Zealand

—

Cheerful Weather for the Wedding first published by The Hogarth Press in 1932; published
in the Holiday Library by John Lehmann 1950; published in Penguin Books 1978
Copyright 1932 by Julia Strachey

An Integrated Man first published as *The Man on the Pier* by John Lehmann in 1951;
published in full under the author's original title in Penguin Books 1978
Copyright © 1951, 1978 by Julia Strachey

—

Made and printed in Great Britain by
Hazell Watson & Viney Ltd,
Aylesbury, Bucks
Set in Linotype Georgian

Contents

Cheerful Weather for the Wedding

1

On March 5th Mrs Thatcham, a middle-class widow, married her eldest daughter, Dolly, who was twenty-three years old, to the Hon. Owen Bigham. He was eight years older than she was, and in the Diplomatic Service.

It had been a short engagement, as engagements are supposed to go – only a month, but Owen was due out in South America at the end of March, to take up a post there for several years, and Dolly had agreed to marry and go out with him.

Owen and Dolly were married from the Thatchams' house in the country. (Owen's parents had a house in that part of the world also, – the other side of the sea bay at Malton.)

At the beginning of the wedding morning it was grey and cold.

It so happened that at five minutes past nine, Dolly, on her way through the drawing-room to breakfast, ran into Millman, the middle-aged parlourmaid.

'So sorry, Millman.'

'Not at all, Miss. Look, here is something Lily found of yours, pressed down behind one of the drawers in your old bureau that used to be in the old nursery.'

Millman handed Dolly a square blue leather bag, faded yellowish in streaks, and with the leather handle swinging loose.

'It must have been there ever since last summer, Miss, when you moved all your things out, you remember? And the bureau was put up in the attic.'

'Good gracious me, Millman. I expect there are all sorts of precious things inside it. Hundreds of lost cheques, my brooch, and that wretched gold thimble of cook's I lost, perhaps.'

'Well, you have a good look, Miss. I'm sure I hope you'll find all the lot of them in there!'

Millman laughed merrily and went out of the drawing-room.

Dolly sat down at a small writing-table just beside her and opened the bag. It was all but empty. A layer of grey fluff and something like biscuit crumbs lay along the bottom, and besides this there was a pink bus-ticket and a folded-up old envelope in her mother's writing. She opened the envelope and pulled out her mother's letter. It was dated last July, and the address at the top was that of their cousin Bob's house at Hadley Hill. (This cousin Bob's full title was Canon Dakin. As Dolly's father was dead, and there were no uncles, it was he who was to give Dolly away at the wedding that afternoon.)

Dolly glanced at the letter. It seemed to be a very fair specimen copy of all her mother's other letters.

She smiled, and began to read the letter through: 'We had such a nasty wet wk-end for your Aunt B., but K. and Ch. and Mr F. and P. all turned to and helped her write out her cards for her M.W.O.S. next Sat. and were a very cheerful busy little party. Would you mind filling up the enclosed p.c. and sending it off to L., letting her know if you ever received the address you wanted and that she sent you? I had lunch with her today and she is so terribly afraid that you never received it as you did not write and thank her for it. Today we have come down to stay with cousin Bob at his new house at Hadley. – Such a cheerful little house right on the top of H. Hill; rather draughty perhaps, but such a cheery cosy little place for the fine weather! All the flowers look so gay, and there is such a pretty view of the little old Saxon church. We are five miles here from Dinsbury, $7\frac{1}{2}$

from Churton' ['Now we're off,' thought Dolly], 'only 10 from Great Broddington (8 from Little Broddington), and 15 from Bell-Hill. C. and M. also the P. and W. McGr's came over from L. and we went for a nice M. drive. If you drive along the Dinsbury Road from here and bear round to the left by Tiggicombe, and cross the main London and Hadley Rd and bear up well to the right you get to Wogsbottom, which is only 2½ miles from Crockdalton (and not above 3 from Pegworth) ...' Dolly skipped the next half-page and began again lower down: 'It is such a trial for Cousin Bob that "K" will drink so heavily, – they tell me such dreadful stories about him. Of course to me all this seems such a pity! So curious of him! with such a *devoted* mother and father ...' Dolly looked up from the letter. She seemed to fall into a kind of trance, – maybe thinking of her dipsomaniac cousin 'K' – as her mother called him – who used often to come and stay with her when they were both children, or maybe thinking of the main London and Hadley Road.

Above the writing-table where Dolly sat was an ancient mirror.

This mirror was rusted over with tiny specks by the hundred, and also the quicksilver at the back had become blackened in the course of ages, so that the drawing-room, as reflected in its corpse-like face, seemed forever swimming in an eerie, dead-looking, metallic twilight, such as is never experienced in the actual world outside. And a strange effect was produced:

It was as if the drawing-room reappeared in this mirror as a familiar room in a dream reappears, ghostly, significant, and wiped free of all signs of humdrum and trivial existence. Two crossed books lying flat, the round top of a table, a carved lizard's head on a clock, the sofa-top and its arms, shone in the grey light from the sky outside; everything else was in shadow. The transparent ferns that stood massed in the window showed up very brightly, and looked fearful. They seemed to have come alive, so to speak. They looked to have just that moment reared up their long backs, arched their jagged and serrated bodies menacingly, twisted and knotted themselves tightly about each other, and darted out long forked and ribboning tongues from one to the other; and all as if under some terrible compulsion ... they brought to mind travellers' descriptions of the jungles in the Congo, – of the silent struggle and strangulation that vegetable life there consists in it seems.

To complete the picture, Dolly's white face, with its thick and heavily curled back lips, above her black speckled wool frock, glimmered palely in front of the ferns, like a phosphorescent orchid blooming alone there in the twilit swamp.

For five or six minutes the pale and luminous orchid remained stationary, in the centre of the mirror's dark surface. The strange thing was the way the eyes kept ceaselessly roaming, shifting, ranging, round and round the room. Round and round again ... this looked queer – the face so passive and remote seeming, and the eyes so restless.

The light perhaps caught the mirrored eyes at a peculiar angle, and this might have caused them to glitter so uncomfortably, it seemed even so wildly – irresponsibly, – like the glittering eyes of a sick woman who is exhausted, yet feverish.

'I can't understand what the maids are thinking of this morning – a quarter past nine and breakfast is not ready yet! They keep the meals behindhand in this way – so funny of them!' exclaimed Mrs Thatcham, who had come into the room behind Dolly's back, and was running round from chair to chair thumping down the cushions and fluffing them up again. She spoke this in tones of cold amazement, her wide-open eyes sparkling like twin glaciers.

'Well, you'd better hurry along and ask cook for *your*

breakfast, dear child, at any rate. Or we'll never get you dressed and ready in all your nice things ... run along will you, dear child?'

Dolly threw letter, bus-ticket, and leather bag all together in the waste-paper basket, and made off for the breakfast-room.

Mrs Thatcham remained behind for a few minutes rushing round the room on tiny feet, snapping off dead daffodil heads from the vases, pulling back window curtains, or pulling them forward, scratching on the carpet with the toe of her tiny shoe where a stain showed up. All this with a sharp anxiety on her long face as usual, – as though she had inadvertently swallowed a packet of live bumble-bees and was now beginning to feel them stirring about inside her. She stopped and looked up at the clock.

'I simply fail to understand it!' burst from her lips.

She trotted briskly out of the drawing-room in the direction of the kitchen.

2

BY twelve o'clock the long hall at the back of the Thatcham's house, where the family was accustomed to sit, was swimming in brilliant sunlight. Also a howling gale had arisen, as usual, for the house was on top of the cliffs. The wedding was to be at two o'clock (the church being just the other side of the garden wall, which was handy).

Sunlight fell in dazzling oblongs through the windows upon the faded wistaria on the cretonne sofas and arm chairs, and lit up the brass Indian tray on trestle legs piled up with magazines and library books. The yellow brilliance was reflected back from the white-and-brown Serbian embroidery hanging on the end of the piano, and from the silver photograph frames, and Moorish paper-knives. And the light of the big log fire was quite eclipsed, – the flames were all but invisible in all this brightness.

Mrs Thatcham always kept a great number of potted flowers growing in this room, daffodils, fuchsias, hydrangeas, cyclamen. Today, besides these, a massed mountain of hyacinths, pink, red, and washed-out mauves of all sorts, stood on a table close by the fire, the steely-blue spring light from the window glittering upon each of the narrow waxen petals.

Thrown out full length on the sofa lay a schoolboy cousin of the bride's, aged thirteen – the black-haired Robert – reading the *Captain* magazine. Robert had eyes that were lustrous as two oily-black stewed prunes, or blackest treacle, and the complexion of a dark-red peach.

Padding up and down in front of the staircase, with something pompous and uncanny about his tread somehow, was Tom, his elder brother.

Tom was fair and pleasant to look at, but at present his blue-china eyes were bulging out of his head like a bullfrog's.

Both boys had just had their hairs brushed neat as satin, and both had changed into black spotless coats for the wedding.

'Robert.'

It was as if a big bubble had suddenly risen from the bottom of a dark water-tank and burst, low and hollow, upon the surface, – there was nothing about the slow padding figure of Tom to indicate that it was he who had spoken.

'Robert.' (Another bubble burst, low and hollow.)

'Robert. Robert.' All the while Tom kept up his padding backwards and forwards.

'Robert.' Now the word came softly from behind the sofa-head, Tom having padded round there unnoticed by his younger brother.

'Robert,' repeated Tom softly. 'Robert. I say, Robert. Robert. Robert.'

Tom leant over the sofa-head and chanted softly, articulating his words very precisely, as hypnotic doctors do:

'YOUR MOTHER WOULD UNDOUBTEDLY DESIRE THAT YOU SHOULD RETIRE UPSTAIRS TO YOUR BEDROOM, ROBERT, IN ORDER THAT YOU MAY CHANGE THOSE IMPOSSIBLE SOCKS.'

There was no sign of life from the patient.

'CHANGE YOUR SOCKS, ROBERT. DO NOT TAKE ADVANTAGE OF YOUR MOTHER'S ABSENCE TO PLAY THE CAD, ROBERT.'

Robert's black shoes sticking up on the arm of the sofa were crossed one over the other, and revealed a gleam of emerald between the shoes and the trousers.

'Robert. Robert. Robert.'

Robert dashed the *Captain* to the ground and, jerking his head up towards Tom, shouted, 'Shut up, you bally idiot, Tom, will you?' There were tears in his voice. 'What *right* have you to keep on bullying? You're an infernal, blithering bully! ...' And snatching up his magazine he started reading it again.

A minute passed in silence. Then Tom said briskly:

'Robert, your mother would desire you to go upstairs instantly to take off those bounder's socks, Robert, and to change into a respectable pair. Will you go, Robert?'

'What the blazes do you mean? I have just changed into a respectable pair of socks, I tell you!' cried Robert, jerking his magazine away in front of his face, and added, 'Go and put your head in a bag.'

He gave a gulp and went on reading.

'THESE ARE NOT PROPER SOCKS FOR A GENTLEMAN TO WEAR AT A WEDDING,' said Tom, bending over the sofa.

'Go and put your head in a bag,' murmured Robert.

Tom paced slowly away across the springy carpet.

'Would you keep *your mother* waiting –'

'Oh, go and put your head inside a bag!' said Robert.

There came a piercing shriek from a female voice half-way up the staircase.

'Lily! Go instantly, Lily, I tell you! Go along! Go now! Go!'

Someone came clattering down the stairway.

'Go to the sewing-room immediately and tell Rose she is to find that brooch for me within five minutes!' and Kitty, Dolly's young sister, bounded down into the hall.

She was a big, bold-looking girl of seventeen; her hands, red and much swollen, perhaps with the cold, looked somewhat like raw meat chops appearing from the delicate yellow gauze sleeves of her bridesmaid's frock. Kitty's big face was powdered so thickly over the cold skin with white rice powder, and then rouged so strongly on top of it all, that she almost looked to be wearing a pale lilac blotting-paper mask, with red ink stains dashed in upon either cheek.

'Oh, Tom, oh dear, oh dear, I know you are thinking that I look utterly and unspeakably stupid and altogether abominable and dreadful in my frock and wreath,' she cried out, making for the looking-glass.

'Not at all. Very charming indeed,' said Tom, bowing stiffly.

'Yes, you do! You do! I know it well. Why bow in that extraordinary fashion? Lily!' she screamed aloud suddenly, 'send that brooch down immediately! Everybody is dressed and ready for lunch!'

A far-distant voice floated down the stairway: 'I can't find it, Miss ...'

'Yes, you can!' thundered Kitty. 'Go fetch Rose, I tell you; don't be such an owl!'

'Really, Kitty, I don't think I can bear it!' said a voice from the drawing-room doorway. 'Don't you think you could go upstairs and talk to them from up there perhaps?'

A small, neat young lady appeared smiling in the drawing-room doorway, her fingers in her ears. It was little Evelyn Graham, a schoolmate and bosom friend of the bride's. Over her yellow bridesmaid's frock was a grey squirrel fur jacket, and her face was muffled up to the ears in a fluffy woollen scarf. Her narrow green eyes danced and gleamed, and all colours of the rainbow seemed to be reflected in them.

'Br-r-r-r-r-r, I am more dead than alive!' said she, coming over to the fire, and with horror in her voice. She chafed her thin hands together rapidly, then knelt down and held them out to the blaze.

'You are like a dear, elegant little fly,' said Kitty, watching her with a passionate look, and at the same time winding up the gramophone handle. 'I wish I were as chic and intellectual as you! *You* must think *me* a kind of great clumsy block-headed rhinoceros in my bridesmaid's frock, I know! Oh, don't speak about it, please! I do beg you!'

'Tut, child, nonsense,' said Evelyn. 'Oh, what will it be like standing in that draughty church! – Without a coat on! Holding a sopping-wet bouquet of flowers! Really, these quaint old customs are no joke after all is said and done.'

'Quaint old ... oh ... really ... Evelyn!' said Kitty, shocked. 'Ah, but one of these days you will be married yourself, and you will see! You will be talking quite differently ... you will make a most wonderful mother, I know. And so will Dolly, too, – in spite of all the things you two say nowadays ...'

'Tut, child. Tut,' said Evelyn. 'Good gracious, what is that?'

A metallic whistling pealed suddenly out of the mouth of the gramophone. It continued, and presently took shape and became a trifling little tune. Tigers seemed to be growling sulkily within the machine also, and it seemed that something like a hyena was faintly laughing too.

Kitty strained her yellow gauze cape tightly round her hips and began darting rapidly here, there, and everywhere, all over the hall in a twinkling, doing some kind of a dance. Her shoulders she held hunched up by her ears. The dance she was performing seemed a mixture between a Scotch reel and a dreamy waltz, for though her legs twinkled briskly like forked lightning all about the floor, yet her body above them seemed perpetually gliding round and round and leisurely revolving, at one and the same time.

'Oh, for Christ's sake stop it, Kitty!' cried Robert from the sofa, staring at his cousin with his glossy-brown cow's eyes. 'You make me absolutely giddy.'

'Lily!' screeched out Kitty with all the full force of her lungs, and with a last dart she switched off the gramophone. '*Bring ... that ... brooch ... down here immediately!*'

Her three companions screamed and put their hands over their ears.

The glass garden door grated and was burst open from outside. A violent gale rushed all round the room. Curtains jumped out and off their rods nearly. Something screeched out 'R-r-r-r-r-r-r-r-r-r!' on a long, virulent, piercing wail from under the passage doorway, and everyone's heart turned over in their chests with a feeling of dismal foreboding.

The big hall carpet reared up its head and undulated softly all along its length, like an angry sea-serpent.

'*Mille diables*,' muttered little Evelyn, slewing her mouth sideways in a demon's grimace, and she turned up her coat collar.

Mrs Thatcham walked in, and shut the door behind her, a rough red cloak thrown over her satin wedding-clothes.

'The tortoise has poked its nose out into the world again,' she said, wiping her little feet briskly on the door-mat, 'in order to bid a last fond farewell to Dolly, I suppose. I think she'll miss that tortoise as much as any of us.' A door slammed somewhere down the passage.

'I think she will,' said Evelyn.

The tortoise had been given to Dolly by a young man friend of hers – Joseph Patten (a student of anthropology at some college in London) – the summer before.

Joseph was, as a matter of fact, sitting alone in the next room that very instant. He had come down for the day from London.

'Half-past twelve already!' said Mrs Thatcham. She stared round the hall with her clear, orange, glassy eyes. 'Has Dolly gone up to dress yet?' she asked, with a haggard look at Kitty.

'Oh, she has been up there untold ages, Mum,' said Kitty. She was busy in front of the mirror arranging her wreath. 'Mum, do you think I look too exceptionally stupid in this get-up?' she asked.

'Half the family not turned up, and the wedding at two!' said Mrs Thatcham. 'We had better (all of us who *are* here) go upstairs and have something to eat. I told Millman to put a cold snack-luncheon up in the nursery, just for the family.' She pattered over to the windows, and began pulling back the chintz curtains and puffing up the cushions on the window-seats.

'Oh, such a beautiful day for Dolly's wedding! Everything looks so cheerful and pretty, the garden looking so gay. You can see right over across to the Malton Downs!' She bustled over to the library door behind the sofa.

'Oh, but what is this?' she cried in dismay. She had opened the library door, and there, laid out on a long table, were dishes of cutlets in pale jelly, big salad bowls, bottles of white wine, piles of sandwiches, and so forth. 'Oh! But then Millman must have laid the snack-luncheon in here!' she exclaimed.

There was a silence. Mrs Thatcham stared frigidly at the cutlets and sandwiches.

'How disappointing of Millman!' she said. 'She is an odd being, really. So funny of her to do that now! When I told her most particularly the nursery ... as we shall want the library kept free ... so very odd of her!'

'Not odd at all, Mum. Considering I heard you tell her most particularly, at tea-time, to be sure and put the cold lunch in the *library* so as not to have to light a fire in the nursery today.'

'Oh no, my dear child. You are utterly wrong, I assure you,' said her mother briskly. 'I particularly said the nursery ... never mind, we will all come along in here now, as it is laid. Robert, dear boy! I don't think those great boots look very well upon my nice sofa cover ... Come along now and have something to eat, dear child; you will make yourself sick lying upside-down there in front of that roaring fire. Is that a nice magazine – the *Captain* – you are reading? I rather thought your mother preferred you not to read magazines during the holidays ...'

Robert sloped in behind Mrs Thatcham to the library. Tom, seeing him disappearing, took three strides and caught hold of Robert by the elbow, in the middle of the doorway.

'My dear man, you have jolly well *got* to go off and change those socks! Why – suppose, my dear chap, that another man from Rugby should be present at the ceremony! Such a thing is possible, you know!'

Robert tried to wrench free of Tom, but Tom only held him the tighter.

'And just think what that man will say when he gets back to school, Robert! Why, it will be all over the shop! It is terrible! Terrible!' He shook Robert's elbow. 'For God's sake go and change before it is too *late*,' he hissed through clenched teeth.

'These are perfectly good socks, my dear man. I fail to grasp what you are talking about,' said Robert. 'Go and put your head in a bag.'

Robert shook himself free and made off towards the lunch table.

In the silent drawing-room, that opened out of the hall, Joseph Patten sat on alone.

The light here, that filtered in through the conservatory with its myriad leafy ferns in pots upon wire stands, was turned to a brilliant green.

Joseph might have been a statue in some green stone, dressed up in a tweed suit, sitting there upon the sofa – his light hair, face, mouth, eyes, wrists, and hands were so motionless, and so green.

Kitty floated into the drawing-room on her way through to fetch her mother's rye biscuits from the dining-room.

Joseph caught hold of her yellow gauze cape as she passed him. 'Isn't Dolly nearly ready to come down *yet*?' he asked, for the sixth time that morning.

'I don't know, I'm sure,' said Kitty, and floated away through the twilight.

Joseph walked into the family hall, and stood pressed up against the glass garden door looking out over the terrace.

Little Evelyn Graham put down a magazine she was looking at upon the brass table, and went and joined him there.

A kind of brassy yellow sunlight flooded all the garden. The arms of the bushes were swinging violently about in a really savage wind. The streaked ribbons from a bush of pampas-grass, immediately outside the door, streamed outwards in all directions. This bush remained squashed down as flat as a pancake to the level of the gravel terrace in a curious way, and it looked unnatural, as if a heavy, invisible person must be sitting down on top of it.

'Have you observed,' began Evelyn with a giggle, 'that Mrs

Thatcham's one criterion of a beautiful day is whether or not it is possible to see across as far as the Malton Downs? "Can you, or can you *not*, see across to the Malton Downs?" – that is the only question. For the farther you can see, – why, the more beautiful the day! And not the day only, either, for the beauties of the landscape, and the countryside also, hinge entirely on the answer to that question.'

Evelyn sniggered, and continued, warming to her subject: 'Thus, if it is possible for Mrs Thatcham to see *two* counties at once from the top of a hill, then the view from there is a fine one, – the country exceedingly lovely. If *three* counties are visible at the same time, it is then more lovely than ever, – the countryside positively magnificent; and so on and so forth.'

The young man gave half a smile, and turning his head farther away from Evelyn, continued staring silently out of the glass door.

Evelyn glanced up at his averted face, then immediately left him and went to join the others in the library.

Joseph, when satisfied that he was alone in the hall, sat down on the sofa, beside the hyacinth table.

Five minutes later Millman, carrying a tray of whisky and soda, halted on her way through into the library.

'Not feeling very well, sir? Would you like me to bring you a drop of brandy? It's sometimes rather a good thing if you are feeling a little bit seedy or anything.'

'No, thank you.'

'Oh, very well, sir. But there's plenty handy if you should want some,' and she passed on.

In the end he got up to go and join the others in the library.

As he passed the red baize swing-door into the passage, it opened, and he found himself close up against a tall, grey-haired man, in black clerical clothes, with a gaunt white face reminiscent of a Pre-Raphaelite painting of Dante. It was Canon Dakin, or Cousin Bob of Hadley Hill as the family called him.

Shaking hands with Joseph with ceremonial politeness, the Canon proceeded along to the library beside him, questioning him cordially as to how he was getting on with his studies in London.

Joseph, blushing a deep red, and smiling broadly the whole while with embarrassment, answered his questions, walking unsteadily along beside the Canon sideways – as a crab walks, stumbling up against the corners of sofas, and of pianos, as he came upon them – as it were from behind, each time. Mrs Thatcham had said in cold surprise once, walking behind Joseph and Dolly down to the bathing-place: 'That young man seems to be walking *backwards* instead of forwards. I really can't imagine how he ever gets anywhere! Such a very quaint person! ...' She disliked Joseph. It seemed to her that he said deliberately disgusting and evil things in front of her young daughter Kitty; in front of the servants too: he very often wounded her feelings; and altogether she experienced a feeling of anxious strain when he was in her presence.

Canon Dakin and Joseph took their places at the snack-luncheon table, where they found that a red-haired cousin, a young man of twenty, nicknamed 'Lob', had already joined the family party.

'Hey! Here comes the Anthro-pop-ologist!' shouted Lob, waving his fork in greeting (he treated this science completely *de haut en bas* always).

'How are your lectures going?' asked Kitty of Joseph, a kind of desperate intenseness in her voice and face. This was her style of the moment with the male sex.

'Very well, thank you,' said Joseph, and added: 'We heard about the practices of the Minoan Islanders upon reaching the age of puberty at the last one.' He started snapping up his cutlet.

'Oh, really? How *terribly* interesting!' said Kitty.

'Yes, very. Like to hear about them?' offered Joseph.

'Kitty, dear child! Kitty! Kitty! Open the window a trifle at the top, will you! The air gets so terribly stuffy in here always!' cried out Mrs Thatcham very loudly.

'We have seen Two Men who are willing to Throw the Bones with reference to Heaven!' recited Lob, pointing his fork upwards into the air, and rolling his *r*'s sonorously.

What he said was merely one of the many passages he had picked up out of Joseph's anthropological textbooks, and which he was fond of reciting aloud at odd moments, and without any apparent rhyme or reason.

Mrs Thatcham called across to Kitty over at the window: 'Bring me that lamp-shade lying on the window-seat there! I'd like to show everybody! It is a wedding present from Dodo Potts-Griffiths, just sent over by the chauffeur. She made the whole thing entirely herself, painted it, put it together, and everything, and it really is so very cheerful and pretty!'

Kitty came back with the lamp-shade. It was a parchment cube, whipped all along the sides with plaited thongs of leather, which gathered themselves together into long tassels depending from the bottom rim at each corner. At the bottom of each tassel hung a knot of discoloured wooden beads – purple and yellow, and some marbled stone ones, and some tiny elephants and monkeys also. On the parchment shade itself was an Elizabethan galleon. Above and below the galleon (forming two bands round the top and bottom rims of the lamp-shade) were heart-shaped leaves.

The galleon and the leaves were not, in any sense, painted from Nature, yet they were not exactly diagrammatic either. Rather it was as though an average had somehow been arrived at of all the Elizabethan galleons and of all the leaves that had ever before been painted on a lamp-shade, and a diagram then drawn to represent this average.

The galleon was tinted rust colour and orange. For the leaves, it seemed that the artist had mixed together one-third blue paint, one-third green paint, one-third dust – and filled in the outlines with this mixture.

'Now, do you not think this is quite wonderful!' cried Mrs Thatcham, holding the shade out to the Canon, and with the look of agony on her face which always accompanied her expressions of admiration for an object. 'A wedding present for Dolly! So nice!' she cried shrilly. Her face was drawn long as a fiddle-stick. 'I really think this is such a nice cheerful pattern she has painted up round the border here! Vine leaves, I suppose ... aren't they?' She was peering with tense anxiety at the leafy border. 'Oh no, though! They cannot be vine leaves! For these are heart-shaped ... perhaps they are periwinkle leaves.' She put on her pince-nez and devoured the pattern rabidly through them from under knitted eyebrows. 'Yes! Why, that is what they must be! – periwinkle leaves – how wonderfully clever!' She withdrew her pince-nez abruptly from her nose.

Everyone gaped at the painted lamp-shade held up in Mrs Thatcham's hand.

There was the sound of a cat's sneeze, and every eye swivelled round in the direction from whence this sound had proceeded.

Joseph, with head bowed over his plate, was quivering violently from head to foot, and every now and then sneezing like a cat – at all events that is how it sounded.

The company soon understood that the young man was attacked by a fit of the giggles, and all looked surprised; excepting Evelyn, to whom giggles and laughter were as water is to a fish. And so, although not understanding very exactly what was the matter, she joined in now with Joseph immediately.

The young man, apparently unaware that the whole table was watching him, kept on shaking his bowed head hysterically, as if flies were bothering his ears; kept hitting his palms softly against the sides of his chair, quivered from head to foot, and bounced up and down on his seat all the time as though riding in a jolting taxi. All this in silence, except for the quick bursts of cat's sneezing.

All of a sudden he tossed up his flushed face boldly and shook the straggling locks out of his eyes with a free gesture. But immediately he seemed to bounce high up off his chair again, and to come down with a bursting sneeze a hundred times more violent than all before.

'Somebody seems amused enough about it at any rate,' said Mrs Thatcham. She picked up the black horn salad spoon and fork, and conveyed a quantity of cubed potatoes and beetroot in mayonnaise on to her plate.

Joseph raised his head, tossed back his locks again, and, throwing out his arm with a lordly gesture, seized the silver salt-pot and swept it through the air to his plate, where, with very free-hand gesturing, he swung showers of salt out of the little perforated silver lighthouse down upon his cutlets, with wide rotating swoops some two feet in diameter.

'And what do *you* think of Miss Dodo Potts-Griffiths's present?' Evelyn asked him, her narrowed eyes reflecting the sunlit greens of the garden outside the window.

With two quite weak sneezes Joseph seized upon the water-jug and wafted it up and down above his tumbler (like a well-bucket rising and dropping), pouring out a thin stream of water all the time as he did so.

'. . . Oh! . . . the lamp-shade?' said he all of a sudden in a startled voice. He shook some loose strands of hair off his forehead. 'Well, it is certainly a most skilfully contrived expression, and gratification, of the herd instinct – must allow that – and, as such, a really most appropriate gift for a wedding.' He popped a thick crust of bread into his mouth, munched it voraciously and, stretching out his hand, caught hold of a giant bowl of trifle, to which he helped himself pretty liberally.

'Disappointing!' said Mrs Thatcham, and drew in her breath with a loud hissing sound. She stretched out her round middle-aged arm for the lamp-shade. 'Miss Griffiths doesn't seem to have found very much appreciation for her talents and arduous labour *here* at all events.' Her breath hissed again, as she drew it in between her almost shut teeth. 'Lob, dear boy, are you all ready for the church, I wonder. The ceremony is at two, you know! I want you all to be in your places ten minutes beforehand. Of course, it always much amuses me to hear you young things discussing the experienced and skilled labours of women of the world – old enough to be your grandmothers – who had been practising their talents since long before *you* were first rocked in your cradles. However; s-s-s-s-s-ssh-sh-s-s-s. Pass your plate along for more trifle, Tom. I really *cannot* get over our good fortune in having such wonderful weather for the wedding!' She sat back, very upright, in her chair, twisting her thin gold bracelets round upon her left wrist, and stared unwinkingly across at Joseph with a blank orange eye.

His little fit was now completely over. While it lasted it had been ecstatic and whole-hearted; and now, like a sparrow that gets up out of its dustbath again, after having fluffed about all over the place with care-free frenzy for three or four minutes, he set to work once more pecking away at his food wherever his eyes could best light upon it.

And now what many of the younger members of the family had been dreading happened. Aunt Bella, an unmarried sister of Mrs Thatcham's, arrived among them.

'So the animals are being fed in the library!' cried Bella, stepping in over the threshold. She laughed heartily, and for some minutes. Aunt Bella's flowered grey lace dress and floating scarf showed up her cinnamon skin and black eyes to advantage. Her diamond earrings which flashed and sparkled and swung about her, her grey snakeskin vanity bag, shoes and gloves, seemed new and expensive, and re-minded one of shop windows. Her eyes wandered round the room of young people as she seated herself in the window. There were not enough chairs to go round now, and the younger ones of the family rose to their feet and wandered uncertainly about here and there nibbling at sandwiches and *petits fours*.

'Oh, I am feeling so wickedly proud of my beautiful new car! You cannot imagine!' she whispered as it were delight-edly, and in confidence, to the glassy-eyed Tom, and laughed very heartily, drawing his arm through hers.

'Oh yes? Really?' he answered, and gave a stiff little bow.

'And oh! – I have got such a perfect pet of a chauffeur! You know, Tom,' she lowered her voice again, 'he simply treats me as though I was – I don't know *what*! –'

'Oh, really?'

'– made of sugar or – or something, that will melt at the least drop of rain! And that must be so wonderfully carefully cherished and looked after!'

'Oh no. How delightful,' murmured Tom, edging away towards the lunch table.

'I cannot help being really rather touched, (and secretly) profoundly amused by him!' went on Bella, her eye wander-ing over to the red-haired Lob. She laughed again mischiev-ously and, getting up, went across to Lob.

'Well, Lob! And how are you these days!'

Very soon she was telling him about her staff of servants in her house across the bay; telling him he must come and stay with her over there, so that they could laugh over the whole *ménage* together. 'And you know, Lob' – her voice sunk to a whisper – 'those three funny old things – the laundrymaid, the parlourmaid, and the cook – have been with me for thirty years. Ever since they first came to me from the village! And oh! they are such very dear, quaint people, – and you know, Lob – though I say it as shouldn't – they simply cherish *me* – I don't know *what* – I might be the Queen of England! Really!'

'My dear lady,' replied the cheerful Lob, speaking unexpectedly loudly, and holding his glass of wine up to the light for a moment, 'I don't care two pins about all that! No! The question, as *I* see it, is quite a different one. The whole thing is simply *this*: Is it possible to be a Reckless Libertine without spending a great deal of money?'

His Aunt Bella looked taken aback.

The fact was that Lob was inconsequent in his conversation at all times, and today he had had the good fortune, before coming across the wine, already to have have laid hold of four glasses of best sherry.

'Because,' he went on, raising his long third finger, 'other things being equal, that is what I intend to be.'

'Pray what do you mean – what other things being equal?' asked little Evelyn Graham, who was standing close behind him in her grey fur jacket.

'Ah – ha! Ha! Ha!' shouted Lob, vague and delighted, and bursting into a guffaw of laughter, he wagged his long finger at her archly.

'I am sorry to hear you have formed such dastardly plans for the future at your age of youthful innocence,' said Aunt Bella. She looked uneasy. She caught hold of Canon Dakin's arm as he passed her.

Mrs Thatcham called to Lob from her seat at the snack-lunch table:

'I think, dear boy, you had better put down that glass for a while ... Why don't you go out and take a turn in the garden? The fresh air will do you good. Go along and show Cousin Bob our beautiful new sensitive plant, down in the lower greenhouse. (Take the boy out into the fresh air, for goodness' sake, Bob, and pray don't let him come into the church in that condition.) Tipsy already. Disappointing!'

Meanwhile, no less a person than the bridegroom himself had appeared upon the scene. There were exclamations of amazement on every side.

Owen was a man who had enormously wide shoulders and a thick neck, like a bull; he had a flushed, simple, affectionate face, although it wore a wary expression at the minute.

'Oh, Mrs Thatcham, this is too dreadful of me! I know this is the last place in the world I ought to be in at the present moment!' He laughed heartily, but was plainly embarrassed. 'The fact is, Dolly has got the ring. She took it to have it made larger at the jeweller's. She promised faithfully she would give it back to the best man, but – er –ah – er – has apparently forgotten to do so.' He looked down, reproachfully, at a tall yellow daffodil that was leaning up sideways out of its pot towards him.

Tom was sent upstairs to Dolly's room to fetch the ring.

The lunch party transferred itself back into the hall. Bella, who had brought over some gramophone records, now put one on the gramophone.

Surrounded by many strange 'in-laws' he had not met before, Owen now went round among them all, his face beaming, his white teeth flashing, crying, 'Splendid! Splendid! Capital! Oh, capital! Splendid!' all through the room.

Somebody started saying 'Hush', and hissing like a snake in order to silence the room for the new gramophone record.

It was Miss Spoon, the girls' one-time governess.

Owen looked frightened, and dropped down instantly on to the sofa to listen.

The record had not been long going before Owen, with an uncomfortable face, began beating time to it. 'Ta, ta, tee-ta!' he whispered, marking the time with one finger and looking with an anxious sidelong glance into Kitty's face, as she sat beside him on the sofa.

He leant forward towards her and whispered, 'Oh, this is the most capital piece! An old favourite!'

Kitty stared back blankly into Owen's flushed face, which she observed shone steely lilac all down the left side in the bright spring light from the window. There was something miserably guilty and anxious endeavouring to hide itself behind his rigid features.

Tom, who soon returned with the ring, went over and joined his younger brother behind the sofa upon which Kitty and Owen were sitting. And these two soon heard an angry whispering behind them.

'Robert! I beg you – I implore you! – I ask you for one moment to imagine something! Will you, Robert? Listen. You are kneeling there in the church, Robert! The ceremony is in full swing: the clergyman is praying, the church is full of flowers, everybody, *everybody*, is as smartly dressed as they can be, Robert. All of a sudden you glance up! You see a man from Rugby staring at you from across the aisle! He has a curious smile on his face, Robert. And he is staring. Staring. *Down at your socks* –' There was a violent scuffle behind the sofa and Robert dashed suddenly through into the drawing-room.

Tom followed upon his heels, colliding with Mrs Thatcham as he rounded the corner.

'What? Never been to Chidworth!' she was exclaiming to a white-moustached stranger beside her. '(Dear child, do look where you are running to, s-s-s-s-sh-s-s-s.) Oh, but you must go to Chidworth! Why, you can see three counties at once from there on a fine day! Then the little village is so pretty!

All the little gardens so cheerful and gay ... It is five miles from there to Waddingchitwold, you know ...' As she piloted her guest up the hall stairway she murmured, 'I have arranged for you to go into the lilac room; you have a rather nice view from there ...'

'The lilac room? Mum, how many more people are to go into the lilac room?' shouted out Kitty from below. 'Cousin Bob! Mr Spigott! Aunt Bella! Miss Spoon! – a pity the bed is such a narrow one!' But her mother and her visitor had already disappeared, and did not hear her.

Kitty flounced off into the drawing-room. She had seen Joseph Patten disappear in there a moment or two before. There he was, alone in the green twilight again; but in a different chair this time. Now his face looked black viewed against the glass fern-filled conservatory.

'Mum makes living in this house unbearable,' Kitty said, and flung herself down in an armchair. 'Yesterday, you know, I began really and truly to fear for her sanity! Well, it is possible to become unbalanced in advancing years, isn't it? Mum would ring the bell for Millman: "Millman! Tell cook to make two extra pots of liver *pâté* for tomorrow's sandwiches." As soon as Millman had left the room, it was: "Kitty! run and tell Millman we will not have the extra *pâté* after all. We will telephone for more sandwiches from Gunter's." Then, later in the day she would go down and row poor old cook up: "Cook!! but where are the two extra pots of liver *pâté*?" "I did not receive orders for extra *pâté*, Madam."'

'Isn't Dolly dressed *yet*?' interrupted Joseph.

'I don't know. "I did not receive orders for extra liver *pâté*, Madam." Then Mum would say, "Do you mean that Millman forgot to give you the order? Well! She is a curious person really!" and she would hiss at poor old cook through her teeth.'

Kitty gave a wild, strange cackle, like a hen who is suddenly caught hold of, and looked up at Joseph.

His face was turned away, and with a large handkerchief he was wiping something off his cheek.

'Aren't you feeling well, Joseph? Oh dear, oh dear, oh dear, I had counted on you as being the one bright spot at this awful family gathering –'

But the young man had risen, and now walked away rapidly out of the room without listening.

'Well, this is all rather gloomy, really!' thought Kitty. 'Lob is such an idiot. Evelyn thinks me provincial – I know she does; I know she does; and doesn't want to talk to me. Tom goes snooping round after Robert the whole time, like an octopus after its prey in deep waters – it really makes one's blood run cold to see them ... But perhaps there will be some naval lieutenants later, at the reception.' And she fell to picturing manly sun-bronzed faces ranged in a semi-circle round her at the buffet, and limpid sea-blue eyes gazing intently into hers. And she began wondering how in the world she was going to keep those limpid eyes from glancing downwards at her swollen hand as it held up her glass ice-platter, – from suddenly noticing with repulsion how huge, coarse, and purple it looked beside the delicate rose-pink pyramid ice ... oh dear, oh dear, her shameful hands! Why, what bad luck it was really! – My God! What bad luck!

3

MEANWHILE the bride-to-be was busy attiring herself for the wedding ceremony.

Dolly's white-enamelled Edwardian bedroom jutted out over the kitchen garden, in a sort of little turret. It was at the top of the house, and reached by a steep and narrow stairway. Coming in at the bedroom door, one might easily imagine one's self to be up in the air in a balloon, or else inside a lighthouse. One saw only dazzling white light coming in at the big windows on all sides, and through the bow window directly opposite the door shone the pale blue sea-bay of Malton.

This morning the countryside, through each and all of the big windows, was bright golden in the sunlight. On the sides of a little hill quite close, beyond the railway cutting, grew a thick hazel copse. Today, with the sun shining through its bare branches, this seemed to be not trees at all, but merely folds of something diaphanous floating along the surface of the hillside – a flock of brown vapours, here dark, there light – lit up in the sunshine.

And all over the countryside this morning the bare copses looked like these brown gossamer scarves; they billowed over the hillsides, here opalescent, there obscure – according to the sunlight and shadow among their bronze and gauzy foldings.

Within doors Dolly stood bent over the wooden washstand, whitening her black eyebrows with frothy lather, her nose bright pink, and dripping with soapy water. As her face came out from behind the sponge each side, it wore a reproachful, stupefied expression.

All about the airy bedroom, maids of different kinds, in dark skirts and white blouses stooped low and searched about for stockings and garters, or stood warming satin shoes and chemises in front of the coal fire.

On a table in the bay window was a glass vase with a bunch of long-stalked narcissi in it. The flower-heads on their thin, giant stalks were no bigger than sixpenny pieces, and each had a frilly orange centre. One or two red dwarf tulips were stuck in among the narcissi.

Cold puffs of wind from the partly opened window fidgeted

all the flower-heads about, and kept up an irritating squeak, squeak, and sharp banging of the loose window-hasp up against the framework. That was unpleasant to the occupants of the room, undoubtedly; but what must have been delicious to them was the fresh, sweet, springlike scent of the narcissi which went wafting round on the air upon each new puff of breeze from the windows.

Dolly finished washing, arranging her black hair with the rust-red strips in it neatly. She dipped something that looked like a limp orange 'Captain' biscuit into a pink bowl on the dressing-table, and afterwards dabbed and smeared it all over her reproachful-looking face, leaving the skin covered over evenly with light corn-coloured powder.

The whole toilet was carried out as a performing elephant might make its toilet sitting up in a circus ring, languidly, clumsily, as though her arms were made of iron.

With Jessop, her mother's elderly lady's-maid, and with her dear friend Rose, the young sewing-maid, Dolly chatted a little, but her voice was like a piano that is played all the while with the soft damper so pressed down that it can barely be heard.

Jessop, dressed in black, with her face as yellow and wrinkled as a grocer's apricot, and with her long nose like an ant-eater's, went travelling round the room on tiptoe as usual, as though she were in an invalid's darkened chamber; and there was now, as always, a pained expression on her yellow face, as though she knew of something very shameful afoot somewhere in the household, which she realized to be none of her business all the same. She moved with a kind of modest majesty, as one imagines royalty must delight to do; and her eyes she kept down-cast upon the carpet.

'I wore my white satin wedding-shoes down to dinner last night, Jessop,' murmured Dolly. 'And they are grey and soiled at the toes now; isn't it dreadful.'

'Tut! Tut! You ought not to have done that, Miss,' breathed Jessop, looking a little offended. Dropping her voice, she whispered in confidence, 'Never mind, Miss! Give them to me, and we will see what we can do with them. You see, Miss, we have spent many, many years over this kind of little matter, and so you see we know one or two little wrinkles by this time ...'

Dolly held up the white satin shoes to her.

'Thank you, Miss,' breathed Jessop in a repressive voice, her eyes cast down upon the carpet.

She received the white shoes in her wrinkled claws, and glided majestically away with them to the bay window.

Rose, a very pretty pale-faced girl with thick black eyelashes, usually in the highest of spirits – a girl who was for ever dropping things on to the sewing-room floor and ejaculating, 'Bang! There go my false teeth!' and exploding into peals of laughter – today was looking very solemn, as she hooked up Dolly's wedding-dress.

'The Princesse Teresa,' said Rose, in her high silvery voice, like a bird singing (she named a foreign royalty who had lately been married to an Englishman and had had her photograph in all the papers). 'The Princesse Teresa had a wonderful beautiful wedding. Didn't she?'

Rose did up the last hook intently. 'When the clergyman asked her, "Who takes this man to be their lawful wedded husband,"' she went on, 'they say the Princesse answered up, in such a clear voice, so that everybody, right away down to the back, could hear her. "I DO!" she said.'

Dolly glanced at Rose. She found her looking emotional; and more solemn than she had ever seen her before.

The woman started to fix the long wedding-veil on to the pearl coronet that was pointed like a starfish, upon Dolly's head. The veil, which had belonged to Dolly's wealthy Portuguese grandmother, seemed unendingly long and bulky in the small bedroom. Gigantic billowing fold upon fold of lacy birds and flowers seemed heaped up over the bed, the rocking-chair, the table, and everywhere.

Dolly knew, as she looked round at the long wedding-veil stretching away forever, and at the women, too, so busy all around her, that something remarkable and upsetting in her life was steadily going forward.

She was aware of this; but it was as if she were reading about it in a book from the circulating library, instead of herself living through it.

'Sweetly pretty flowers, aren't they?' said Rose, nodding towards the bridal bouquet of lilies and white carnations that stood in a blue jug of water in the corner.

'Dolly!' shouted a male voice up the stairway.

The door was open. Dolly recognized Joseph's voice. 'What! Again?' she said to herself.

'Hulloa!' she echoed back, faintly.

There was a silence.

'Hulloa!' she called again, but in her present mood it sounded only as loud as a dying kitten's mew.

Silence again.

'Are you coming down soon?' called up Joseph at last.

'I don't know,' she answered. 'I'm not dressed yet.'

A considerable pause followed.

'Do come down,' came Joseph's voice at last.

'Oh, indeed! Pray, why in the world *should* I?' whispered Dolly loudly to herself. Aloud she repeated, languidly, 'Well, you see ... I am not dressed yet.'

A long pause followed, and Dolly took it that he had gone away again.

'Will you be finished soon?' presently came Joseph's voice once more.

Dolly waited, and then said, in a careless sing-song voice: 'Oh, I don't know at all ... I'm afraid ... No, I really have not the faintest notion.'

'Well, I will be in the drawing-room,' croaked Joseph, but

something seemed to muffle his voice this time and Dolly did not catch what he had said. His footsteps retreated down the passage.

Dolly was now dressed and ready for the wedding. She told the handmaids they might go. When she was alone she rustled in her long skirts over to the bay window and sat down on the window-seat in the sunlight.

Out on the croquet lawn a short figure was standing alone, a scarlet cloak billowing up in the wind behind her. It was Mrs Thatcham, and she was examining a black dot on the grass at her feet.

Seeing Whitstable, the gardener, with his white Panama hat and yellow waxed moustache, walking along the path between the cabbages below her, Dolly opened the window and shouted down to him.

'Whitstable! Can that be the tortoise come back again? Out there on the croquet lawn?'

'Yes, Miss!' shouted back Whitstable. 'Yes! Oh, I knew he'd be somewhere about! I seen him once or twice during the winter season, snuggling up against the glass-house stove-pipe; – and I don't blame him neither.'

'Please tell Millman to get the girls to pack him up immediately,' shouted Dolly. 'I shall take him with me to South America! He will enjoy himself out there much better than in this windy climate.'

'Yes, Miss.' Whitstable trudged off towards the kitchen.

He heard Dolly's voice in waves upon the gusts of the wind behind him: '... rye biscuit tin ... big holes punched in the lid ... lettuce leaves!'

'Very good, Miss!'

He turned the corner.

Hearing a tap at the open door, Dolly turned her head and saw little Evelyn stepping up warily into the room with a glass of red port wine in her hand. Behind her was Kitty.

The girls came in and shut the door. Evelyn sat down in the rocking-chair.

Dolly quaffed off the wine. 'Not that I stand much in need of it,' she remarked. She put her plump white hand behind the window curtains and drew out a tall bottle labelled 'Jamaica Rum', and showed it to Evelyn.

'You certainly do *not* need it – by the look of things.' said Evelyn. She had noticed that the rum-bottle was half empty.

Kitty, who had opened her wide scarlet-lipped mouth to burst out into praise of Dolly's beauty as she sat there in the sunlight in her wedding-clothes, remained with it open, paralysed, upon seeing the bottle.

'Oh! how very, very awful,' she said at last. 'I couldn't have imagined such a thing possible! A bride sitting upstairs in the bedroom swigging rum! – out of a bottle! – just before entering the church for her wedding ceremony!'

'Really!' murmured Dolly, raising her black eyebrows, surprised. 'Well, yes, you've still got a lot to learn, my child, it is true,' she added, sighing.

Kitty balanced herself in her yellow satin high-heeled shoes upon the brass fender. 'I'm sorry to say it, Dolly,' she said, 'but in some ways it will be a good thing when you are no longer in the house. It will not be so demoralizing for the servants, at any rate.'

Dolly gave a weak laugh.

'Well, well, that is a pleasant thing to say to your sister on the eve of her departure for South America,' she murmured.

'I admire you and your set frightfully, Dolly!' shouted Kitty, slipping off the fender sharply, and then clambering up on to it again. 'I know you are marvellously clever! And interesting! and witty too. But I do think the way you look at certain things is absolutely BEASTLY – there is no other word for it. You know what I mean ... And even on your own wedding-day! ... And there's Joseph down there been saying such stupid, awful things again ...'

'What things?' whispered Dolly, faintly.

'Oh, what does it matter. You will only think them funny.'

'You must tell us!' said Evelyn.

'Oh, very well then – well – I told Joseph that an Englishman in love lacked poetry ... that is how it started. I told him about that awful Robinson youth down at Malton: how, when his car broke down as he was bringing me home after a dance in the early hours, and we had to walk up the hill at five o'clock in the morning, instead of looking at the sunrise, or at me, all he could do was to stump along with a face black as thunder, muttering, "After tonight my name is mud in Malton! My name is mud in Malton!" "My dear chap," I said to him, "really! What *does* it matter *what* your name is in a place like Malton?" I told Joseph I envied Barbara McKenzie her Spanish naval officer, who plays to her on his ukulele in the moonlight, and is not ashamed of his love for her. I'm going to Spain next autumn, by the way, Doll, with Ursula MacTavish and her family, if Mum will let me.'

Kitty broke off and examined the heel of her shoe carefully on both sides.

'I told Joseph I thought *he* would play a ukulele beautifully,' she added, 'and that I couldn't imagine *him* ever being ashamed of his love for a woman, – well! I don't think he *would* be. Oh, well – but he shut me up and became quite ratty for some reason, and began telling me: "You must know, Kitty, that I don't at all care for all this snobbish Continental talk of yours about foreigners, love, poetry, and ukuleles. You must understand that there are still some of us left who don't appreciate that attitude in our womenfolk. We aren't accustomed to it, and we don't want it. It's un-English. My own aim is still the clean-limbed, dirty-minded, thorough English gentleman, and I still have hopes of being

one. Yes, I hope to achieve great things," and all the rest of
it.'

Kitty stamped her foot and turned pink. 'I *loathe* you all
when you start to talk in this way! ... An English gentleman
is *not* dirty-minded, I tell you! He may lack poetry and be a
bit on the stiff side, certainly, but dirty-minded is just what
he is *not*!'

'How do you know this?' inquired Evelyn from the rocking-chair.

'How do I know?' shouted out Kitty, slipping off the fender with a bang and clambering up on to it again. 'Is Cousin
Bob dirty-minded?' (She alluded to the Canon.) 'Was *Dad*
dirty-minded?'

'Terribly. Terribly,' murmered Dolly, looking depressed,
her forehead resting on a limp hand, her plump elbow on the
window-sill.

'You are drunk!' said Kitty.

Dolly did not deny it.

'Well, anyway, *I* think it is all utterly disgusting!' shouted
Kitty, and ran out of the room, her cheeks red and burning.

'I don't mind telling you, Evelyn, that we have been
treated to these lectures every single day for the last twelve
months now.' Dolly poured some more rum into a tooth-
glass. '"Dirty", "Clean", "English gentleman", "Spanish
guitar". The whole house rocks with it. And the worst of it
is one suffers a terrible revulsion after a bit, like that time
when we were all given boiled cabbage cut up into squares
every lunch-time and dinner for a month, do you remember? ... That miserable Joseph cannot resist baiting Kitty on
these subjects.' Dolly sighed. 'He likes to stir up the wasps'
nest a little with a stick, and then run away and hide, and
then, of course, the wasps fly straight upstairs and sting innocent people ...' She swallowed down the rum. 'There has
been such a desolating muddle with the Pall Mall Deposito-

ries,' she went on in a whisper, her forehead piled on her languid hand again, her eyes cast down upon the floor.

'The Pall Mall Depositories! Why! – what has happened?'

'Well, you know old Aunt Minnie died a little while ago.'

'What?' said Evelyn.

Dolly's voice was now too soft to be audible. It had been slowly fading away for some time, and in talking to Dolly now, Evelyn felt as if she were trying hard to telephone to somebody up at the Firth of Forth, on a very bad line, in thundery weather.

'... I told you, Aunt Minnie died a few months ago,' repeated Dolly in a whisper.

'What? Oh yes?'

'She left several cabinets of curios (if you know what they are) that she had collected, to be divided between Kitty and me.'

'M-m-m?'

'Well, Mother made a list out of all the different objects in the cabinet before sending them to the Depository to be stored, in accordance with the Depository regulations. You see, I was busy buying things for South America myself.'

There was a silence. Only the hum of the fire burning and the occasional squawk of the loose window-hasp could be heard.

Dolly sighed heavily.

She continued: 'It seemed the list did not correspond with the contents of the cabinets. That brute at the Depository – Humble, or Gumble, or whatever his name is – sent back the whole lot of these cases of curios last Friday. With the result that I have been sitting on the cellar floor surrounded by lighted candles, sorting all the objects ever since – old Spanish coins, keys, and goodness knows what all, knee-deep around me.'

A moan burst from Evelyn's lips. Dolly went on, almost inaudibly: 'Mum would pick up a filthy little embroidered Indian bag, eaten away by moths and hanging in ribbons and tatters. "Now here's rather a useful little object. I like these nice curly-wigs all over it. I wonder what they used *that* for? I dare say they keep their turban-pins inside them – quite a good idea. I suppose this clip passes through the ring here. But how neat!" and so on, and all the time one's back was aching as if knives were being jabbed into it.'

'Oh dear, I am so sorry!' burst out Evelyn. 'Why didn't you wire to me to come and do it, dearest? You must be completely worn out, with all your packing to do as well, and–' She looked with dismay at the expression on Dolly's down-bent face. 'Oh, how miserable, dearest creature.'

Dolly sat with bent head, silent. And Evelyn saw with despair that tears began to splash down on to her white satin knee.

'You are tired, Dolly dear. And no wonder. How I wish you hadn't drunk all that rum! But that can't be helped now. Cheer up, dearest, you will soon be bathing under blue skies. And then resting in the shade of fanning palm trees.'

Dolly blew her nose. 'You will faithfully promise to come out and stay with us; won't you?' she whispered. 'Owen insists on paying for your passage. (And he can well afford it, I assure you.) I could not possibly exist there for long without you.' Dolly gave a hiccough. 'Oh, God. Now I've got the hiccoughs. Oh, dear. And Owen says no more could he either. Oh! oh dear, oh dear.'

Evelyn promised faithfully she would go, and gave Dolly a glass of water to sip.

And now, seeing that it was a quarter to two, and Mrs Thatcham had made everyone promise that they would be in the church ten minutes before the ceremony was due to begin, Evelyn reluctantly got up and left Dolly.

'Ready, dear child?' shouted Mrs Thatcham, outside the bedroom door. She had just passed Evelyn upon the narrow staircase.

She came in, rearranged Dolly's veil, stroked her hair once or twice, and kissed her.

'I am proud of my beautiful daughter,' she said.

On hearing these soft and – as it might be – tenderly playful words, at such a moment, from such a person, Dolly turned sharply away and, with her back to her mother, leant down and began fumbling loudly with the loose and squeaking window-hasp.

'Do go down, Mother dear,' she mumbled. 'I have one or two last things to finish off. Do go down. I must really.'

Her mother hesitated, but when Dolly continued to rattle and thump on the window-hasp and then suddenly burst out (still leaning out of the window), 'Oh, blast this bloody thing! Mother, *do* go *down*!' – she bustled away down the staircase after all.

Dolly stood holding tightly on to the window-hasp, the sunlit country outside shivering as a golden, heaving blur through her tears.

She remembered a letter she had received that morning from a certain German lady, a friend who lived in Munich. Half-way down one of the pages her friend had written: 'I am haunted all the time by the feeling that my last years are upon me. I *cannot* resign myself to this, try as I may. I love fire, vitality, beauty, and movement in all things ... and *loathe* sitting still in armchairs, aching all over, one's teeth dropping out one by one ... Do, dearest Dolly, I implore you, enjoy yourself as hard as ever you can, while you are still so young and lovely ...'

'She is on the wrong tack in this last sentence. I must write and tell her,' thought Dolly. 'Neither youth nor loveliness makes people happy. It takes something utterly different to do that.'

She sat down on the window-seat and began to think, yet once again, of the last summer, spent almost entirely, minute by minute, with Joseph ... building a summer-house together, floating up and down along the coast in his boat ...

'Never a word! Never one single word the whole time!' she suddenly burst out, aloud. She jumped to her feet. Drawing in a long breath she began smiling – if smiling it could be called. 'All is well! He does not care for me, and therefore will not miss me!'

The cold wind blowing on her from the window had made her face seem swollen, chilled, and grey and patchy-looking. She went over to the mahogany chest, and, opening the deep top drawer, fetched out a handkerchief, and after a few minutes, 'He is an odd fish, all the same! ...' she muttered aloud in a doubtful voice. She began remembering certain incidents, more especially once at a large dinner party at the hotel in Malton one time. There had been a discussion about a certain kind of crackly biscuit made with treacle, and looking like stiff brown lace, called a 'jumbly'. 'What, never tasted a jumbly!' Joseph beside her had said, quite suddenly, peering in underneath her large summer hat. 'But you must taste a jumbly! You would adore them!' But the point was, that through his face, and most especially his eyes, Joseph's whole being had announced, plainly, and with a violent fervour, not 'You would adore them,' but 'I adore you.'

(Exactly in the same way that the hero in Tolstoi's *Family Happiness* turns and speaks to the heroine suddenly of frogs, and she understands, as he speaks, that he is telling her he loves her. Dolly had read that story shortly afterwards.) 'Only Tolstoi's hero had not just had an *apéritif* and a couple of glasses of wine, one presumes,' reflected Dolly.

'Supposing, just supposing,' went on Dolly, 'that Joseph came up to me now, five minutes before the wedding though it is, and confessed, at last, that he had loved me all along, begged me to run off with him, by the back door, across the fields, while everyone was sitting waiting in the church for me, now what should I do after all?'

'Dolly!' called up the Canon from the passage. He was waiting below to take her to the church.

'Only five more minutes, you know!' he cried. 'All going smoothly?'

Everybody else had left the house by this time, excepting these two.

And also a third : Joseph.

4

JOSEPH was standing beside a bamboo table in his bedroom, staring at the white wall-paper covered with its bunches of dark violets tied up with pink twist. His pale cheeks were wet, and he could not stop shivering from head to foot, steadily, like an iron spring which is vibrating.

In the turmoil of feelings which had descended upon him, quite unexpectedly, during the last half-hour, and which he was utterly powerless to disentangle or make the least head or tail of, one idea had now come up to the surface at last, and beat like a little hammer all the while in his terrified mind.

'Stop the wedding! Stop the wedding! Stop the wedding! Stop the wedding!' it went.

What for, exactly, he couldn't imagine – but there would be time enough afterwards to reflect upon that. But now! in five more minutes it would be too late! It would be too late!

Suddenly he rushed to the door and flew out of the room, crying 'Dolly! Dolly!' in a panic, and ran down the staircase into the hall three steps at a time.

At this moment Dolly was trailing slowly down the back staircase (which was nearer to her part of the house than the main one), her lace train wound round and round her arm. From out of the voluminous folds of this there peeped a cork and the top of the neck of a bottle. In her other hand was her large bunch of carnations and lilies.

At the bottom of the stairway, in the shadows, Whitstable, the gardener, was waiting for her, his Panama hat in his hand.

'Excuse me, Miss, but could you spare time to step into the kitchen and let my old mother see you afore the ceremony! Half a minute only would suffice, if you could see your way to it ...'

Dolly looked anxiously up at the clock and hurriedly rustled through into the kitchen.

Old Mrs Whitstable was sitting in a farther room, the cook's tiny sitting-room, in a wicker armchair. She resembled the blackish knobbled ad twisted stump of an old elm tree very much more nearly than she did a human being. Although she was all but blind, and all but deaf also, and no longer had many wits in her possession, she had set her heart on seeing Dolly (whom she had known from a child) in her wedding-clothes; and Whitstable had accordingly wheeled her along, in a Bath chair borrowed from the blacksmith for the purpose.

'Don't get up, Mrs Whitstable, please! Stay where you are!' cried Dolly from the doorway, but the old creature had already tottered to her feet.

'Of course, she isn't as young as she were, now, and she do think of you as being quite a little tiny kid, Ma'am. We never can get her to understand, not properly, as how you have growed up into a young lady since her time,' remarked Whitstable, as usual.

Interviews between Dolly and old Mrs Whitstable ran

their due course as smoothly as does a familiar gramophone record – not one note ever being varied during the process.

Dolly, who was already markedly late for her wedding, was wondering at what point she was going to be able to remove the needle from the disc, so to speak, this time.

Meanwhile the old lady was droning ahead in a low voice, not much louder than the evening wind playing through a withered holly bush:

'Oh, I remember you, when you come back to me bringing our little doggie Patch in your arms after that motor-car accident. He weren't troubled a bit by it! Not a bit! Saving only just a sore scratch on the end of 'is tail. No need to worry about old Patchy!'

This was her opening speech, always. The dog referred to had not been brought back to her by Dolly, but by a neighbouring farmer's daughter; and, in fact, the accident had nothing to do with Dolly whatsoever.

'Her memory isn't quite what is used to be . . . ,' muttered Whitstable here.

The old lady fixed her clouded eyes upon Dolly's white satin-covered knees.

'And now you are growed up into a fine handsome woman,' she went on in her sing-song.

'Oh, Lord,' thought Dolly, her eyes on the clock.

'And your husband will be a fine handsome man. And you be proud of him, and he be proud of you, and you be proud of one another.' (This last speech had often embarrassed Dolly in the past if she had chanced to have a young man along with her whom she was at all sweet on, when she dropped in at the old lady's cottage with some message from her mother. Whitstable would hastily chime in at this point, 'She ain't got her wits about her nowadays, Miss!')

Dolly always tried to keep her eyes off Mrs Whitstable's hands during these interviews, the flesh of which was already black as ebony with extreme age – this blackness of the flesh does not usually occur until after death – and the bones and joints of which, as before-mentioned, were so beknobbled and twisted about as to be literally unrecognizable as human hands at all.

'Of course, I lost my eyesight nowadays,' whispered the wind in the holly bush, 'and something seems to rise up inside my head all on a sudden and everything turns black and purple in front of my eyes, and I do fall over on to my back on the floor, with the dizziness. Oh, nobody do know! Nobody do know what I do feel rising up within my head sometimes! And that come upon me all of a sudden! And I can't fancy nothing to eat now, you know! – only just bread and water, only just bread and water; or if anyone has got a nice rabbit's head or anything, I do enjoy a nice broth out of *that*: I can always eat a broth off of a nice rabbit's head–'

'Well, Mother,' interrupted Whitstable, anxiously, 'Miss Dolly has got to be going.'

'This is the end, fortunately,' thought Dolly.

'Well, you be a fine handsome woman, my dear. And your husband be a fine handsome man. And he be proud of you, and you be proud of him, and you both be proud of one another – but, Laws! you have shot up something *terrible*!' she finished off unexpectedly. She was staring upwards towards Dolly's neck and chin with a horrified and dumbfounded expression on her face.

This was quite a new ending for once.

'Oh, she be remembering all the time when you were nothing more than a little tiny thing,' explained Whitstable. 'I expect she have just noticed how much taller you be grown.' He turned round as he said this to the retreating Dolly, but she was already through the door before he could properly twist his neck round.

Joseph, meanwhile, hearing voices somewhere in another

part of the house, began rushing through all the rooms, his face as white as paper, searching everywhere for Dolly. At last he bounded up the backstairs, and on, up Dolly's private stairway, to her bedroom. The door was open. The room was empty. A pink box of orange powder lay overturned upon the carpet. A strong small of narcissi filled his nostrils.

On the bed, a heap of blue tissue paper kept wafting up and down at the corners in the draught from the open door. The empty, deserted room! What is more deadly depressing?

The clock on the dressing-table said five and a half minutes past two. Maybe she had left the house then? For certainly the ceremony was due to begin at two.

He turned round and tumbled like a maniac down the narrow staircase, and then along the narrow passage to the main stairs.

'Dolly!' he heard the Canon's faint faraway shout to his niece, from down below somewhere.

So she was still in the house. He clattered off down the main stairway. The landing was empty. He ran despairingly, first to the right, into the sewing-room; then to the left, into the nursery; then back and on down the main stairs into the big hall. There, at last, was Dolly.

She was standing in the middle of the hall, her head bent, regarding something black upon the front of her white wedding-dress. She looked up at Joseph, and her face was red as a radish and wore a frantic expression of horror. Her eyes were staring insanely.

'For Heaven's sake, what am I to do! What am I to do! I cannot go into the church like this!' she screamed up at him. She held out her skirt towards him; her small hand was dark blue, and upon the white satin was a black stain as big as a tea-pot.

By her toes lay an overturned ink-bottle.

Joseph ran down to her. 'Oh, Dolly! Do for pity's sake listen–'

'Suggest something! Suggest something!' screamed Dolly, her eyes flashing. 'I know! Run upstairs and get a scarf out of mother's drawer, will you!'

'One moment! Dolly! Dearest!'

'Do go! Please don't stop!' shouted Dolly, stamping her foot. 'In the bottom drawer! A white lace scarf! Quickly!' And she pushed him away towards the staircase.

Joseph bounded up the stairs. He managed to rout out the scarf from the drawer.

When he came down Dolly was half-way up on the turn of the staircase, to meet him.

'Dolly!' came the Canon's voice sharply from the drawing-room. 'You must positively come, my dear!'

'Coming, Cousin Bob.'

'Help me tie it round my waist, Joseph, round here, round here,' Dolly, with fingers of forked lightning, was fastening the lace scarf so that it hung down and covered the ink-stain.

Joseph snatched her left wrist, and clutching it tightly, held it up in the air, a long way from him, as though it were a viper that was trying to dart its forked tongue into his flesh. His face now had changed, seemed to have gone to pieces; it showed strain, and a kind of convulsions upon it, as though some frightful change and combustion were taking place just inside it. His mouth was drawn, and he laboured under a choking in his windpipe.

'For God's sake, tell me one thing,' a queer voice was saying from his throat.

'I will tell you anything in the world you like *afterwards*,' wailed Dolly, and her wrist wriggled so sharply in his hand that he was obliged to let go of it.

'Dolly! Dolly!' bellowed the Canon.

'Coming!' she shrieked back. 'Pin this!'

She shoved something small and knobbled into Joseph's fingers.

He looked down and saw it was a round emerald brooch set in pearls.

'Against the stain, in front of the stain! Oh, do hurry!' wailed Dolly.

Choking, and shaking his head in a gesture of despair, Joseph knelt down to pin the lace scarf over the ink stain on Dolly's skirt.

Staring at the ink-stained stitches of some white flowers embroidered on the satin, he mumbled, 'How did you manage to do this?' all the time trying to fasten the brooch.

'I was trying to fix the cork back into my rum-bottle over there on the writing-table, with one hand only – the other was holding my bouquet. The damned thing slipped, and ink-bottle and all fell over on to my dress. Was ever anybody so unfortunate before?' Dolly began laughing hopelessly.

'Dolly!' shouted the Canon.

'Here,' cried Dolly, and brushing rudely out of Joseph's hands, she disappeared into the drawing-room. There was a rustling of skirts, and then the door at the far end of the drawing-room banged.

'Well. It is over now,' said Joseph aloud.

In scarcely a minute Joseph saw the top of Mrs Thatcham's old Sunbeam car gliding along, upon the other side of the garden wall, towards the church. He then remembered that he, too, should long ago have taken his departure in the same direction.

He sat down on the sofa.

In front of him, hanging over the banisters crookedly and as though just about to slip down on to the floor, was a voluminous red Chinese robe covered all over with a complicated network of creases. The sun from the window fell on this garment and threw up each crease into sharp relief. Dim-looking dust fogged the surface of the cloth all over. More-over it all looked sticky to the touch; somehow, altogether the garment looked fusty and repulsive beyond words.

Joseph leant back against the sofa and heaved an ele-phant's sigh.

'Thanks be to Goodness that she wouldn't let me tell her anything!' he ejaculated. 'Who knows but that she might really have postponed the wedding! – and what in the world should I have done about it afterwards!'

The church organ sounded clearly through the hall.

That meant the bride was advancing down the aisle upon the arm of her cousin, the Canon.

5

JOSEPH, who expected to have the next twenty minutes in which partially to recover himself, upon the sofa, was sur-prised and annoyed to see the red baize door swing open after only three or four minutes had passed.

There came in a midget of a village woman, like a mos-quito, wearing a blouse and a skirt. She wore an enormous apron, but instead of a servant's white cap, she had on a shiny black hat with a few discoloured forget-me-nots fixed up against one side of it. She staggered in under the weight of a deep wooden tray piled up with gilded china.

Panting and grunting, her face round and red and glossy as a polished apple, she put the tray down upon the Turkey carpet, in the centre of the room, under the chandelier.

Going over to the little writing-table, she picked up the red blotting-pad, the pen-holders, the china stamp-box and so forth, two by two, went over to the piano and dotted them all about on top of it. When the writing-table was cleared, she spread an embroidered tea-cloth upon it.

'Oh ... curse and drat it!' she growled immediately, and, whisking it off, respread it, but with the other side uppermost.

Standing back a pace and staring at her handiwork, she exploded into a torrent of giggles, which made a husky reverberation down in her chest.

Meanwhile Joseph might have been a fly on the ceiling, for all the notice she took of him.

'This is the first time ever *I* fussed round a droring-room tea-table then! Believe me, or believe me not. All them little cakes in jelly and all of it. Oh no! Very decidedly not!' said she, addressing the tea-tray upon the floor.

She trotted out of the room again. She was soon back, carrying a cake-stand and some teaspoons. When she had rid herself of these, she came over to the middle of the room, and standing with her hands on her hips, addressed the tea-tray upon the floor again.

'The gentleman that come to see about the hot pipes out in the lobby, said to me, "*I* have two of my own," he said, "what are both of them big strapping great boys by now. And oh ... good golly! – what devils and demons they do be!" he said. "Well," I said to him, "my son Teddy is exactly the very same thing over again," I said. "All the time this cigarette-smoking, they pointed boots, and all of it, why, devils and demons isn't in it with such as *they* are," I said. No. Very decidedly not!'

'Will she ever go out of the room again?' thought Joseph.

The little woman stooped down and began taking up the cups and saucers off the tray. 'Yes! They come down and asked me if I would help with the wedding teas and all of it. If you ask *me* (now I don't know what manner of a gentleman I am addressing at the present moment – mark me well), but if you ask *me* – well, then in my opinion, marriage is a totally mistaken idea.' She breathed heavily and scowled at the tea-cups in her hands. 'My husband has been dead seven years. *Thanks be for that then.* And never no more nothink of anythink of that again for me!' There was a silence during which the woman got on with laying the tea-cups. The organ started playing again down in the church.

'Go. Go. Go,' said a loud voice in Joseph's head to the little woman.

'Teddy came home late last Friday night again,' she started, and Joseph saw she was talking to the tea-tray on the floor once more.

'I was lying in bed at the time. Mark me well. He came right in and began the selfsame song all over again: "Mum, are you going to let me have half a crown this week, please?" "No, TEDDY. Why should I give you what I up and earn by the sweat of my brow to go merely spending on cigarette-smoking, and the gees, and all of it? – most emphatically I AM NOT." And he up and emptied a bucketful of cold water over me as I lay. Sopping the bedclothes and everything. "CURSE YOU, MY BOY," I said.'

'Strange doings!' thought Joseph dimly. He had hardly heard her recital though; he was wondering if he would be able to get a talk with Dolly.

The little creature was staring up into Joseph's face, he suddenly noticed.

'Have you got the face-ache?' she asked.

'The face-ache? Yes . . . I have.'

'Oh! I wondered! Oh! Well, you're a gentleman what has got a capital set of teeth, if ever there was one!' she exclaimed, and immediately bustled over to the tea-table. 'Now, Teddy was keeping on tying a piece of thread to his tooth all last week. He'd tied the other end on to the door-handle–'

'Here come the people from the church. Look,' pointed out Joseph.

She stood up on tiptoe. Sure enough, cars were beginning to glide along the other side of the garden wall, conveying the bride and the guests back again to the house for the reception.

'Oh!' said the little woman. She seemed disappointed.

'They'll be coming in here in a minute,' warned Joseph.

'I'd best be getting along then,' muttered the little one, uncertainly. She gathered up her tray and left him in peace.

Now the regular wedding crush began – but at the farther end of the house, in the large front drawing-room, and in the study.

One or two of the guests had evidently strayed through into the small drawing-room opening out of the hall, however.

For Joseph heard, in a lady's hushed and cautious tones: 'Of course, I know one shouldn't mention such subjects on an occasion of *this* sort, but really!' – here she dropped her voice too low for it to be audible in the hall – 'as big as a *cartwheel* ... I assure you! ... and entirely composed of violets ... truly! ...'

'... But how did he afford ...? *Surely?* ...' came in a different huskier female voice.

'Oh, my dear, but didn't you know? – *umbrella handles!*' hissed the first voice. 'Mints of money!' There was a subdued giggle.

'Mrs Drayton!' This was a third voice, and Joseph recognized it as belonging to little Jimmy Dakin. He was the seven-year-old bearer of the bride's train and youngest son of the Canon. His voice was very low-pitched, deliberate, and slow. 'Have you heard this riddle, I wonder?' asked Jimmy.

'What riddle, dear?'

There was a pause.

Jimmy's voice said, 'Tell me, please: What is the difference between a honey-*comb* and a honey-*moon*?'

'Good gracious! I'm sure I don't know.'

'It is this: A honey-comb has one *million* cells, and a honey-moon has *one*. Rather good, isn't it?'

'What? My dear child! Really!'

'Lily told that one. Good, isn't it?'

'Well, don't go and tell it to the bridegroom, that is all I ask you.'

Joseph heard sounds of stifled laughter.

Mrs Thatcham suddenly pushed in backwards at the baize door, and piloted into the room an aged aunt of hers, whom she settled upon the sofa by the tea-table.

'I had a special little tea put in here for you, Aunt Katie, so as you could be out of the crush. Oh! – *that's* not very nice!' Mrs Thatcham's eye had caught sight of the stamp-box, pens, envelope holder, etc., studded about over the top of the piano. 'Now, why are the writing things on top of the piano? Oh! Why, she must have used the *writing*-table for the tea things instead of the tea-table! Now, how funny of her! Can you imagine her doing such a thing? S-s-s-s-s-s-s-s. So odd!'

'Well, it was mad Nellie up from the village, Mum,' brayed Kitty, who had come into the room behind her mother. 'I told you she would make a muddle of everything; look, here's the jam-pot nestling among the scones at the bottom of the cake-basket. Can you conceive of anything more idiotic?'

'Well, you certainly would think she could unfold a tea-table at her time of life. S-s-s-s-s-s-s-s-sh-sh. What a very curious person,' said Mrs Thatcham in a tone of reserve.

'The tea looks perfectly delicious, and that is the only thing that matters,' cooed old Aunt Katie. 'I'm simply *dyin'* for some of that lovely Cape gooseberry jam!'

Aunt Katie was a thin, sly-looking old lady, who sat very upright, and who had round, black boot-button eyes, brilliantly lit up with some very enigmatic expression – whether intense merriment, or malice, or what, it was difficult to decide. She was dressed in three shades of violet, with many slender gold and silver chains round her neck. The nose on her pale astute face was red as a cherry. White lace, finely written all over in loops and squirls with a thin black snaky velvet ribbon, made a yoke to the top of her dress. Her gauze scarf, pink as a cyclamen, and marked like a butterfly's wings, had hundreds of little tucks upon it, and was edged with lace.

Aunt Katie's hats were like Mediterranean gardens in full blossom. Today her hat was strangely wide and flat, and supported along its brim a regular shrubbery of black cherries, purple and scarlet geraniums, yellow speckled pansies, spiky green sprays of something – oats, or ospreys, and heaven knows what besides. Some pallid silvery-pink roses stood up from all the rest, and looked like refined, blonde English peeresses amongst a horde of gipsies. In looking upon their large, crinkled, ashy-pink faces, one felt the cool relief of evening superimposed upon the meridian glare.

Aunt Katie leaned forward. 'Are you coming to have some tea with your old Aunt Katie?' she asked little Jimmy Dakin, who stood hesitating, in his white satin jacket and knickers, in the drawing-room doorway.

Jimmy came and sat down by his great-aunt, and the pair began their tea.

'And you took tea with your cousins at Boxbridge last week, I hear,' said the old lady, handing the boy a cup of tea.

'I hope your Cousin Roger was nice to you. He is gettin' such a grand person nowadays; captain of his cricket team at school, they tell me!'

Jimmy's face was round, and brown as a hen's egg. He was

a tiny little boy. As for his features, they were so small they could hardly be seen, bunched up together as they were in the middle of his face, like the currants in a penny bun when they all run into the centre together for some reason. Two velvety-brown eyes were always on the watch above these tiny features, and if the curious glance of another got caught up for an instant in the beam of their penetrating gaze, they would be lowered instantly, leaving the spectator gazing, baffled, at this very demure, reserved, *comme il faut* brown currant bun.

Joseph, on the sofa, looked in despair at this couple at the tea-table. Impossible to say good-bye to Dolly in any of the other rooms, surrounded by strange people! And now, here in the hall also, was Jimmy and his aunt, and Jimmy eating and talking so maddeningly slowly that it was clear that the couple would be there for a good two or three hours at least.

'Then Roger offered me a plate with some scones on it,' Jimmy was saying slowly. 'I took one of those. The scone I took was just about the size (just about) – or rather just about the *tallness* – of a whistle.'

'What is the tallness of a whistle, my dear?' asked his great-aunt.

'Well, I believe I should have said – just about the tallness of a whistle with a marble laid on top of it, or perhaps a fountain-pen (on its side, of course!) laid on top of a whistle. Well, after I had finished that scone, he offered me a plate of cocoa-nut cakes. "Oh no," I said. "I cannot eat another cocoa-nut cake." "Well, then, will you have some bread and butter to finish with?" he said. "Oh no," I said. "I really could not do *that*. No. I cannot eat any more bread and butter."'

Jimmy's brown eyes kept a systematic look-out over the room as he talked. It was clear that he was only relating his story in order to keep his aunt entertained. 'Well *then*, (even *then*) he tried to persuade me to eat something further! He handed me a plate with only one biscuit on it. It was about the size, I should say – let me see now – of the end of that tea-spoon with a bus ticket beside it . . .'

Joseph sprang up, and opened the door into the library. The library was empty. Quickly shutting the door again, he went off to fetch Dolly.

Aunt Katie stared out of the glass garden door on to the terrace, where a semicircle of bridesmaids could be seen, their yellow dresses whipping up and down in the wind, their hair streaming. Two men in billowing mackintoshes kept running round a camera on a tall tripod in front of them. The whole party looked more dead than alive.

'Those poor girls must be simply shiverin' in the icy blast! I wouldn't care to have *my* photograph taken in such a costume, on a day like this!'

'B-r-r-r-r,' cried Mrs Thatcham, bursting open the garden door from the outside. 'Rather fresh out today!' She rubbed her little feet cheerfully on the mat and bustled through into the drawing-room.

At the same moment, unnoticed by her or Aunt Katie, or Jimmy either, Dolly (dressed now in her dark going-away costume, and looking, with her hair untidied under a jaunty pink velvet hat, a trifle vulgar) glided along the wall behind the tea-table and in at the library door. Joseph was close at her heels.

Joseph shut the library door softly to, behind them.

6

THERE was not much light in the library, for where there were no shelves filled with dark leather volumes, there was heavy wood panelling painted chocolate brown, and massive plush curtains shrouded the windows.

The remains of the family 'snack lunch' still stood upon the long table. Crumpled-up napkins, and cloudy wine-glasses half filled with yellow wine, stood about higgledy-piggledy among the bowls of half-finished trifle.

'Why, what is this?' cried Dolly, in a very high, airy, very amused tone of voice, and she picked up a dark mass of material from the wooden window-seat. It was a green tartan kilt and sporran. A rose-pink canvas mask dropped to the floor from out its folds.

Joseph and Dolly looked down at the mask. A pair of square gelatine spectacles with vermilion rims was placed over two goggling blue-china eyes; a frayed ginger moustache and false teeth were sticking out in all directions. To the forehead was fastened a pale blue cricketing-cap.

'Oh, that is just something that Lob and Tom and a lot of them dressed up in, to have their photographs taken,' said Joseph.

'Why?'

'Oh, to send to Kitty. Don't let's talk about that now.'

There was a pause.

'Why *did* they have their photographs taken in such garments,' inquired Dolly in her high, airy-sounding voice.

'Oh, it was to be a practical joke on Kitty. They were each going to send her their photograph with a different inscription underneath, as Kitty's admirers always do, you know:

"To Kitty – because of a glorious afternoon in an orchard at Hove . . . ," and so on – you know the sort of thing Kitty's room is filled with . . .'

'I see.' Dolly sat down on the window-seat and stared out at the garden, her face devoid of expression. When, at length, she glanced up at Joseph, she saw a face the colour of a beetroot gazing meaningly and imploringly at her. She hastily dropped her eyes.

'Have you settled your mother comfortably in up at Liverpool?' she asked.

'Yes.'

'And your course of lectures up there, – they take six months, don't they?'

'Yes.'

'And you are proposing to go to another set there?'

'Yes.'

'And will you really enjoy them – or are you rather dreading the whole business?'

'It will be all right.'

'Do you know anybody up there?'

'No.'

Dolly felt him looking imploringly at her face.

'But I suppose you will be able to get introductions?' she said.

'Oh, don't let us go on talking like this!' he burst out.

Dolly glanced up sideways. He was blushing redder than ever, and now gave her a miserable forced smile.

Dolly bit her lip and turned her head quickly towards the garden; her own face now flooded with colour also.

'But, really, though, why not? I seriously do want to know all about it . . . ,' she said. After a moment she slightly turned her head and gave an uneasy, curious glance at him.

He immediately gave her another miserable-looking smile, only half a smile this time, and immediately turned away, with his back to her, and leant up against the brown panelling.

As he leant there, she saw he was shivering all over. Dolly jumped up and put an arm around his shoulders.

'Dearest Joseph. Dear Joseph. Do come and sit down, dear,' she said.

They both sat down on the window-seat together.

Dolly kept her arm round his shoulders. She could see that tears were rolling down his pale face, but he turned it half away, towards the wall, and kept wiping away the tears with his handkerchief.

'But what is it all, really? You must tell me what you are feeling,' said Dolly.

Dolly looked painfully strained and uncomfortable. She was feeling that something had gone wrong somewhere now, that something false had crept into the situation, as they sat there on the window-seat, her arm round the shoulders of the weeping Joseph.

Joseph shook his head silently in answer to her questions, and continued shivering.

'It's no good ...,' he said, and waved his hands. Soon his shivering got worse, and sobs began to shake him. 'It's no earthly use asking me what is the matter,' he said roughly, gasping for breath as if he had been plunged into iced water. 'I don't know myself.'

After quite a long time he added, 'Evelyn said some time ago (not to me) that you were in love with me, she thought.'

'Well, perhaps I was some time ago. But I am not now; I haven't been for a good while.'

Joseph waited a second, and then removed himself from the seat, and went over to the farther window by himself. 'Why do you never tell anybody anything?' he said angrily. 'You always like to make out that you are on top of the wave. That *you* can never be in need of anyone else's help ...'

'Why did you never mention to me that you were going to be married?' said Joseph, looking at her with some sort of direct feeling in his face now.

'Not mention it! What can you mean? You got my letter from Albania?' cried Dolly.

'Well, good gracious, dear. That letter from Albania! Of course I never dreamt from *that* that you would really do it!'

'I'm sure I don't know why not,' said Dolly coldly.

'Tut! – and then why so late in the day! – barely a month ago!'

'But if I only decided I was going to marry a month ago!' said Dolly heatedly. 'But, anyway, why all this fuss, good gracious me! You don't want to marry me yourself! *You* are not in love with me.'

'No ... No ... I know that ... ,' said Joseph.

All of a sudden he turned sharply away from her, began breathing in heavy long-drawn gasps and sobs again as though he were choking over an enormous chicken-bone, and coughing.

Dolly sprang up and put her arm around his waist.

Joseph this time turned, and put his arm round her shoulder. He looked down at her; his cheeks were wet, and he gave a smile. 'Darling!' he said, and there was real warmth suddenly in his voice

As he said the word, the door handle rattled and the library door was burst open.

They both looked round with startled faces.

There stood Owen, the bridegroom, in a bowler hat, and with a travelling-rug over his arm. A look of fright came into his face as he took in the interlocked couple standing before him in the dim light, with their guilty faces, and Joseph's cheeks so plainly wet with tears.

'Sorry!' he said, after a short pause.

The couple dropped apart from each other.

'But it's time to go, dear. Everybody is standing out on the doorstep waiting to bid us a fond farewell.' Owen stepped instantly backwards across the threshold, and shut the door again.

'That has done it,' said Dolly.

The door opened again, but only two inches.

'I'm sorry to interrupt, dear, but what is all this about taking a tortoise along or something or other – on board the liner with us – something – I can't understand it quite … Millman handed me a biscuit tin, which she said had a tortoise inside it …'

'That's all right. That's my tortoise.'

'It may be your tortoise, dear, but what is it going to eat crossing over – on the boat – is what I'm thinking!'

'Why, good gracious me! (Do come in, Owen! What's the matter with you?) Surely there must be *something* on a huge big boat like that that a tortoise can eat. Good gracious me!'

'That's all very well. But I'm afraid *not*, dear, all the same.'

'What! Can it not eat dried peas?'

'I'm afraid not, dear.'

'At all events, it likes to eat ice wafers, I know that. And these big boats are always stacked with *them*.'

'Well … but if you will forgive me for doing so … I'm afraid I have told Millman we are *not* going to take the tortoise. They have let it loose by this time. I'm sorry. It's probably half-way over the fields to Malton by now – where, believe me, it will be much happier than–'

'My goodness, it's perfectly insufferable!' cried out Dolly, snatching up her bag and gloves from the table.

Mrs Thatcham poked her nose round the corner of the door.

'Oh, there you are!' she cried. 'We could not think where on earth you had got to. Come along, child; everybody's waiting out on the doorstep; you'll miss your boat if you're not careful.' She shooed Dolly out of the library.

On the front doorstep a huge crowd was waiting: relations, guests, and (all in a group at one side) the servants – Mad Nellie, her face flushed, and looking ready to burst with excitement and pleasure, – in spite of all her principles. The motor was ready, with baggage piled all over it, and a white satin shoe could be seen dangling from beneath a gladstone bag.

Kitty was crying, and little Evelyn was weeping quietly in the background. Red-haired Lob was standing by with a strange white paper hat on his head with long upstanding ears to it like a rabbit's; he was rolling his eyes and looking very devilish, and guarding something secret hidden under his jacket.

Out in the drive there, standing about round the motor-car in the furious March gale, everyone felt as though they were being beaten on the back of the head and on the nose with heavy carpets and having cold steel knives thrust up inside their nostrils, and when they opened their mouths to avoid the pain of this, big wads of iced cotton-wool seemed to be forced against the insides of their throats immediately, so that they choked, and could not draw any breath in.

In this cutting, furiously buffeting wind, amid the cries of good-bye, and bowing down before the storms of rice and confetti, the lack of high spirits on the part of the bride and bridegroom passed unnoticed. Away they drove, out of sight round the drive corner, and without wasting another moment the whole crowd made for shelter again as hurriedly as might be.

Everyone but those few who were staying in the house now took their departure.

Aunt Bella started back in her new motor to her loyal household across the bay.

Mrs Thatcham, Kitty, little Evelyn, Lob, and the two schoolboys filtered back into the hall, one by one.

7

IN the hall they found Aunt Katie and Joseph, who had been sitting facing each other, at opposite ends of the room, in silence for the last ten minutes. Aunt Katie had taken out her little pack of patience cards and was playing 'Emperor' on her basketwork patience tray.

Little Jimmy Dakin sat silently on the sofa beside her. Joseph, with legs crossed and arms folded, sat with a white face, glaring in front of him.

Suddenly a scuffle started up behind the hydrangeas.

'What did I tell you? What did I tell you? *Two men from Rugby* present at the ceremony!' chattered a voice behind the flowers, practically sobbing with nervous vexation.

There was some more sharp whispering, and the pallid, stained white globes of the hydrangeas swayed forward dangerously in their pots.

'Children, what is the matter? Come out from behind there!'

'That fat man was Arbuthnot major!' hissed the angry voice behind the flower ... All up with us now, all up! Damn you, Robert, damn you!'

Heavy breathing, and 'Blast you!' shrieked Robert, tumbling out from behind the hydrangeas holding on to his left wrist, which was scarlet, and with tears pouring down his cheeks. 'You are a bully!' he shouted.

'Go out of the room immediately,' commanded Mrs Thatcham, and added, quite astounded, 'What extraordinary manners! Odd beings, you are! Really!' Her voice was freezing.

The boys sloped out of the room.

Mrs Thatcham turned to Joseph. 'Why not go upstairs and have a good lie down, Joseph? I would. Run along, dear boy. Go along.'

'No, thank you. I'm starting for the station in ten minutes.'

'Well. Why not go up even if only for ten minutes? You're not doing yourself or anybody else any good by moping round in here with a face like that, you know, child. Run upstairs. *I* should.'

Joseph made no movement.

'Hetty!' shouted a deep bass voice from the top of the stairway. It was Mrs Thatcham's Christian name.

Everyone glanced upwards.

An exceedingly elegant male figure, in a wine-coloured silk dressing-gown, which was patterned over with a design of little grey-and-white feathers, stood holding on to the banisters. It was Canon Dakin. His grey curly hair was tumbled, and his face looked pale and beautiful in the white light from the upper landing.

'I apologize for shouting down the stairway thus attired.' He cleared his throat. 'But a rather awkward thing has happened. I ran up to my bedroom and undressed in rather a hurry, hoping to be able to get a bath in before catching my train back to Birmingham; er – h'm – when I returned from the bathroom I found – er – apparently a woman's underclothes scattered over my bed. My own clothes I discovered had slipped down behind the armchair (and so, of course, had not been visible to the lady who had evidently mistaken my bedroom for hers). Er-r-r – h'm! I don't quite know. What is the best thing to do under the circumstances? ...'

Whilst the Canon had been speaking, Mrs Thatcham's eye had wandered to a mysterious figure in a grey Japanese kimono with big black storks printed on it, that was lurking bashfully in the drawing-room doorway. Two long plaits of hair hung down over the shoulders. The lady had been waving a tiny white pocket-handkerchief up and down in order to attract her attention.

'But how extraordinary!' cried out Mrs Thatcham to the Canon. 'Half a moment, Bob, and I will be with you,' and she hurried in and joined the lady in the drawing-room.

It was Miss Spoon, the girls' one-time governess.

'Mrs Thatcham, it is really extraordinarily embarrassing!' those in the hall heard the latter whispering in a low voice. 'I went to have a bath . . . returned to my room for a moment . . . bending down over the armchair! . . . and you see all my things in the drawers in there . . .'

'What room are you in?' demanded Mrs Thatcham very loudly, and putting on her pince-nez. She could be seen, through the drawing-room doorway, staring down at the black storks on Miss Spoon's dressing-gown through her pince-nez, as though the storks and the storks alone were to blame for the whole distasteful incident.

'The lilac room, where you yourself put me,' said Miss Spoon anxiously.

'Oh, Mum!' screamed out Kitty from the hall. 'What did I tell you! You *would* put them all into the lilac room. I knew this would happen!'

However, when this little matter had been set right at last, Mrs Thatcham returned to the hall again. The sun had gone down behind the trees now.

Robert had returned to the hall, and was sitting in the window-seat reading the *Captain*.

Joseph had not moved a muscle.

'Poor Aunt Katie, with nobody at all to look after you or help you with your patience!' exclaimed Mrs Thatcham, with a glittering stare at Joseph. She began pattering roughly about the room, thumping the cushions and fluffing them out again. 'Do you young men *never* think of anybody but yourselves nowadays, I wonder? To me that seems so curious!' There was, as the saying goes, a knife-edge on her voice.

Kitty, Joseph, and Aunt Katie all turned their heads and looked inquiringly at Mrs Thatcham. She was looking interested in her subject, and seemed just about to say something further, but no, instead she whipped an open box of chocolates off the little table beside her.

'Have a chocolate, Robert?' She went across and handed the box to Robert in the window.

'Evelyn, a chocolate?' She waved the box at her.

'Aunt Kate? They are so very delicious! Joseph, help yourself, child.' So saying, she put down the chocolate-box on the table again.

Jimmy Dakin, the only person who had not been offered a chocolate, cast his eyes down upon the carpet, blushing hotly, and looked with very great concentration at the Turkish arabesques beneath his dangling feet.

A few minutes went by of general crunching and munching.

Mrs Thatcham ate her chocolate standing in front of the window, her orange eyes staring out through the little lead bars connecting the panes, across at the rapidly tossing branches of the elm trees opposite, her neck rising very upright from her brown silk-covered shoulders.

'Excellent chocolates!' mumbled Aunt Katie with satisfaction.

'Oh, but Jimmy!' cried out Evelyn in dismay from her armchair. She had just noticed the expression on the little boy's crimson face. 'Have you not been offered a chocolate?'

'Well, now! I was just waiting for somebody or other to say

that!' said Jimmy with slow jocoseness, his cheeks red as fire.

'How dreadful!' cried Evelyn, and quickly handed him the chocolates, urging him to take several of them to make up for lost chances.

'Well, I had to have a laugh to myself about it, I must say!' replied Jimmy, smiling, and feeling for a chocolate. But when everyone had looked away from him again, he bent down his head and softly wiped away a tear from either eye with the lace corner of the tea-cloth beside him.

Mrs Thatcham went and stood in front of Joseph, upon the shallow stone fender, and looked over his head away out of the window.

'You know you young men nowadays seem to mope about the place all anyhow,' she said. 'Never seeming to care to pull yourselves together, to stand up nice and square, or walk along properly. Or to join in with other people's fun ... don't you know what I mean?'

No one answered.

'And yet you're never lagging behindhand, I notice, when it comes to raising your voices in criticism of people old enough to be your grandmother.' She pointed a finger down at Joseph. 'Now, *you*, Joseph–'

'Oh, Mum!' cried Kitty from the corner.

'*You*, Joseph, have got everything you want from life: the profession you wanted, a first-rate education, all the money you want, a most devoted mother and family, and yet here you seem to be – all up against everybody! S-s-s-s-s-s-sh-sh.'

In the south of France, when the *mistral* has been blowing for some time across the water, the even healthy blue complexion of the sea turns to streaks of biliousness, and to congested violet patches – shocking sight indeed. Something of the sort had now happened upon Joseph's face. Had it not been for the uncomfortable streaks of yellow, and the dark patches, now apparent over his neck and on the sides of his cheeks, no one would have guessed that in Joseph, during the last few minutes, a *mistral* had started up, and that deep waters were being severely ruffled.

'Nothing seems good enough for you!' said Mrs Thatcham wonderingly. 'Of course I may be very dense – but I freely confess – I utterly fail to understand it!'

Joseph, sitting back in his chair with his arms folded, raised his head and looked up into Mrs Thatcham's eyes.

'Of course you may be very dense – that might be the reason, I suppose,' he murmured thoughtfully, 'that you do, as you say, so utterly fail to understand it. You can't understand why the two boys have such extraordinary manners either, can you? And then you can't understand why Mad Nellie lays the drawing-room tea incorrectly, or why the Canon and Miss Spoon come to be sharing a bedroom. You couldn't grasp how it was Millman could have been such an odd person as to lay the lunch in the library instead of the nursery! In fact, you don't really understand anyone or anything about you, do you? "How odd of her!" "How strange!" "I may be dense but I fail to understand it!" How many times an hour are you obliged to confess that?'

Mrs Thatcham stared at him as though he were reciting the multiplication table to her all of a sudden.

'Why not set to work,' said Joseph, 'by way of a change, and determine to find out a little about these things that puzzle you so? M-m? It would be interesting, wouldn't it?'

Joseph's voice was as quiet when he finished this peroration as when he began it, his face as expressionless.

He turned his head away now, and transferred his fixed gaze slightly to the left of Mrs Thatcham, in the direction of the library door. There was a silence. The lady seemed in a trance. All gazed at the couple with – to use a vulgar expression – their eyes fairly popping out on stalks.

'As for where your own daughters are concerned, of course, you know less than that fly upon the ceiling,' said Joseph, without turning his head at all. 'I ought not to tell you this, I suppose,' he went on reflectively, 'but I'm going to. *You* didn't know, did you, that when Dolly was out in Albania last autumn she gave birth to a child out there?'

'Oh, JOSEPH!' bawled out Kitty.

Mrs Thatcham started.

'You're mad!' she shouted, after a moment.

Joseph shook his head. 'No, I'm not mad, believe me! It's true right enough, but of course *you* would be the last person to know it.'

'What?'

'I say *you* would be the last person to know about it. Why! It would seem so *very* odd to you! So very curious! You would think Dolly such a "very strange person" for doing such a thing! – that of course she must have despaired of even attempting to explain about it!'

Tears were rolling down Mrs Thatcham's uncomprehending face.

'Oh, no need to be alarmed about it,' said Joseph, watching her. 'She has farmed it out with the midwife's sister in the country there. It is perfectly happy, I assure you.'

Kitty sprang forward into the middle of the room and stood there uncertainly.

'What are you talking about?' shouted Mrs Thatcham.

'Why, I am telling you that you are a grandmother. In fact, that you are doubly a grandmother – if you really want the truth! It was twins! Only I didn't like to say so. So now you have two little Albanian grandchildren, like little white mice, with pink eyes, to write letters to asking them why they haven't thanked you for the presents, and telling them how far you are from Cocklebank and Niggybottom. I must go now, or I shall lose my train. Thank you for a most delightful day.' Joseph jumped up and ran away up the stairs to his bedroom.

Tears were rolling down Mrs Thatcham's cheeks and her face looked drawn and bemused; she kept blowing her nose on a tiny little handkerchief. 'But what is wrong with him? What made him speak to me like that?' she kept on and on repeating. 'You can't possibly suppose ...?' she added in a shaking voice.

'Of *course* not! Don't pay any attention, Mum! He's drunk! That's what's the matter with him!' said Kitty, putting her arm round her mamma.

'Outrageous way of talkin',' said Aunt Katie in her mild, pleasant-sounding voice. 'I knew there was something a trifle fishy as soon as he mentioned that they were two little *Albanians*–with pink eyes and long white tails. Well I said to myself, she was only in Albania five weeks all told! Rather quick work that.'

'Katie!' breathed Mrs Thatcham warningly, and indicated young Robert in the window-seat with a nod of her neatly waved grey head.

Joseph, still with his strangely impassive face, but with his heart bounding up and down in his chest with such force that he could barely draw his breath in, strode along the oil-cloth passage to his bedroom.

Here he stood in the window, and looked out over the wintry rose arches and cabbages of the now twilit kitchen garden. Somebody came and took his suitcase away, and went out again. He began to feel calmer.

He thought of what a number of times and what a number of different weathers he had stood looking out there, and thinking of Dolly, since first he had met her.

Something strange seemed to have happened in their relationship; but he couldn't for the life of him make out what it had been ...

Last summer, for example, they had been inseparable, building a new summer-house together, trailing about everywhere in his boat, him teaching her how to play croquet, and so on ... all of a sudden off she had gone to Albania, of all unheard-of places, with some stupid girl friend or other, and no sooner did she get back than, Jack Robinson! there she was engaged to be married to old Owen Bigham! Yes, there was something very strange about it all somewhere. He remembered a dinner party there had been one time down in Malton before going to the cinema.

It had been a burningly hot summer day and the dinner-table had been fixed for their party up against the open hotel window. He and Dolly had sat side by side, looking out at the sea front, which at that hour was nearly deserted. And what a melancholy, bewildered feeling stole over him as he conjured up that scene. He remembered it very clearly. Small knots of young men shop-assistants and clerks had stood about, smoking and chatting, on the pavement beneath the window. Short men they all were, he remembered, with unusually low foreheads; and many had orange or brown scarves round their necks (in spite of the August weather). Guffaws of laughter kept drifting in at the open window from these groups, cigarette smoke also, and the little men kept perpetually turning up their faces towards the dinner party. A few tousle-headed girls, with stout forms like pillar-boxes, or bolsters, wandered slowly arm-in-arm along the sea front, upon the other side of the street. The sea front, the pavement below the window, and all this side of the bay lay steeped in the late evening shadow; but the sea itself was full in the sunlight and was a startling spectacle, the whole sea-bay looking like a sheet of palest blue glass laid out gleaming underneath the pink sunset sky.

A lilac band of heat haze spread all along the horizon line, and out of this dim region a few upward-curling, clotted-cream clouds had half emerged, got caught in the pink sun-set rays, and remained suspended, voluptuous-looking and completely motionless, all through dinner-time. And he remembered he had taken the white roses pinned on Dolly's shoulder for brilliant salmon-pink ones in the late sunshine; and Dolly's fascinating, melancholy face, and long plump neck beneath her straw hat, had seemed made of flame, like the glowing end of a cigarette.

They had been given fried whiting and other uneatable foods, but the wine, red burgundy, had not been at all too bad; perhaps it was on account of the latter that he had felt so extraordinarily happy – so desperate, so wild! After din-ner they all set off walking to the cinema through the narrow Malton streets. Standing on the hotel steps after the meal, they observed that now all the people, the houses, the pave-ments and everything had turned a bright, uniform violet in the dusk. The air felt hot on their faces, and smelt strongly of syringa or heliotrope or something of the sort. Joseph and Dolly dropped behind the others. And finally lost them alto-gether ... Anyway the point was he had felt he loved her, and, though he *said* nothing, he knew that she knew this very well. She loved him too.

And yet it hadn't been love, but some depressing kind of swindle after all, it seemed.

Standing at his bedroom window by the bamboo table, and looking out at the cold March cabbages and the gravel paths, he felt that the Dolly he had walked with in the street that evening last summer was not the Dolly who had just been married this afternoon at all, and that he himself bore very little relation to the young man at Malton of that evening. And he understood that something had gone queer and awry between them since that time and the present; something was wrong, and he felt swindled. But as he was in danger of missing his train, there was no time to unravel it all just at present.

He walked off down the passage.

''Tis better to have loved and lost than never to have loved at all,' he thought with bitterness.

'Next August who shall I be taking with me in my boat?' he wondered.

A horrible feeling of depression seemed to rise up from inside him somewhere. It crept along every nerve, and kept growing deeper and deeper, like a strong physical nausea. His stomach began to turn into lead; in fact all his inside seemed to be congesting, and suffocating him with this strange, cold, heavy, physical gloom. When he reached the head of the stairway he heard the telephone bell ring down in the hall below.

'Oh, it's *you*, is it, Dodo!' shouted Mrs Thatcham into the telephone.

Hearing Mrs Thatcham's voice, Joseph instinctively paused at the top of the stairway.

'Oh, thank you very much! Yes indeed! everything went off quite splendidly!' Mrs Thatcham was saying down the telephone, evidently to Miss Dodo Potts-Griffiths.

Joseph's head felt heavy as a cannon-ball, and his neck as weak as worsted. He leant up against the flowered wall-paper for a moment, and rested the back of his head against the wall. He heard Mrs Thatcham shouting cheerfully into the telephone:

'It couldn't have gone better! Yes – so dreadfully disappointing you were not able to get over. But your lampshade was very much appreciated! Yes indeed! Everybody admired it! Everybody. Quite enormously! So wonderfully clever! and so pretty and gay. S-s-s-s-sh-sh-sh ... Thank you very much, dear. Yes – well, of course, we had such wonderful cheerful weather for it all! The little old church

77

looked so pretty lit up with the sunshine, don't you know – the girls' yellow frocks looked so pleasant and gay. S-s-s-s-s-sh-sh-sh.'

The hall there below, Mrs Thatcham, the whole house, and everything in it, suddenly seemed profoundly uninteresting to Joseph. It had nothing to do with him really, at all – he saw that in a flash. He looked at the scene – himself sitting there on the top stair, and the family in the hall below – as if through the wrong end of a long telescope. The buzzing in his ears got louder. A clear voice, inside his head, gave him a piece of information, above the worrying buzzing. 'What you need is some brandy,' said the voice. 'Some brandy, yes, a good idea,' he thought, and remembered that Millman had said something about it earlier in the afternoon to him. What would be the best way to get hold of Millman? On second thoughts he went along to hunt round in the dining-room himself for it.

An Integrated Man

To
Frances and Ralph

1

'Everything in my life is well ordered and serene. I wake up in the mornings rested and refreshed! And above all with a feeling of virtue. My days are spent unharassed by pressures that torture and distort. At the age of forty-one, I'm bound to admit that I have become that fabulous beast an "integrated man"!'

So spoke out Ned Moon, lying alone in the yellow spare-room bed at Flitchcombe Manor.

It was eight o'clock on a Wednesday morning in July 1936.

Opposite Ned were two windows, draped in muslin, open wide.

A knock came on the bedroom door. This would be his host, a man with the strange name of Reamur Cedar.

'Come in.'

Reamur, without a sound, glided in.

Ned, who had been an intimate since Cambridge – eighteen years before – said nothing, but lay back vaguely on his pillow. One did not look inquiringly at Reamur. No results were to be got that way. Instead, Ned made to ignore the tall, pale figure, who now passed across the carpet wearing his London overcoat and clasping a briefcase under his arm like a vision glimpsed from a train at night, moving under a naphtha flare far away, and reached the spare-room window.

Reamur, who had got up and breakfasted early, remained for some time with his back to the window, contemplating Ned; standing, with his white face, uncannily still.

Reamur was always uncannily still. No one ever observed him either leaving, or entering, a room. He was merely there.

Or else he was seen to be surprisingly not there. Like the lady in the conjurer's cabinet: 'Now you see her. Now you don't.'

'Yes, at the age of forty-one I have become an integrated man,' Ned repeated, looking up at the ceiling.

'Furthermore,' he added, 'I have developed a digestive apparatus. I am now able to, so to speak, appropriate life. I carve it, masticate it, digest it, and use it for my nourishment. I am even able to hand round slices to other people. In fact I do with it what I want. Marvellous, that!' he finished mournfully, as if he were displaying to his friend an enormous yellow and purple bruise with regretful pride.

Then he turned himself sideways in the bed and looked affectionately at the chest of drawers, upon which the cascade of bills and envelopes, tags of coloured tape and rolls of tracing paper seemed momently about to slip on to the floor in a shower, but which by some miracle in fact remained motionless.

'You see that mountain of papers on the chest of drawers? I have answered every one of those letters on that chest, although some of them came only yesterday afternoon, believe it or not. I have dealt exhaustively, on behalf of both Aron and myself, with each of those forms; you can't see them, but there are shoals of them I assure you – insurance forms and so on you know, in connection with our new school of course. I have studied, passed, or else rejected, all those architects' blueprints. Filed all receipted bills! And in that red box' – Ned pointed a finger – 'are collected all the letters in answer to our advertisements for staff, both teachers and servants – but under separate clips. Then again the question of medical attendance ... Aron has delegated to me – however I won't bore you. The point is d'you see ... the point I want to make is that one should feel master of oneself. And I do! One should become the disciplined instrument of one's purpose. And I have. How many people can honestly say the same?'

His soft voice melted into silence, and he sank back with a wistful look on to his pillow.

Reamur answered, as usual, nothing; but continued regarding Ned, or rather the end of Ned's nose above the bed-clothes.

Ned did not have to look at his friend in order to know what expression would be in that well-known face. Reamur, he knew, although enjoying the best of health, would have in his eyes the look of someone mortally ill and very near the border of the next world. A look at once remote, haunted, and serenely benign – the look of the man in the conjuror's box.

'So there it is,' said the voice from the bed. 'That's how it is. In fact I may say, Reamur, at my late age I have become – what I never before envisaged in my wildest moments – even a *happy* man!'

Reamur continued to contemplate him with ill-looking serenity.

Ned lay fluttering his eyelids drowsily and looking up at the ceiling.

'Yes, yes. There's little doubt that you see before you now a happy and integrated man,' he repeated and added, 'You think my words boastful?'

Reamur laughed.

Every week, on the Monday, Reamur travelled up to London and there spent the day; returning in time for a late supper. Nobody knew exactly what it was he did there, apart from sitting alone in the British Museum looking things up. What was he looking up? That he would tell nobody. But he certainly brought back notes and diagrams with him. These he made use of in some mysterious fashion, out of sight of prying eyes, locked up alone in the library.

'She hasn't brought in your tea yet,' said Reamur. 'I have come in here and bothered you before you have been woken up even!'

'Not a bit. Doreen is simply very late in calling me. It's long after eight. As a matter of fact I particularly wanted to see you, Reamur, before you went up to London. Would you be able to buy a box of geometry instruments for your son, during the day, and bring them back with you? At present we have to manage in our lessons with a tape measure, drawing-pins and swivelling bits of string, and we don't get on very fast. Geometry boxes can be got at Hamleys, if you're going to be near Regent Street at all.'

Reamur took out a notebook and made a note about the compass box.

'"Stationary blast of waterfalls!" ...' came a mumbling from the bed.

'What's that?'

'I'm saying that happiness is really a kind of tranquillity in motion.'

Reamur shut up his notebook and looked expectantly at the bed.

'A happy man is like Wordsworth's "Stationary blast of waterfalls". From the distance only this motionless white thread in its niche in the scenery – apparently harmless enough. Even turning a mill wheel perhaps.' Ned paused; and continued sadly, 'Yet put your ear to the ground, and (if you are a Red Indian) you will become aware of a murderous cataract of violences quaking the land for miles around. There you have your waterfall – and your happy man.'

Ned met Reamur's eyes over the bedclothes fixed on him with their strange languor, and, as always, as the minutes ticked by under his contemplative gaze, the familiar feeling came over Ned of being subjected to some sort of a human tuning-fork. What's more, of being accounted spiritually off-key.

He said, confused, 'One makes these remarks ... pro-nouncements about waterfalls ... and it's true that tomorrow one will be declaring that a happy man is after all, simply a kangaroo – a hop to the side and three shuffles backwards! Or something of that sort ... You mustn't hold me to it!'

Reamur put his notebook away into his breast pocket. Then he asked:

'And how long has Octavia been married?'

'*Octavia?*'

Ned jerked his shoulders up abruptly and peered at Reamur over the bedclothes.

'Yes. I mean, how long now since you have seen her?'

Silence.

'Three years, I suppose. Yes, three years. More.'

No movement came from the bed for a little while.

A cow bellowed out in the fields.

'Mmm ... yes, it's true, I had a very rough passage with Octavia all those years. And what a long time it seemed! It seemed as if it was going on for ever.'

'But it didn't.'

'No, it didn't. She married that creature.'

'Yes.'

'Afterwards it became perfectly obvious that it was really *he* whom she had loved all through that long hectic time.'

'Perhaps so,' agreed Reamur.

'But then, why make such a peculiarly elaborate pretence to me all those years about it?'

No answer.

'Hmm? What?'

'At any rate you must admit you're well out of it now, Ned.'

'Oh, well out of it now! Well out of it now. Well out of it now.'

A car hooted close on the main road. Reamur began feeling about inside his pockets for something.

Through the shut window a child's voice floated up from the garden.

'Ned Moon! Ned Moon! I say, Ned Moon!'

Reamur turned round to the window and pushed it up. He leant out. Co-Co, his son, a small boy of nine, stood below, holding a silver chain.

'Is Chadwick up there with you?'

Reamur turned round to the bed.

'Is Chadwick in here, do you suppose, Ned?'

'Certainly not.'

'No,' he called down, 'Chadwick is not up here.'

'She *is* up there.'

'No, she's not here.'

'Are you sure she's not under the bed?'

'Are you sure she's not under the bed, Ned?'

'Quite sure.'

'No. Co-Co, not under the bed.'

'Isn't she in the chimney place?'

'No.'

'Quite sure?'

'Quite sure.'

'I wonder where she is, then?'

A pause.

Reamur said: 'I expect she's round in the orchard eating the chickens' breakfast. Isn't this the hour they dish it out? And she always goes punctually. You can see her every morning with her head in the steam gollaping it all down.'

Co-Co turned on his heel and, tossing back his head much offended, ran round the corner in search of his Siamese pet.

Reamur shut the window but remained standing staring out over the garden.

'I fancy I can hear the car.'

A car had stopped outside the house, round the corner by the front door.

'I must fly, then.'

But Reamur still remained standing silhouetted in front of the window.

'And so you are going to bring Aron's wife down with you from London this evening? ... Or was it not this evening, but Thursday?'

Reamur did not answer questions. He remained silent.

At this moment there came a hesitant scuffle outside the door. Then a pause. And again a scuffle. Horror spread over Ned's face and he submerged beneath the bedclothes.

'Doreen! Reamur, save me! Can't you take the tea-tray from her? Tell her at any rate I don't want anything else done ...'

Dismayed, he looked round the room for his friend. Reamur had disappeared.

Ned shrank down into the bed again and covered his head with the clothes. 'Spectral serpent!' he muttered with annoyance.

A knock. He pretended, even to himself, that he was asleep.

As he lay in the stifling dark with shut eyes, he was soon aware that something was shambling about close by. Then suddenly Doreen let the morning tea-tray fall with a crash on the table at Ned's bedside.

This girl's morning hesitancies and bogglings with the towels and the curtains and the other things in his bedroom daily appalled Ned, and they seemed to last for ever.

He waited patiently. An infinity went by during which he heard nothing. Stifled at last by the bedclothes he peeped out. Doreen was wavering round the window doing something with the chintz curtains. He shut his eyes and withdrew below.

It was the girl's personality which upset him. Weak, vacillating, sulky, yet artificially ingratiating; and with something violent and savage-looking just beneath the surface. Treacherous! In the same way that something else was treacherous also – what was it? He thought of a candle flame in a draughty passage.

When he looked out next, Doreen was coming in his direction.

Yet after all not quite that! Uncertain as a dandelion fluff, she wafted hither and thither on pin-point heels, her face unhealthy and scarred with cosmetics, her figure lax as a curtain.

Ned forced himself to relax and lie back in patience. And there followed another interminable period of Doreen's capricious hesitancies. At the towel rail for instance – what could she be doing? A peep disclosed that she was not folding towels. Nor was she unfolding them. She was merely tentatively fidgeting. And all this havering was accompanied by uneven breathing; whilst repeated pistol reports would come from her otherwise phantom-silent shoes.

All of a sudden a searing hiss! Ned looked out. She was standing still and simply fingering his yellow sponge-bag. He lay down under the sheet again and gave himself up to despair.

It was much later that a scratching began somewhere over by the armchair at the window. She must be doing something or other to his clothes there. Should he look out again and see what? Unexpectedly he heard the bedroom door shut.

Silence.

Doreen was gone!

Ned shot up from beneath the bedclothes and grasped the teapot.

As he drank his first cup of tea he caught sight of himself in the dressing-table mirror. A large man with dark skin, and a masculine moulding of feature. But what was that leprosy – a kind of phosphorescent mould on his head, above his left ear? He paused, startled, teacup in air, and stared.

It was merely the greying patch over his temple, of course, but the light from the window had caught it so that it glittered. And it had dreadfully looked what it was: the place upon which a supernatural finger had been laid, under whose steel touch the warmth of life had fled, never to return again.

He felt horror and repulsion, yet a satisfying pleasure in that repulsion.

He took a drink of tea and looked in the glass again.

This time he marked how thin his hair was getting, and how limply it hung down where before it used to spring youthfully upward. His hair, he thought, was spent weed, left lying flaccid now that the midday tide had turned. He felt despair at the notion, but again this was accompanied by pleasure in the corruption of himself. He took another sip of his tea. His mind detached itself. All that sort of thing seemed so far away nowadays, in any case. The visible body of the present hardly concerned him. He lived so remote from what he thought of as 'surface', nowadays.

Turning his head, he glanced at the mound of papers upon the chest of drawers. If he gazed greedily at those bills, at those typed letters, rolls of tracing paper, and orange and buff-coloured portfolios and files, it was because they hid from view the only reality in life. All his ambitions lay amongst those papers there. What he would do with the school that he and his friend Aron had just purchased. Oaklands, as the place was called. How they would reorganize it. Rebuild it. All that was going to happen there in the years ahead.

A month before they had bought this school – a going concern with some forty small boys and a handful of staff attached to it, and the plan was to take over and expand it, add to these boys fifty more by degrees, and even perhaps fifty more again. Meanwhile, during these summer holidays, carpenters, builders and plumbers were on the precincts, heavily engaged; a new gymnasium and larger changing rooms being the first improvements on the list.

Policy would change gradually; but many material circumstances were already long overdue – so Ned and his friend felt – for a change. Some of the school tradesmen, for instance, and the visiting doctor in particular.

He jumped out of bed.

Air from the garden filled the bedroom, chiefly the sour smell from the dew-soaked yew tree, standing just outside and touching the sill with the ends of its branches.

Ned picked up his socks. Going to the open window he put them on, standing first upon one foot and then the other.

Outside, a vast summer confusion was going on. Beetles, spiders, caterpillars, ladybirds, insects innumerable were crawling in and out of flower-pots, and leaping off the tops of grasses. Hedgehogs were stealing cautiously through the long clover in the fields. Amongst the corn, field-mice, rabbits and young partridges were scuttling, where already binding-machines joggled along, clogging the air with petrol vapour. In the little orchard, beyond the yew tree, thistles were seeding, and the thistle seeds and the white butterflies came floating about over everything, whilst cows coughed grassily, cats sneezed fishily, and all of this and more besides was being recorded on the air in sound and smell.

An immense vigour filled Ned as he listened and sniffed, and the thought came to him that even if everything else in his life were to crumble into ruins – which at present was very far from being the case – this early-morning rumour, countrified, fresh, and always a little different every day of the year, would still provide enough enjoyment to live for entirely of itself.

Whilst wriggling into his trousers, he kept looking about

for his belt, which he could nowhere see. At last he spied it, under the armchair, and stooping down, found also a small key. He placed the key on the dressing-table and started to put on his tie (grey linen matching his shirt material – a fashion at that time), and his mind returned to the train of thought it had been pursuing even before Reamur had come into his room.

As a young man he had been poor and had worked in London, teaching at a county council school. Although living in a houseful of students in Soho where things were far removed from the humdrum, he yet remembered how revolted he was at that time by the routine hours that are without inspiration in a day – those spent in buying stamps for letters, in filing receipts, in the dreary wuthering of machineries, in the changings from place to place – that had drowned all his courage. Life had manifested itself as a slow-moving lava of heavy cinders bearing down on the head. But now the fact had dawned on him, and he could hardly believe his good luck, that at last he had reached a time of life when that interminable grind embittered him no longer, when trivialities served merely as a measuring tape lying between one chosen project and the next.

For the first time in his life he felt a sense of permanent happiness.

This visit to his friends here at Flitchcombe. He had been here now three weeks. And in this household of old friends, during the whole month of July, what had happened? Merely flies had buzzed, there had been desultory chat, tedious walks – and work. Take, for instance, the day before, Tuesday. It had, of course, been the same as all other days at Flitchcombe.

It had started as usual with that farce the 'daily' housemaid, Doreen, all the business with the early-morning tea which everyone so disliked. Then had come breakfast with its letters, bills, circulars and catalogues. After breakfast Reamur, the host, had, as usual, locked himself into his study for the morning. Reamur's wife, Gwen, had put on her gum-boots and begun to plod round the fruit cages and hen houses with the gardener, and had also rummaged among those sheds in which were the electric-light engine, the an-thracite stove, the stored apples and the bicycles, and all the time giving orders to the 'man', Wilkes. Later she had walked down and given orders at the farm. (Both the farm and the Manor House were hers, for it was she who had the money, as well as all the 'interest' in the 'place'.)

Co-Co, the small son of the house, had finished his lessons with Ned Moon as usual at twelve-thirty and had gone to bounce a tennis ball on the back of the house until the lunch bell rang. Once the lesson was over one had begun to notice the flies. At ten minutes to one the postman had appeared bringing hundreds more catalogues. And certain cows, those that had lost their calves, on perceiving his red bicycle from afar, charged joyfully across the field in a bunch, imagining he was bringing back to them their stolen children. When they had realized their mistake, they had stood and trum-peted shrilly as usual for half an hour.

Then luncheon. And a massed rendezvous of flies!

During lunch the family had of course kept up a conver-sation, but each was in reality far away, absorbed in his own affairs.

After lunch the cows had suddenly begun to bellow again. The flies, however, had dropped off to sleep. Then coffee on the terrace, while the party had watched someone come out to the field and lead the cows away. There had followed the customary silence of two or three hours, during which the house-party went for its afternoon walks – not all together, but in shifts. When they got home again, and just before tea, they had seen the afternoon postman rounding the corner of the drive on his red bicycle, bringing a stack of London, but also country, catalogues, and attracting more galloping cows across the field.

Trumpeting of cows.

Then, after tea, homework for Co-Co. The study again for Reamur. While Gwen had taken one of the cars and dashed off to a rural committee meeting – something to do with the new bridge on the turnpike road – and afterwards had visited friends. During this last period Ned had been at last free to discuss with Aron – his chief friend and now his fellow partner – all their plans for the new school they had bought, and also to do some work on a chapter of his little botany book. After dinner, reading. And at last bed, with much discussion as to who would, and who would not, have a bath. Finally, Agatha Christie, owls, and the sounds, through the dark corridors, of gushing bath-taps behind locked doors, together with innumerable clickings and latchings of bedroom doors both near and far and ... sleep.

The day before that, on the Monday, the very same thing: cows, flies, catalogues, walks, lessons, discussions about the school plans with Aron, flies, cows, more catalogues ... And yet he had never enjoyed a visit here so much before.

He leant forward over the dressing-table, his head turned to the side, and gazing down with one eye into the looking-glass as a bird into water he began brushing the side of his greying temple with a brush.

'Tut! What a power over life one acquires in middle life to be sure!'

Ned slipped into his jacket. Again he stared into the glass absentmindedly, and for the fifth time that morning murmuring: 'A happy man!' he went downstairs to breakfast.

NED came into the dining-room and was greeted with silence. He said 'Good morning' to the couple seated there – and it was not answered.

He went over to the sideboard and surveyed the foods. Besides porridge and cereals three silver chafing dishes held haddock, kidneys, and scrambled eggs on long pieces of toast.

He helped himself to porridge, aware of the strange stillness in the room.

He poured out coffee and hot milk and then looked round at the breakfast-table.

Gwen sat at the head, quiet, poised over her haddock. On her right was the empty chair of her son Co-Co, which had been pushed roughly aside, a crumpled napkin lay beside it on the floor. Beyond that sat Ned's great friend Aron, who was also, incidentally, a cousin of Gwen's. The cousins were dark, handsome persons in their late thirties.

There was certainly something odd in the atmosphere. Ned concluded that they must be having a sort of tiff. He could tell from their faces.

If in Gwen's aspect there was something rigidly pinioned, if, there bent over her haddock, she was sitting sealed away, entombed, manacled, and in duress, if she appeared to glimmer palely through dark glutinous depths that bore heavily down on her and kept her jammed, this effect of being upon some private ocean floor and pressed upon by twilit miles was only the usual thing with her. Was in fact her *métier*.

What interested Ned was to find his friend Aron also, momentarily, in the same wedged condition.

Ned took up his porridge bowl and his coffee and, passing beside Gwen, sat down at the table. Gwen raised her eyes to him.

As one who, staring up through groundswell, water-blindness and refraction, guesses a seagull circling overhead – he saw her take him in.

'Good morning.'

'Good morning.'

Silence again.

Aron was plump and heavily built, swarthily dark, and with great black giglamps for eyes covered with horn spectacles even larger. Always stylish in the *ne plus ultra* of quietly miraculous tweeds, he was, above all, and because he had made himself such, a compact man.

If Gwen was a deep-sea turtle, swayingly imprisoned in striated shell, Aron was merely a sturdy land mole, hampered only by his *embonpoint*. A mole by figure, a mole in snug richness of apparel, and a mole in the strength and silence with which he constructed his formidable works.

Yet he loved to burst through from his labyrinths below, up into the air, at all available intervals, to sniff the breezes and to enjoy the day if possible – and, if not, at least to keep the surface of things on his visiting list. Not so Gwen.

Their cousinship lay in their swarthy colouring, not in the distance of the bases from which they operated – she from the weaving mirages of an ocean bed, he from so much closer to the ordinary humdrum.

Anxious though Ned was to understand what the conversation of these two had been about, he judged it best to remain silent. He ate his porridge without a word.

Suddenly Aron said, rapidly fluffing up the back of his hair:

'But, my dear Gwen, surely you don't imagine I up and

bought this school one fine morning and announced myself headmaster without Marina – well, without having thoroughly discussed the matter with my own wife!'

Gwen looked up.

'You imagine the arrangements were made without consulting her,' continued Aron, 'and that she will be amazed when she learns of the part she has to take ...! All the lessons she has to give; the beatings she has to administer ... You must think your young friend Marina has gone and married a madman, in that case!'

His voice had swollen to a grating tone.

Gwen began to struggle.

'No, Aron, I don't imagine my young friend is married to a madman at all. You know I think you, or rather I know you to be, an unusually able man, and a most original thinker ...' She sounded exhausted. 'I have the deepest respect for any school, any plan of yours.' She paused. 'A most original thinker ... And that is just *it*. Just the trouble. So original – but is originality so much required in every instance?'

'What on earth are you trying to say, Gwen? The question of originality is quite off the point! I'm trying to tell you that Marina has decided this: that apart from getting to know the boys in a private capacity, taking meals with them and so on, she will lead her own life entirely! Nothing more or less! You know she has the child Violet, my little stepdaughter, to look after; then her music to keep up, as you know – her own singing; and ... and so on, as I have just explained.'

'I know. I understand. My point merely being,' said Gwen, sinking deep into a gloom, 'that Marina may still have not fully taken in what her position will, *in fact*, turn out to be in this affair. I know you have both settled everything up "on paper", as it were: you are the headmaster and his wife, but you are going to be different. Yet how different *can* one be?

Has Marina been able to visualize her impact ... well, on the staff, shall we say, for instance? She can hardly cut them all dead, I suppose ...'

'Cut them all dead? Why should she cut them all dead?'

'But where is she going to draw the line? She is bound to be on friendly terms with them, of course. One can't fly in the face of simply everything. Let us see ... she will probably ask them to tea. And so on and so forth ... Well, it won't be long, for instance, before they all realize that she has a voice. That she sings. Very well! They will pester her to sing at the concerts without a doubt.'

'I hope they may.'

'She will sing at half-term concerts,' said Gwen in a hollow tone.

'Why not?'

Aron sighed, again fluffed up his hair rapidly behind his ears. He felt in his hip pocket, brought out a pipe, laid it on the table beside his plate. Putting his hand – which was oddly small and helpless looking – into his breast pocket, he produced some pigeon feathers – five or six – these he laid on the table in a semi-circle above the pipe, a kind of *aurora borealis*. After contemplating them for a moment, he gathered the pigeon feathers up again one by one and stuffed them back again into his breast pocket. His pipe went into the jacket pocket on his hip.

'You must forgive me,' he said, 'if I pretend to know a little about the running of a school after all these years at the game.'

'You must remember that our Aron is an educationist of some repute! His book on the subject is, I suppose you know dear Gwen, a household word,' interpolated Ned.

'I am not talking about *Aron*. I am talking about Marina. And about what kind of a headmistress she is going to make.'

'But I have explained that she will not be headmistress! Our house will not be in the grounds even!'

'I didn't mean headmistress. I am sorry. I meant to say, headmaster's wife. What sort of headmaster's wife?'

Aron sighed noisily, took a single pigeon's feather from his pocket this time, and, turning away, started to clean out his pipe.

Gwen bent again over her haddock plate. Slowly and deliberately she gathered and swept up together a bundle of the fish – pieces of flesh attached, or half attached, to bones. With fastidious care she disentangled completely, one by one, these bones from their white flesh, laying the bones on one side of her plate and fish flesh in a small heap on the other. Next she concentrated upon the grilled tomato. With a hovering unwillingness, her fork for some time hesitating reluctantly above the tomato fragments, she began to pile them on the top of the white fish flesh. After this, in due course, it became apparent that she was sprinkling the little tomato mound with drops of the milky juice in which the haddock had been stewed; this was slow work again on account of the difficulty of shifting the liquid with a knife and fork. Next, with a certain hesitation, she began dismantling the tiny heap, pausing to scrape, every so often, places on her plate where the milk had escaped and collected.

After a little Gwen spoke again.

'I feel I must draw your attention to the end-of-term tea parties. What of *them*?'

'Well, what of them?'

'There Marina will be surrounded by the parents.'

'Certainly.'

'Let us then imagine her walking down the herbaceous border with Mrs Simkins. Or Mrs Tomkins. Or Lord Pepperpot. Or Lady Decanter ... Well, Lady Decanter shall we say?'

'Lady Decanter, if you like.'

Gwen set aside her empty haddock plate. Stretching forward to a bowl which bore the name of a famous potter beneath, an article that had survived from a phase she had gone through three years before when every vessel in the house had been replaced with this type of heavy pottery, she opened up the white napkin in it and took out a hot scone.

'Now then: Lady Decanter's son has been very poorly of late.'

'I don't see why.'

Gwen looked searchingly at Aron.

'That's the trouble! He *has* been very poorly – yet nobody can see why!'

She stretched out for a china pot with a knob on its top representing a cupid, fussy and mean in a Dresden style. She helped herself, pondering, to honey and to butter, and continued:

'Marina will not have visited the boy in the sickroom. She won't know the first thing about him. His temperature or anything else. How should she know? But Lady Decanter will be appalled! She'll go back home and she'll tell Lord Pepperpot. She'll say, "That poor little mite was in the sickroom all those weeks and the headmaster's wife never once visited him!"'

'It won't be like that at all.'

'And, by the way,' said Gwen, looking anxious, 'have you heard from Marina yet what day she is going to arrive? I had half expected her yesterday.'

'I've heard nothing. She is a naughty girl.'

'I hope she will let us know in good time because of sending the car. If she were to come tomorrow evening I should arrange for the car to drop Co-Co at his music lesson over at Softon a little early, or, on the other hand, it *could* go later, and take Co-Co with it to the station to pick her up.'

'If she doesn't let us know in time she can't expect to be met. Don't dream of putting yourself out. She can well look after herself. She can take a taxi, can't she?'

'Oh no, she mustn't do that! Why we are fourteen miles from the station out here, you know.'

Ned let the conversation flow over him, he did not wish to be involved. He had helped himself to more hot scones after the kidneys, and to plenty of honey. This he followed up by a peach. At the end, after all of these things, he broke off a piece of Ryvita from a packet on the sideboard and thereafter spent all his attention attempting to pile on to it the shrimps which he had dug out, with the long-handled spoon supplied for the purpose, from a stone jar blurrily inscribed 'Morecambe Bay'. The shrimps kept tumbling off again, and scattering everywhere over the red and gold pattern on his plate.

Satisfaction filled him at this time of day. Not only at the good breakfast inside him, but at the scene in general, and he was loath to spoil it.

Breakfast conversation at Flitchcombe Manor varied very much, as was natural, from day to day. Often the prevailing mood was very sluggish, and the conversation quite a bore. Or sometimes some queer bug seemed to have bitten one of the party and a hostile element ran round the table, one person catching it from the next. Or it might be that everyone was in good spirits, laughing and boisterous, trying to shout each other down as at a large cocktail party. But in any case, and whatever the prevailing mood, Ned had always felt at this breakfast hour, and more especially during these last summer weeks at Flitchcombe, for he had been here all the holidays coaching the boy, a kind of bliss, a taking of everything, no matter what, in his stride. Every day he had congratulated himself at being so ensconced amongst these friends, these tried old favourites, and at having the fun of watching the facets of their several personalities striking sparks off one another as they revolved.

He had enjoyed also, particularly this year, the spectacle, outside the window, of the fruit trees, the lawns and the fields – also all at variance one with another under the changing morning skies. He had enjoyed, while drinking his coffee, the view from the window, even when it had been woebegone in drizzling dampness, or when it had seemed all metal, yet shifty and rebarbative under a northerly wind – his two least favourite kinds of weather. Today it was quiet, with early sunlight on the lawns.

By the sundial Ned caught sight of Co-Co bending over, calling aloud downwards, and brandishing his silver chain. At his feet, like pastry rolled out carelessly and burnt and blackened at both ends, lay Chadwick, the Siamese cat, washing its ears and refusing him attention.

Ned finished his shrimps, leant back and lighted a cigarette.

A cow started to bellow out in the fields, and buckets could be heard slapped down on to the cobbles behind the house.

Gwen and Aron had been quiet for a while; Gwen rustling the pages of the catalogues sent down from London, Aron smoking his pipe and pointing his nose first up at one corner of the ceiling and then at the other, as if looking for cobwebs, which meant that he was thinking.

The shouts of men sounded in the farm close by, across the squeaking of the hand pump over there. A tractor made its way across the hidden fields. Ned took up *The Times* and started the leading article. As he did so he began to feel the strongly turning wheels of his digestion travelling satisfactorily round and round. He was aware of something noble in the process, resembling a mighty bass accompaniment to some majestic concerto played deep within, sturdily, and with aplomb.

But through all of this, and through the article in *The Times* on which his eyes were directed, Ned's mind was occupied with thoughts of his own work; that work which he shared now with Aron – the new school which was about to spring into being.

As he read on down the newspaper column, these two embryos within him, his school and his digestion, began together to kick and quicken, and finishing the article in rather a hurry he rose from the table and went to the door. With his hand on the handle he turned, for he heard Gwen addressing him.

'And what do *you* think, Ned, about all of this?'

'All of what?'

'All this about Marina not joining in with the life at Oaklands. Is it feasible? Do you think that Marina herself has the required muscle for standing poised in such a pre-carious position – half in and half out of the coils? How do *you* judge her?'

'Well, I haven't even met her yet, Gwen!'

'Haven't–?'

'No! Don't you remember, I was still teaching in America when Aron got married last year? And when I returned Marina was in Switzerland with – with the child – what's her name? – Violet. At the sanatorium.'

(Aron had married a young woman still in her twenties, but already with a daughter, Violet, a little girl of eight.)

'Oh, how stupid of me! Of course! How extraordinary! Ah well, you will make each other's acquaintance before the week is out – I hope!'

Ned slid his hand over the door-knob and filtered unob-trusively from the room.

3

In the afternoon of the following day, whilst waiting for tea, Co-Co took his tennis ball to bounce it on the back of the house. The wall he threw the ball against was the school-room wall, inside which Ned Moon and Aron were sitting together at the round table covered with red felt.

Ned, in blue shirtsleeves (he had hung his coat on the back of the chair), was mending Co-Co's white linen box kite. Grasping the linen comfortably in his left fist, he dug with his right into the material with a darning needle and white thread. One had only to look at his large and articulate hands to see that they belonged to a sensitive and well-educated person, who, at the same time, felt at home in the world of physical things.

Aron, on the contrary, with his narrow helpless hands (unexpected on a man of his bulk) awkwardly plucking off papers from a pile beside him and pressing them one by one upon a jellygraph (they were some kind of rough syllabus to be used in connection with the new school), looked out of his element; he was pale, and concentrated, but in his mole-ish earthworks far away, and all these coarse machinations with the jellygraph seemed to be some sort of patent *tour de force* whereby the papers were being manipulated from a distance by remote control, not directly by him at all.

'What is so characteristic of our northern summers,' said Aron, who was looking out of the open garden doors, 'is just this dull, tepid weather when the upper airs are shut away by clouds; when cats and dogs and human beings, and even hens, hide themselves out of sight; when all day long no living sound is heard, and deadness lies on the land like a stifling eiderdown.'

'Yes,' answered Ned. 'Deadness, as you say.'

Aron put another paper on to the jelly and smoothed it awkwardly.

'I am English enough to like it,' he said. 'But just look at it out there now!'

They both looked through the garden doors at the end of the schoolroom.

On the lawn outside stood an ugly summerhouse of creosoted planks, intended for the children. Co-Co had an elder brother, away at school, and this part of the garden was kept for them. Beyond it, enclosing an orchard, ran a wire fence half shrouded in mangy nettles. A starling perched on the fence.

Summerhouse, nettles, wire fence and starling, all looked dull and dispirited. And the clouds overhead seemed bored. Too bored and heavy to move away again.

'*I* am English enough to like it all too,' said Ned. 'I was just reflecting upon all the grey days, drowsy and tepid and boring, just like this, that I have spent here these last three weeks tutoring Co-Co. And how I have felt myself to be an egg stifled under the weight of this dowdy, great, bourgeois, grey mother hen of an English July. Yes ... I have been enabled to remain happily hatching out my plans here, quite undisturbed by anything from outside that wriggles, squawks, or prowls.'

Both heads bent over their work again. Ned's face, ruddy and English, was roughly pitted, showed hairs (shaved that morning but coming through again), and sweat. Aron's bent down over his jellygraph, was olive-smooth, cool and intellectual.

Ned got up and walked over to stand in the garden doorway. From there he could see grey-trousered legs, and the front half of a deck-chair protruding amongst the trunks of the apple trees in the orchard. It was Reamur. Beside him, on the grass, could be seen piles of books. Even from here the strips of paper flowing out at all angles from them were visible, which Ned knew to be crowded with pencil jottings.

'The first time this afternoon I noticed Reamur's legs they were quite close here you know – beside the door. Next time I looked they were farther away, behind the yew tree. Only five minutes ago, when Co-Co went out with his ball, I could see them glimmering inside the summerhouse. But now, look, there they are at the far end of the orchard! Really, life with our friend Reamur is a long game of "grandmother's steps" in reverse. Every time one looks at Reamur he is a step further away.'

'Yes,' answered Aron. 'With all this occultation he must be near to vanishing point. Any day now I'm afraid it will be *spurlos versenek.*'

From the sash window in the side wall came the voice of Gwen, who had been for the last ten minutes haranguing somebody outside there, in the queer, hollow and courtly tone she had adopted for her own. It fell with a numb sound upon the leaden afternoon.

'... One can hardly over-estimate the importance of a semi-circle;' came the voice. 'At the top of some steep acclivity. At the top of a *slope*, I should say, perhaps. A crescent formation ensures that all – *all!* can get a good view. They like to see the world. They like the sun. And the fresh air of course. But chiefly to *see*. To see each other. To see the view. To know what is going forward all about them. A width of outlook ... people simply don't realise ...'

'Who is she talking to?' asked Aron.

Ned took a few steps out of doors on to the grass, from where he could see round the corner of the house to the farm footpath, whence proceeded the voice. Gwen stood there in loud purple tweeds and a lad of about fourteen stood facing her. He had a wide heliotrope cap resting on the tips of his ears and was clasping a basket of red fruit against his stomach.

'Garden boy, I think.'

'What on earth is it all about?'

Aron put his jellygraph tin on one side and started to unfurl a large roll of tracing paper with an architect's plan in pencil upon it. 'She is putting him into touch with the contemporary trends of his time in art, I suppose. Or else politics.'

Ned stood on the grass watching for a few moments.

Gwen, facing the youth with the heliotrope cap, stood with her arms held forth like a swimmer, palm to palm. As Ned watched, she raised them higher. And again higher; till they were above her head. It struck him, then, that any stranger seeing Gwen there in that posture with the words pouring so monotonously out of her mouth would take her to be in a trance, by something exalted and psychic possessed.

He called back softly to Aron, 'She may be describing her trip to Brighton. It's all about crescents. Or perhaps expounding to him about model cities, and all that . . .'

'Health. And not merely of the body,' came the voice. 'Happiness! The glandular tissues, everything, responds to it. Very well then. Let us make a résumé of it all: a crescent-shaped formation; self-respect, above all a *good* view . . . and of course a very wide mesh of netting. Why, rabbit pie can be every *bit* as good as chicken if things are properly managed.'

Silence.

Ned came softly back into the schoolroom again.

'Why, I believe it was about the new rabbit hutches.'

He went back to the table. He stood looking down at the kite. The cows started trumpeting on a high, hysterical note in the field.

'I saw the postman rounding the bend. Bringing more seed

catalogues, no doubt. That means it is tea-time. Oh, devil take this safety-pin! It must be rusty. I have tried to pull it through the kite fabric but it will *not* budge.'

'Leave it in. It won't hurt.'

But Ned sat down and began again wrenching at the pin.

'Oh, those wretched cows! Why *must* they?'

Aron rummaged amongst the papers on the table and took out a packet of carbon papers.

All of a sudden the flies on the window-pane woke up and started to rage together with a venomous zizzing. One amongst them began to boom deafeningly and to throw its scaly body repeatedly against the glass. Others, too, began to boom in the same echoing manner, and soon all of them together were hurling their scaly bodies against the pane. One could imagine that packets of tintacks were being showered again and again at the glass.

Meanwhile, Gwen's voice had risen up on to the air again and flowed on and on and on.

Aron now, dropping his rolls of paper, tiptoed to the window and with great caution slid up the sash. Hiding behind the curtain, he listened to what was going on, and peeped round cautiously to see what was happening out there.

Gwen still faced the gardener's boy with his basket of fruit against his chest. '... you invariably go to the Geisha Café and order a couple of poached eggs on toast!' she was saying reproachfully.

Ned called out from the table. 'After tea, Aron, we positively must go through that mountain of correspondence on my chest of drawers upstairs.'

'Yes.' Aron left the window and came back into the room. 'I'd like to polish it off one day before my wife arrives. For afterwards it may be more difficult to find the time. She is bringing the child, you know, Violet, and the whole house will be upside down, if I know anything about it, by the time Vi and Co-Co get together.'

'Oh dear. Ah well, I have already answered every letter in that lot! Only I would not post them before they were passed by you. I kept everything here to await your arrival as I knew you wouldn't want to bother with it in London, what with Marina's return from Switzerland, and so on. I am hoping you will not be offended at my criticisms on the letter you composed to the headmaster of our rival establishment at Upper Oakley ... I have had to cross three-quarters of your letter out.'

'What!'

'I can explain more easily when we come to it. There's tea.'

The tea bell had rung. And immediately Co-Co's tennis ball stopped, and there followed a shrill yapping-yodelling sound, evidently some kind of comic interlude.

Gwen walked in at the garden door. The effect of the conventional black waves, hard, glossy and smug-looking, of her rather provincial hair style, was cancelled out by the face beneath, which betrayed someone lost and anxiously uncertain.

She stood by the table sorting over some letters in her hand. Then she looked up at Aron.

'What are we going to do about meeting Marina tomorrow if we hear nothing? No news of her by this afternoon's post again! Yet she certainly said she was crossing on the twenty-third; and that is tomorrow. You see, the trouble is, if she *wasn't* coming on the twenty-third we could have sent Co-Co in by car to the skating rink at Malton ...'

She was on edge and trying not to betray it. Yet she fixed Aron with such a sharp eye that he felt nervous.

'It is very naughty of her. I do apologize for my wife's behaviour.'

'Oh, it doesn't *matter* at all. It is only that we are such a long way from the station that, as I say, I shouldn't like her to find herself there with no one to bring her out. It's a good fourteen miles.'

'She can well look after herself.'

'Yes, but *Violet* will be so tired. After the long journey the night before.'

'Don't give them a thought. They can perfectly well come out by taxi.'

Gwen had now taken a seat on a painted Norwegian stool between the geography globe and the piano.

'Was that the tea bell?' asked Ned.

'Yes, and I must go and wash.'

But she didn't go and wash. She sat still on the stool. Ned, glancing at her, saw that her face was masked, every muscle engaged in pulling her personality warily inwards and backwards into herself again.

'I suppose one is much to blame,' she said, in a low tone, after a moment, 'that still, after all these years, one so completely fails to find the key ... with all these people.'

They both looked up at this and noticed her troubled flush.

'What people?' Aron asked her. 'The gardener's boy, you mean?'

'Him. *And* all the others. I've had a most unpleasant scene with the girls in the kitchen, and with that stick Wilkes. They none of them have any glimmering of the kind of world they live in.' She checked herself. 'I know it's not their fault. They haven't had the opportunity. But they're completely uninterested when those who *have* had opportunities attempt to show them things ... Well, frankly, they're furious.'

Ned pinched his nose several times in order not to have to answer.

'Perhaps one should be like everybody else,' Gwen continued. 'Simply tell them: "Do this! Do that! Light the fire in the sitting-room! Lay the table! Make the bed! Then on your day off you can go and see the latest Hollywood crooner at the Majestic, followed by pastries and poached eggs at the Geisha Café ..." But it's all wrong! Can *nobody* help them?'

'Well, the borough councils are arranging these cultural cinemas and lectures we've been reading of,' said Aron, to tease her.

Gwen's face grew stormy.

'Oh yes, that's a very good idea,' she said, as if from a tomb. 'But I don't agree with Plato about state nurseries – for whatever age. County council houses are quite enough. We don't want county council souls as well.'

Aron put down his papers and, pushing back his chair from the table, leant back, smiling and waving round in the air his horn spectacles. His bulk, his well-kept head of jetty, luxuriant hair, his expensive tweeds (which today were caramel, adorned with a bloomy petunia in the buttonhole) – all this debonair amplitude gave him a buoyant air, which set his cousin at a disadvantage.

For Gwen, on the contrary, was giving forth an impression of being tangled, dejected and wet. All the more so for the way her own, reckless-looking clothes (clothes so brand new that one expected to see the price ticket at the back of the neck) stood up in the world – defiantly jolly and, as it were, apart from her. For the last year she had engaged in mortal combat, so to speak, in the matter of dress, with Jauntiness, investing in racy, staring sulphurs, insolent cherries and piercing copper-verdigris. Yet these ribald clothes merely seemed to show up all the more her own personal, sub-merged quality.

'But what happened in the kitchen?' asked Ned.

'I tried to give them all some idea of what the new art society at Malton is trying to do. For instance, to tell them of this new movement in sculpture of which there is a demonstration now on view in the Malton Galleries.'

'My hat!' said Aron, and put his spectacles back on his nose.

'I offered to send them all in the car and treat them to tea afterwards, if only they would visit the society's exhibition,' added Gwen.

'How did they take it?'

'Oh, they stared. You could have heard a pin drop. Not one of them would give a straight answer about going in the car on Friday to the gallery exhibition.'

Ned began pinching his nose again.

'In order to ... in order to interest them in the exhibition I endeavoured to show them some photographs. Quite suddenly the kitchen maid – who was at the sink – seemed to disintegrate. She dashed the Spode cake-plate on to the brick floor with a high yelp, breaking it into just about a hundred pieces. So that was that.'

'Oh, good God!'

'Yes. So what do you think?'

'You did your best, Gwen,' murmured Aron. He rose from his chair and started tidying up the pens, carbons and odd papers scattered about.

'If they are not up to it it is not your fault. But the plate is a catastrophe. However, I think Ned can mend that for you so it doesn't show. He works miracles in that line.'

Aron was now rubbing his carbon-stained fingers with a crumpled yellow silk Paisley handkerchief and looking at Gwen owlishly over the tops of his horn spectacles.

'You're looking a little bit guilty, Gwen,' said Aron. 'I wonder why?'

Gwen pondered a moment.

'I have to admit I *am* feeling guilty,' she muttered at last. 'I haven't told you quite everything. Unhappily I ...' Her voice faded. She began again with an effort. 'My attitude was hectoring! Yes, it really was hectoring. In the end I *forced* them to look at the photographs. They tried to cast me off, poor things – laughed insultingly and broke plates in order to free themselves. But I fixed my corroding eye upon them, and I could see them shrinking beneath my juggernaut chariot wheels ...'

Ned laughed.

'And,' she added, 'funnily enough, I know that I don't really feel, and didn't even *at the time* feel, that what I was telling them was any of it true! But it is true ...! I feel so harassed. Something tells me that it is all a frame-up! It was *not* a frame-up.'

She leant forward, picked up a tail of yellow wool from the floor, and began winding it into a miniature yellow drum, which, when neat enough, she placed on the rim of the geography globe.

Then she nervously undid her jacket. 'I'm really so bothered and distracted,' she said. 'My attitude, and my opinions, and even my conscience – most of all my conscience, – but, anyway, the whole machinery of my personality has gone so askew. I can't seem to remedy it.'

She walked over to the french windows; halfway across the threshold she stopped.

'My clothes aren't right either. Look at this infernal coat and skirt. It's wrong. I know quite well I look like a bedraggled old cat that's been dressed up to have its photograph taken. And you see it's the same trouble everywhere. All over the house. It suddenly dawned on me yesterday that every room is an experiment that has failed! And outside the house too.'

Stepping out on to the grass she regarded the roof for a few moments. When she spoke again her voice had grown dreamy.

'This house was, when we built it, I remember, to be the very latest thing out. I think it was taken from a Gold Coast city. Then, at the last moment, I idiotically insisted on clapping on this fussy thatched roof, in spite of all the architect said, because I'd read an article about thatching being the best system of controlling the temperature, which I'm much afraid really does cancel the effect out just as he said it would ... But, worst thing of all, I carry at the back all the time this inexplicable sensation of guilt ... *Why?* What is it all about?'

A small boy, thin and dark, wearing a polo sweater, landed abruptly on the grass outside the garden doorway beside Gwen, as if shot from an air-gun.

'Why on *earth* don't you come and have tea? You are horrible, *really*. You know perfectly well how the tea spoils standing there hour after hour, and everything is getting absolutely *ruined*!'

'Don't roar at her, Co-Co!' said Ned. 'You're not a tiger, I hope.'

'Will you come and have tea!'

Seeing the boy's mother bemused and at a loss, Ned spoke again.

'Co-Co, go back and wait for us quietly, please.'

Ned's voice, always soft and deprecatory – almost private – nevertheless had an effect . The child, red with passion, shot out of sight again.

Gwen started to walk slowly off after him. She stopped. 'My very face has gone wrong. It doesn't belong to me. Nor, of course, my hair style. You know I think *that* is really the trouble – I simply can't make all these things *belong* to me the way other people do. When I look in the glass I think of what Groucho Marx said to the lady he met in the restaurant: "Your face reminds me of you. Your neck reminds me of you. Every little thing about you reminds me of you –

excepting *you*!" Well, everything about me rather reminds me of me, but never *me*.'

Ned and Aron, still sitting at the table, meditated this.

The fact was that her strange struggle, to both their knowledge, had continued without pause for the last fifteen years. Ned felt that there was some kind of a glorying, incantatory routine about her processes of thought; it was as if she were not so much simply struggling up through dark waters towards the light, as glumly and gleefully performing fishy rites, in some octopoid saraband of a tribal kind, in which she alternately welcomed, then exorcized, then welcomed again, some fascinating brindled and bridling Kraken which was to mere surface eyes invisible.

In Ned's case it was for precisely that – for Gwen's absorbed abandonment to the marine drama of it all, for all the phosphorescent humours perpetually licking up and down her sides, that he had chosen her, long ago, for a friend. And these things were congenial to him today as they had been in the beginning, and he couldn't picture her changed.

She was looking toward them for an answer, though. What could they say?

'It's your conscience, Gwen,' said Aron. 'It's putting too great a strain upon you.'

'How do you mean?'

'Don't you keep a bigger conscience than you can afford? *Your* conscience, Gwen, is a miraculous machine, doing overtime, never resting, reaching conclusions, exacting loyalties and demanding obediences which are perfectly independent of your nature as a whole–'

A thin wailing sounded upon the air outside the garden door. It was obviously Co-Co wailing for his tea.

'What I mean is, don't you set yourself tasks that your nature is quite uninterested in achieving, Gwen?' finished Aron.

Gwen's expression relaxed, as if she might be rather pleased with Aron's notion.

'All the same, I don't quite see. How am I to tell what *is* my nature?'

'I don't know, Gwen. Somehow one has to acquire a sense of conviction, I suppose. It is certainly not an easy trick. Don't ask me how it's done.'

'I'm lacking in conviction!' Gwen repeated. 'I believe you're right!' Her face cleared.

He has given her a delicious tit-bit for her precious Kraken! thought Ned.

'*Will you come and begin your tea!*' wailed Co-Co's voice in the distance. He was evidently leaning out of the drawing-room window round the corner of the house.

'Oh yes, we really must,' said Ned, jumping up. 'Poor Co-Co will cut his throat with the bread knife if we don't go.'

'Or ours,' said Aron, jumping up.

Ned stepped out of the schoolroom on to the grass, and taking Gwen's arm drew her away and round the corner of the house. Aron followed.

4

THE next day, Friday, was the same as all the others. Cows, flies, tennis balls, catalogues, meals and walks.

At one o'clock the schoolroom door opened. It revealed the 'man', Wilkes, standing there stiffly, with his scornful stare directed at Ned, who was alone.

'Luncheon is served, sir.'

'Thank you.'

The man disappeared again, shutting the door noisily behind him.

In the dining-room only the tall manservant stood, silent, like a poker, by the sideboard. Through the window, thrown open to the rose garden, Co-Co was to be seen balancing on the base of the sundial.

Ned sat down on the window-seat and putting his head out of the window called to Co-Co.

'Luncheon!'

'*I* know!'

Co-Co gave a heave backwards off the ledge, his legs landed bent and wide apart on the grass in the same position in which they had just been straddled round the pillar of the sundial.

'Are you all ready? Hands washed? Hair brushed and everything?'

'*Of course.* What do you suppose?'

'All right. Come along.'

Co-Co sauntered across the grass to the side door. In his grey flannel jacket his arms, as he strolled, dangled loosely and as it were hopelessly, that is to say Co-Co intended to convey by them that he had given up hope and faith. By this, and by the way in which he held his nose scornfully in the air and looked down it towards the tip, he expressed his ennui at his tutor's footling question.

Ned withdrew his head. He and the serving-man were waiting for the others to come in for luncheon.

A fly was buzzing languidly on one corner of the window-pane. It was hot, yet there was still the same grey ceiling of cloud over the countryside. In the surrounding fields and woods, and in the garden itself, not a leaf flickered. Heat and stillness. The fly stopped buzzing. Then the dining-room and the outdoor world beyond, everything, seemed plunged together into the bottom of a well of stifling inertia and vacuum.

Wilkes stood motionless at the sideboard. Ned on the

window-seat would not look at him, for he feared his malicious staring. He leant back against the panes, looking obliquely out.

All the time, in spite of the so-called dull weather, there was no mistaking how the fierce and savage glare of summertime dominated everything. From somewhere high up beyond the veil of moving clouds it came, with its mighty radiance killing the small furniture of the earth – cottages, the railway bridges, the trees, the cows – and all these things Ned felt showed up as dead; dead, and also buried, in its might; so many dark and petty knots of material heaviness untidying the incandescence of summer in the air.

The great glare was inside the dining-room, too. It stared rudely upon the mahogany chair-legs and the grained sideboard; at the knives, spoons and forks, at the wood panels on the wall with the whorls of dust in their beading, and on the recently polished fire-irons, denuding all these things of mystery, showing them up as lifeless, senseless sticks and stones, and increasing Ned's sense that everything vital and pure was without body and all the rest heavy clay.

In the silent dining-room he began to feel disturbed by the cumbrous machinery round him; fire-irons, lamp-standards, chairs, tables, the wine bin, footstools; everything clutched and clattered at Ned's senses and he knew himself powerless in their grip.

Then something familiar began its attack: it was as if a hidden catastrophe was in the process of materializing and impregnating the air. An ill wind was blowing through the room. A dreadful reality, blanched and purposefully long forgotten, was imposing its livid snow-glare through the artificial lighting of this pantomime set. Five minutes before he had been surrounded by props: tables, footstools, lamps and chairs – and the illusion had been complete. Now things were making themselves clearer, stepping up closer, as inexplicit as a nightmare and as convincing as the waking up. First he began to understand that he was surrounded by something merely gimcrack, something accepted as a temporally useful way of viewing things, and then afterwards he knew where he really was. This substance walling him, this adamant tomb, this dining-room, what was it but that formidable prison cell the present moment? That gaol where each finds himself locked without reprieve for evermore?

In that moment, sitting on the window-seat, Ned knew himself to be looking from the cell of his gaol at its few accoutrements – at the straw pallet, bucket, and wash bowl – alternatively the lamp-standards, fire-irons, and chairs.

A step crossed the threshold. He looked up. Gwen had come in.

After her followed Aron; there was a pause, and then Co-Co made an explosive entrance, all flapping hands and grimaces, in the rear.

They all sat down.

Co-Co took his place on the opposite side from Ned, and at once fell into his customary meal-time reverie, somewhere far out of reach of the grown-up animals around.

And today, again, they all went through luncheon as they had gone through it every day for the last fortnight. They talked of the plans for the day, they gossiped, they referred to something they had read in the papers, and this finally turned into an argument. And under the talk, as usual, each was occupied with his private affairs. Through Ned's head ceaselessly revolved thoughts of the new school. Gwen was centred at heaven knows what point in her domestic and emotional web; while Aron was evidently thinking of his wife, for at times he would break into the talk: 'Gwen, I really think I had better order a taxi to meet Marina and Vi. I'm sure they will arrive tonight on the eight-fifteen. Something tells me they will come by that.'

'If you like,' Gwen would reply. Once she said, 'But Reamur is trying to catch Marina up in London, that was his latest plan, you know. They may easily come back with him in the car.'

'Oh ... well. Then I don't quite know what to do.'

Ned, who had found cold salmon waiting for him on his plate, took a spoonful of miniature new potatoes scattered with parsley from the dish handed to him by the scornful 'man'. Afterwards he helped himself to the somewhat globulated mayonnaise which stood in a white sauce-boat with a dark-blue rim in front of him. Later again, a salad bowl came round with a branching green leaf in it like tiny stags' horns, glistening in oil.

Co-Co sat on his chair twisted sideways away from his mother and Ned. Not only was his plate pushed on one side, away from them, but he kept his face resolutely turned sideways, in the direction of the garden, as he shovelled each mouthful in. He looked angry and was making a plain point of refusing their companionship.

At last he broke out: 'Oh, good heavens, *can't* I go roller-skating on the pier Kursaal this afternoon? Just for *once* in a way? How on earth am I to get up to competition standard if I only go on Saturdays?'

'You can make up later on when Ned goes home and you haven't so many lessons.'

'But the regatta competition is in three weeks' time, I tell you, you fool! And James is coming home specially to skate with me in it!'

James was an older friend of Co-Co's who lived close by, but who was at present at a cramming establishment in Somerset.

'James is not coming home, I'm afraid. He happens to be in quarantine.'

'He's not!'

'Now, Co-Co' – Gwen leant forward and whispered low – 'remember what I said.'

Co-Co whizzed round on his chair away from her with violence.

'Sit round on your chair properly!'

But it was evident that Co-Co would not retire from his position. His emotion was as usual too heavy for such instructions to register.

Ned put out his hand to his glass of cider. As he sipped it he studied Co-Co. He still had, it seemed, gaols and gaolbirds on the brain, for he said in a low voice:

'To be imprisoned to that extent in the present emotion is my definition of hell! I thank God I am, at any rate, no longer a little boy!'

On hearing a definition of hell, Gwen was all attention, and steered herself immediately on to the field.

'Perhaps it is only hell if you have nowhere you want to escape to,' she said. 'For is not unhappiness being without a sense of direction?'

'Yes, but to be a child is to be always at the bottom of the valley. Always the frog in the gorge. Without a hope of seeing the lie of the land outside. Not even dreaming that there *is* any other place but that one dark cleft at the bottom of which he himself scrabbles around panting.'

Wilkes started collecting up the dirty plates. He leant down beside each person slowly and waited a moment before removing his plate, as if he were casting an evil spell.

'To be imprisoned in the present moment ...' said Gwen, half startling Ned with this echo of his former thought. 'Yes, it's true.'

She regarded Co-Co from her end of the table. 'And how plainly one can *see* that prison, deep in the architecture of the prisoner himself.'

It was because Co-Co in his rage had completely cut himself off from them, not hearing what they said, that they were able to discuss him in front of his face.

'Gwen, are you saying that you think of your son as separate from his desire?' enquired Aron, 'and merely attached to it by some machinery – bolts, bars, and what not? Surely a person's desires are a part of his personality? Why should you seek to separate the desirer from his feeling of desire?'

'Well, you're going to make a very peculiar kind of schoolmaster if you don't,' said Gwen; and added after a moment: 'I think I think of a person as being divided into any number of parts, but chiefly as being divided into two parts: the experiencer and the experienced. And I think of the experiencer as being very decidedly imprisoned by the experience! Whether the experience come in the form of a desire, a moment in time, as Ned says, or whatever.'

'What's the pudding?' cried Co-Co, in a loud voice.

'Hush!'

'But I ask you *what is the pudding*?'

'Apple fritters.'

'I agree with you to this extent, Gwen,' said Aron: 'I think Co-Co is different from, because larger than, this desire which grips him. *He* is *larger*, but *it* is *stronger*. In fact, it alters him. That's the point.'

'Yes, in fact he's rather like some large animal – a horse or mule – being eaten by a boa constrictor,' sad Ned huskily. 'First the bones are crushed to jelly and then – my God, he can't escape!'

'Oh, stop it. You're spoiling my appetite. I never heard such a conversation!' protested Aron, helping himself optimistically to butter and a digestive biscuit from a wooden platter in front of him.

But Gwen and Ned seemed to have found a congenial vein. 'And the sinister thing is this,' said Gwen: 'where *one* python desire comes out to grip and feed, others steal up from nowhere and join the feast. Here Co-Co's desire has been thwarted, yet, maddened, it grips him still, whilst other desires all come snaking up to join the fray – desires to escape from us, to get even with us, to smash us all up, to get power for the snakes at all costs, until he becomes a regular wriggling Laocoon writhing there in hundreds at the last.'

' "Wriggling and writhing and fainting in coils",' assented Ned.

Gwen here turned round to the 'man', Wilkes.

'Has the plumber been given something to eat?'

There was silence.

'I really couldn't say, madam.'

It was as if she had asked him if he had washed his ears properly that morning, he sounded so affronted.

'That was his motor-cycle I saw out in the yard, I suppose?'

Again silence.

Gwen repeated her question.

'I really couldn't say, madam.'

'Lily tells me it has broken down.'

The man turned about and stared hard at her. But he said nothing, and turning his back again abruptly started rattling the cutlery on the sideboard.

'Well, if the poor man's motor-cycle has broken down …'

'I presume he can mend it.'

The 'man' wore a linen jacket striped finely with mauve, like the flower of the asphodel. The back of it expressed outrage, as he stood piling up plates.

There was an uncomfortable silence.

Ned poured himself out some beer and said, smiling, 'Aron and I are going to give classes in plumbing when we get our school started.'

'Indeed?'

'Yes. We shall have a demonstration cloakroom with a lavatory and wash-basin and a nest of pipes in the corner in which the visiting plumber can give the boys weekly classes. I've always thought life is insupportable when one is helpless just because a pipe leaks.'

'That sounds to me a most sensible idea.'

There now followed a prolonged wait while the 'man' stood beside the hatch with nothing happening. Then he left the dining-room.

'I think it's only because he's so deaf that he sometimes answers oddly,' said Gwen, a shade paler. 'It gives him a sinister air. But I think it's really only that, *being* so deaf, he's a little out of touch with things.'

Aron laughed and fluffed up his hair rapidly.

'Out of touch. I don't know about that!' he said. 'At any rate if looks could kill I wouldn't answer for the consequences.'

A little later the 'man' came back into the room and stood stiffly beside Gwen at the head of the table. There was an anxious silence.

'Madam, there will be no pudding,' at last he said.

Gwen looked up at him enquiringly into his black, malicious eyes.

'There's an upset in there,' he said.

Gwen hesitated. 'Oh … perhaps I'd better go and see.' She got up and went out of the room. The 'man' followed her.

'*No pudding! Why* is there no pudding?' Co-Co shouted. He had been stunned on first hearing the news but had come to again. From his heavy voice and passionate face it was evident that he took the news as a personal humiliation and wanted to pay back the insult with violence.

'It's this awful business of the cook's cousin,' said Aron.

'What business?'

'Oh, good lord, haven't you heard?' Aron glanced at Co-Co. '*Le chef de police a visité la cousine.*' He jerked his head towards the hatch, '*Ce matin il lui a posé des questions*

...regardant ce qu'on a trouvé dans le jardin, cette affaire du four ... enfin! No, no, it's really *not* a lunch-time subject.'

But Co-Co was over beside the open hatch standing on tiptoe and trying to see what was taking place in the kitchen.

'Something that was found in the garden of the cook's cousin?' Ned murmured.

'Cet enfant mort qui était brûle dans le four ou fond du jardin.'

'*What?* Good God!'

Co-Co ran out of the room to investigate the problem of the pudding more fully. Ned leant out of his chair and called out:

'Co-Co! *Co-Co!* Don't go and worry them in the kitchen, Co-Co!'

But Co-Co did not return.

'But what did you say – a burnt baby in the incinerator?' Ned raised his hand as if to ward off a blow.

'Yes.'

'Whose?'

'The story is that a month or two ago the neighbours began to get very excited ...'

'Oh, but I don't wish to hear! I'm sure it's all lies ... What do you say?'

'There was a wagging of tongues, everyone whispering in corners, because Mrs Haste – that's the cook's cousin's name, – had obviously been huge with child for months but had suddenly reappeared one day completely slim again, yet having said never a word to anyone. Making out in fact that nothing had happened.'

'A bastard, I suppose?'

'That was what everyone began saying. That the baby had been by the man from the radio shop at Malton, they said. But what had become of it? Then some nosy parker discovered this dead baby in the incinerator at the end of the Hastes' garden.'

'Oh no! no! no! no!'

'And now, this very morning, the village policeman came up here on his bicycle to "make inquiries". After Mrs Haste had told him her story, he came on here and talked to Gwen's cook. The cousin, that is. It seems they're going to charge Mrs Haste.'

'And what was Mrs Haste's own story?'

'Her story was that it was true she had produced a still-born infant. Had a miscarriage, in fact, but that the child was by her own husband. She gave an agonizing account ... apparently it had all happened on the stairs ... Having no idea that a still-born birth should be registered she said nothing and finally they got rid of the body in the incinerator. She said that she thought that as it had been born dead it was nobody's official business.'

'These things do appear so very private. At the time.'

'Poor devils. And now her cousin, here, the cook, can't get over the disgrace to the family and keeps falling down among the saucepans every half-hour. That is why there is no pudding, of course.'

'We shan't get any more meals this week, by the look of things.' Ned covered his eyes. 'But on the stairs! Hideous! And having to answer to her husband about the whole question. Wretched man. Poor devils.'

Ned, in his snug retreat, regretted a window having been forced open like this, letting in suddenly all the racket, the foul fumes and the screeched curses of a thoroughfare he knew to be locked from end to end in one excruciating traffic-jam.

I've finished with all that sort of thing, he told himself, once and for all, thank God. Thank God. He rose to his feet.

'Let's change the subject,' he said.

The two friends left the dining-room and wandered off on to the terrace to wait for coffee.

5

NEXT day, though there were several hours of fitful sun in the earlier part of the morning, by lunch-time the wind had brought a covering of clouds again over the sky, in a series of billowing ridges. These banks of grey-rimmed clouds were high overhead, however, and in between them blue sky still showed at intervals.

It was hot and chilly by turns. Ned didn't like all this changeableness, and when it came to after-luncheon coffee begged Gwen to dispense it not on the terrace, as usual, but in the drawing-room.

Ned put down his coffee suddenly, half-way through his cup.

'My gold pencil! I quite forgot. I must go and find it. I must have left it somewhere on the cliff-top during yesterday's walk. I shall have to go up to the ledges again this afternoon and look for it. Yesterday I laid down up there and had a snooze. It must have tumbled out, for the clip is loose.'

'I shall go up to the ledges with you if you'll let me,' said Aron.

'And may I come too?' asked Gwen. 'But do you mind stopping at the village shop on the way? I want some rusks, and a new wick for the little stove. Afterwards I can walk on to the meeting in Fosditch.'

In the end Co-Co also accompanied them. Reamur, however, went upstairs to his study to work.

So, after a long delay, while Co-Co chased over the house

looking for his dry pair of shoes, and with also one or two retracings of the steps back into the house for walking-sticks and forgotten shopping lists, they all four set off at last up the steep laurel-bounded drive. Flitchcombe house lay below the roadway, in a hollow.

Co-Co went capering up the hill ahead.

The drive wound round about in the shrubberies several times before it reached the lodge gates. (The lodge was 'let off' to this unfortunate Haste family, whose incinerator at the bottom of the garden had caused so much trouble in the village.)

Aron stepped ahead and opened the tall iron gates on to the road. Gwen went through the gates, and as Ned followed her he glanced furtively at the windows of the little grey-stone lodge with its Gothic windows.

There were no signs of life about the house, and nobody in its untidy, weedy garden. Only on the window-sill of the living-room, a long cat, white with tortoise-shell markings, lay asleep. The cat shared the window-sill with three or four ripening tomatoes and a vase of marguerites.

At the creaking of the heavy iron gate the cat opened its yellow eyes and stared into Ned's face. It opened its mouth, but no sound could be heard. When it shut its mouth again, Ned saw what an ugly face it had, with small eyes too close together, and a long, bulbous yet flattened nose, and dreary spinsterish expression.

Co-Co had gone crashing through the belt of nettles that crowded beside the boundary wall here, and had clambered up on to the wall itself, from which he took a flying leap on to the road.

They all met upon the tarmac and turned to the left.

Up here on the main road could be seen the sea, a silver gleam under the dark clouds.

They had not taken a few steps before the wind from the

bay struck at them. It hissed in the tops of the trees with the loudness of racing pebbles on a beach.

Almost immediately however the road dipped down again into another little valley, at the bottom of which they would find Flitchcombe village; and Ned was relieved to escape down into the quiet again, away from the hissing in the trees and their slapping, whipping scarves against their cheeks.

Co-Co pranced down the hill with uneven gait, stopping often to examine moles or frogs that had been flattened by motorists upon the surface of the road, and also to pick up old cigarette boxes and other things.

Aron, Gwen and Ned followed some twenty yards behind, walking three abreast; Ned keeping a little apart from the other two and not attending to their conversation. The fact was that Marina had sent a letter that morning informing Aron of her arrival that very night, after dinner. And since that moment, Ned, without realizing it, had adopted a defensive position towards Aron in view of the approaching arrival of his wife.

His close intimacy with his friend was about to be in some degree severed; and, from pride, he preferred to withdraw himself into isolation first, of his own accord, rather than cling to his friend till the last second, only to be shaken off in favour of the newcomer.

The grass verge beside the road was crowded out with a jungle of tall green stalks bearing masses of soiled-looking white flowers; and there were leaves and wild nettles growing between; and the fields everywhere round were blowsy with such a muddle of weeds and unkempt herbage that the whole countryside resembled nothing so much as a great bowl of salad lying tangled there, tough and rank in the hot afternoon glare.

Co-Co suddenly spun up from close beside in the ditch,

where he had been kicking a chestnut along, and fixing Ned with his eyes said, at the same time skipping along backwards in front of him toe to toe:

'An Arabian chieftain on his deathbed called his three sons to him and spoke thus: "It is my wish that our beautiful herd of camels be divided into three portions between you, my sons. And I wish them to be divided as follows: one half to go to my eldest son, one third to my second son, and one ninth to my youngest son!" So saying he immediately died. There were seventeen camels. The question is, how did they do it?'

'But, my dear, you must *not* interrupt when other people are speaking,' said Gwen.

'I'm afraid I've got the story wrong,' said Co-Co. 'Wait a minute. Let me think a little.'

Frowning and pressing his lower lip out over the top one, Co-Co slipped along, sideways now, between Ned and Gwen. All three friends maintained silence. While Co-Co mumbled to himself, 'Half ... No, wait a minute ... No, *one*! ... No, I mean *half* ...'

Soon Co-Co flung away to the edge of the road again, faintly muttering.

Now they were passing the cottage of the washerwoman, a popular person, very fat, a Mrs Dodden. Her house, like most of the old cottages, was more like a small animal than a house – a hedgehog, perhaps, squatting beside the road – with its roof of thatch reaching nearly to the ground and its wavy skirt of ancient wall running all round the bottom, and the two tiny windows, dark boot-button eyes, staring on to the road.

Now the road twisted out of sight round the corner, following round the wall that bounded the garden of Major Crumple. Once round this corner and the triangular village green would come into sight. This twist in the roadway was shady from an ancient arbutus tree which leant far out across the road from Major Crumple's garden.

Co-Co stopped in front of the major's white iron gate, and stared in between the bars. The major was a recluse, a grass-widower whose wife and daughter had run away and deserted him, nobody knew why. Once he had invited Gwen and Co-Co into the house to look at a picture he was hoping to sell, for he had heard that at Flitchcombe Manor they knew about pictures and that sort of thing, and at any rate could give him some advice. They had found his little Queen Anne house, so elegantly serene viewed from outside, in a surprising chaos, with the sitting-room furniture – chairs, chests of drawers and so on – facing the walls, with their backs towards the centre of the room for some reason. In the kitchen there had been eight or nine cheeses on the dresser and sink, and all buried deep within a blue upstanding fuzz of mould. The picture he had wanted to sell had been a small sporting print of no value.

'Don't stand and stare, Co-Co. Come along.'

They all passed on round the corner.

In front of them lay the three-cornered patch of tussocky grass, with the signpost on it, which was Flitchcombe Green. On the farther side stood the inn. Beside it was the village shop, which sold everything and was also a post office. Between them and the green there was now only an oblong box of creosoted planks – the village hall.

Gwen suddenly stood still in the road.

'By the way, wasn't it today that Sally invited you to spend the afternoon and have tea, Co-Co?'

'I believe it was.'

'Well, I never! What time did she ask you to come?'

'After lunch – about three.'

'I thought so. And it's ten minutes past now! Hadn't you better run along?'

Co-Co's friend, Sally Smith, lived in the other direction, on the other side of Flitchcombe Manor.

Co-Co's face had gone pink with the sudden shock. He hesitated in the roadway, the toe of his gym-shoe tracing circles among the loose flints in the dust.

'I'm afraid you'll *have* to go.'

Co-Co opened both eyes wide as if swimming under water, and, wheeling about, rushed full tilt back down the road whence they had just come.

The other three continued down the road towards the shop.

A small garden separated the road from the shop, with a path leading to the door. As the three approached the little gate, a man shot past them on a bicycle, brought himself up with a jerk, jumped off, leaned his bicycle against the ivied fence round the shop and started fumbling in the pockets of his jacket. Ned recognized him at once, with his narrow shoulders and his close-shorn head with its top of greased glittering strings, as one of the clerks at Gwen's grocer in the neighbouring town of Malton. Why was he here in the middle of the day? But it was, of course, Thursday – Malton's early-closing day. Obviously the man lived in one of the houses here at Flitchcombe, and probably bicycled into his work each day.

As the grocer's clerk entered the little gate, having extracted a sealing-waxed packet from his pocket, he ran into two women coming out of the shop door. They were Mrs Hornet, the vinegary chicken-farmer's wife, and, behind her, fat Mrs Dodden, the washerwoman. Ned noticed that both women had identical frocks and hats. Each had a frock like a thin paper bag in shape and colour, with some kind of frayed markings stamped all over it, and each a hat folded over envelope-wise yet rising at the same time upwards like a thimble. This hat looked on Mrs Dodden inadequately small, whilst on little Mrs Horner it showed as weighty and cumbrous as a bucket. This identicalness of clothing was due, Ned knew, not to any similarity in taste between the two women, but to the fact that both wardrobes had come off the same conveyor belt – the one that fed that part of the country.

Both women carried baskets crowded with things they had just bought inside the shop, things that could be seen standing on display in the shop window: that is, cardboard containers of a queer bright purple, and tins, also purple, filled with patented substitute food products for the week, powders tinted differently, and square blocks which were, so the printing on them said, in reality puddings, cakes, soups, trifles, junkets and stews – enough for the whole week's meals.

Meanwhile Ned could not take his eyes off the clerk from Malton. He had noticed that he was in a suit of that very purple, and so tight, narrow and rigid that he himself resembled one of the purple cartons of substitute food mixture that stood in the grocery window.

In the shop Gwen was given her rusks, but was told that they had not got the size of wick that she required. After this they came out of the shop again and stood blinking for a moment on the flagged path outside, for the inside of the shop was dark, and by contrast the village green, with its white signpost and the white chalky road running all round it, dazzled their eyes.

An old dog, big, black and woolly as a hearthrug, lay in the middle of the road with his eyes shut. An ancient labourer in faded corduroy trousers and with a small felt hat shrunken by many winters so that it was little more than a crinkly frill perched over his forehead to keep the sun out of his eyes, came hobbling past them. He called out 'Good morning' in a deaf man's voice; his round old face had been smiling a happy sleep-walker's smile to himself before he saw them, and continued in the same smile after he had passed them by.

They walked down the flagged pathway and passed along the privet hedge to the low gate. Out in the road a young woman, with dark hair, slender (for she was still quite young), crossed over the road with some pennies held in her hand, bound for the baker's shop opposite, out of sight at the moment behind some elder bushes. Behind the baker's shop, set back down a pebbly lane, the vicarage showed, and behind that again the grey flint church. The young woman looked round at the three friends coming out of the shop gateway with the same sleep-walker's look as the old labourer's. She looked neither happy nor sad, and she was wearing the same dress that the washerwoman and Mrs Hornet had worn.

'Down in the village here, locked in this little windless valley, nature seems to have wrapped herself in a rug and dropped off to sleep long ago,' observed Ned, as the three walked off up the road to the right towards the cliffs.

'I was thinking the same thing,' said Aron. 'When I come face to face with it, a village street makes my flesh creep. This is a village of somnambulists.'

'These people *accept* too much. They have been brought up in a philosophy of acceptance. They accept everything that comes without inquiring – no matter what. Food substitutes, clothes substitutes, graven images of every kind. No matter what government comes in – labour, conservative or communist – they'll take everything that's coming to them without inquiry – that's the point. We must not let our boys get like that, Aron.'

The road had turned into a small path and they were climbing the steep cliffside now.

'I know it is fashionable nowadays,' said Gwen in a grey voice, 'amongst so-called progressive and intelligent people, to call aloud for every Tom, Dick and Harry to evaluate, and to revalue, all our ancient practices and faiths upon every conceivable occasion. You all think that the veriest snippet of a schoolgirl and the most unlettered farm-worker can tell us better what is good than can the accumulated wisdom of the ages. Thinking people, and countries too, for that matter, are apt to start out with the idea that they can change everything for the better before you can say Jack Robinson. But they always come back to the old traditions in their maturity.'

'I really don't know quite what we're talking about,' said Ned.

'*I'm* talking about whether it is better to seem alive or half dead,' said Aron.

'I'm talking about the philosophy of acceptance,' said Gwen. 'In order to live the good life one *has* to be half dead. People who are alive all round find it too difficult. Mutilation is called for. One must be prepared to make that sacrifice. One has to accept it. And it should of course be a *graceful* acceptance.'

'Oh, a graceful mutilation is just the thing, I'm sure!' said Ned.

'But does one really have to patrol round the village in a dress like a paper bag, wear a tall envelope on one's head, and feed upon substitute custards?' asked Aron.

'It may well be that that sacrifice, too, is demanded of one at any particular moment in history.'

'I don't know that the term "graceful" exactly describes this type of mutilation, all the same,' he replied.

'I may be very stupid, but I'm not sure if I quite follow the argument,' said Ned. 'However, as we seem to be shaking out our bonnets in the wind and letting the bees come out, I must say that I am finding nowadays, as I said to Aron this morning, all this sleepiness in the air very soothing. I look

forward now to many happy years ahead of quiet preoccupa-
tion with my own little concerns, while dowdy old dears like
Mrs Dodden and Mrs Hornet pass and re-pass monotonously
in front of my eyes.'

'And substitute custard tablets pass and re-pass down your
throat; "washing-up" music passes in and out of your ears . . .'

'Certainly! I'm on Gwen's side. Most heartily I accept our
English phlegm!'

'I prefer *substitute* phlegm,' murmured Aron, looking
towards the sea, which had now appeared, 'as being much
more graceful. Real phlegm I find *dis*graceful.'

'Rather disgusting conversation,' said Gwen. 'But it is, all
the same, quite true . . . Wait a minute, Aron – let me do it.'

They had reached the gate to the pathway up the cliff, and
Aron's overcoat, which had belonged to his grandmother,
and hung upon him like a collapsed bell-tent, had got caught
in the barbed wire that ran along the top. As they unhooked
the coat from the wire a yellow classroom ruler tumbled out
of one of the pockets and fell over on to the wrong side of the
gate.

At last they were safely through the gate.

The change of atmosphere from the village in the valley
was complete, as they walked up the hill.

There was a dropping away, first, of things familiar.

The absence of boundaries – of all hedges and fences, made
itself felt. Instead, there was nothing but solitariness and sky,
and the cliff grasses coming up against the forward-swerving
clouds nakedly. Trees had disappeared as being a race too
sophisticated and delicate to exist in this rough crucible,
where was only a lunatic pandemonium of rushing and shud-
dering, with foam and seagulls tearing over everything and
screaming.

The spit of land on which they walked protruded unexpectedly from the rocky coastline which runs between the

large seaside town of Spatchampton and the smaller resort of Malton. From a distance this cliff resembles a tortoise sticking up its head from its shell, and locally, indeed, it was in fact called Tortoise Head. But to Ned and his companions as they stood upon its summit, which was over a hundred feet high and dropped sheer down into the water, it looked merely what it was – a chunk of slaty bitumen with the cold sea-water ceaselessly pounding it. Down below, round the rock's foot, white gulls floated, their mouths opening and shutting, although nothing of their cries could be heard because of the deafening sound (like the perpetual rending of giant tissue paper) in the air – the ceaseless clatter of the sea. All down the years, mutilating forces had laid waste this place. On both sides of the grassy patch where they stood the black rock – the inner substance of the land – dropped down into the water, showing like a vast wound grinningly exposed, kept fresh and raw without respite.

Ned turned to Gwen and shouted against the wind: 'I'm sure my pencil is up on the ledges somewhere ... I am going to look ...' But the words were blown backwards, and it sounded as though someone were tapping a tin kettle high up in the air above.

Ned turned round and gathered his coat to him in preparation for a further climb, and instantly his scarf shot out a long arm and started beating Aron robustly on the face. Putting up a hand to pull it away he found his coat had blown upwards mushroom-wise all round his head, so he threw up his arms and tried wrestling with it, to force it down. Everyone was laughing and fighting with their billowing clothes, their own as well as other people's. Finally Ned bent himself double and with his head in the gale's stomach, made his way upwards to the top. The others started to descend the cliff again, meaning to meet Ned later at the foot of the hill, out of the gale.

The ledges were a series of natural connecting terraces on the topmost part of the cliff, where the grass grew longer and was filled full of golden guineas, those claw-like flowers.

The rock walls of the ledges formed sheltering bays, some of which were, and some of which were not, protected from the wind. Once among them Ned began to search the grasses carefully for his pencil. The tumult in the air all round continued without cease. As he walked round about the corners of the rocks he became the victim of an invisible savagery in the air which would not let him alone. Titanic shoulderings and heavings alternately mauled him and fawned upon him unwieldily. Yet when he most braced himself against the enemy it would drop slithering to the ground, leaving him abandoned. This alternating passion and treachery directed towards him was tiring and awkward; so that when he reached a spot under the cliff face where the wind did not penetrate at all he sat down for a moment, thankful to be left in peace.

After a minute he spread himself flat on his stomach and looked down upon the torpid bay.

It seemed a stable enough monster, at first sight, the silvery scales on its back shimmering placidly under its even breathing in the dull afternoon light.

But after watching a few moments he became aware, at a spot directly below him, of a queer revolving squirm, a circular ravelling and unravelling, as if the elastic skin, tickled by an unseen finger, were recoiling nervously at that spot with a convulsive, rotatory twitch, and he reflected how strongly the cross current must be running at that spot, and remembered, then, having heard about the dangerous undertow that spun round the base of these cliffs.

As he lay there on his stomach he reflected what he had always reflected whenever he saw the sea: that there, laid out flat in front of his eyes, was the inconceivable. Salt water

– yes! But of a weight, a depth, a size, a power unthinkable!

How to assess the sea? One seems to see it, he thought, yet it is really a secret, hidden from one almost entirely. It is our past, he reflected, that we look at. And now it is incompatible and inaccessible to us, as the past always is. He could not take his eyes off the flat and monstrous tracts of water. Somehow to assess it, to judge it, to force it down into an intelligible scale of values had always been a crying necessity. How often in the past, he reflected, this vital need of man to assess the frame in which he lives his life out must have been abandoned in sheer appal! For, however much man instinctively loves the fascinating and restless sea, and however much he feels himself to be a part of the land also, and inclined to worship its beauty, there is still something in this universe that makes it a stranger to him – worse – an enemy – cruel and stony beyond all measuring.

Above the sea the wind kept the clouds billowing up from the horizon, and every moment the sky was changing. On the other side of the bay lay Spatchampton. Ned could see the crowded houses of the town, white and red, no bigger than coloured hundreds-and-thousands on a cake – he could even see the pier, lying under a vast dark arch of cloud. For a semi-circular mountain range of cloud, peak behind peak, now stood massed solidly in the upper air. The clouds looked angry, inkily fulminating, and where their darkness was pierced or torn, gushed out glistening shafts of light, many-edged, and all these rays threw pencil and hair shadows down cloud mountainsides and on to the sea.

In the past, in his youth, Ned had been unhappy, stultified, – so it had seemed to him – between impossibly conflicting stresses. Deprived of clear-cut golds and blacks he had always had the feeling that in our cloud-impeded northern atmosphere the genius of the scene was tragic. So in the past, when brought face to face, as at the present moment, with a theatrical effect of this thunderous sort – this panoramic kind of dark sea and rocks with its mountainous architecture of the upper airs all looped about with livid diamond illuminations, split by the knife rays that cut and the rain-slanting shadows that hide – he would have deemed the setting of rue and desolation fit enough for the play. He would perhaps have wept tears and asked aloud that old question: What in heaven's name is the plot? Who will tell us the point of the play?

But some mechanism had freed him now. And he could afford to sit fatly in a place apart, content merely to admire the fearful show. He felt no urgency to ask that old question today. Happy people don't ask questions.

All the same, it was getting cold up here. It would quite possibly begin to rain.

He got up, took a firm hold on his scarf ends, and went down the cliff to join his friends.

They reached the village again almost without speaking. Except Ned, to confess his pencil was lost. After the din of the wind and the waves, how silent the inland valley! The empty roadway outside the inn, with its triangle of grass and its signpost, and the grey flint cottages scattered behind the blackberry hedges round about, all stood blank and bored in the tepid four o'clock air.

A bicycle bell sounded smartly. Round the corner dashed a man they had seen before, with his narrow shoulders and his shorn head smeared with grease on top. His bicycle had come down the hill and he sped along without being obliged to pedal. Ned remembered his clothes, a chemical mauve, too narrow for him, stiff as carton paper – yet suddenly Ned saw that it was after all a different man! He didn't stop, but shot round the corner, going inland, and was lost to view.

'Not the clerk from Malton,' he murmured.

'No, the radio shop at Spatchampton,' answered Gwen, after a moment's recollection.

A woman came out of the post office and walked towards them wearing a tall envelope hat and a gown cut like a paper bag with frayed markings on it. She was the new cowman's wife from another farm, and she passed on, her shopping basket filled with substitute food mixtures, done up in cartons of electric blue.

Soon they were passing the village hall again on their way home. They came to the curved pink walls of Major Crumple's house rounding the corner, with its arbutus tree hanging out over the roadway.

They passed the deserted builders' yard and, opposite, the washerwoman's hedgehog cottage. In the middle of the chicken farm they saw Mrs Hornet leading along three goats across the field. The row of council houses they repassed, and afterwards the village school, tall, narrow, and red, with the stone motto like a waving scarf above the doorway: I AM KNOWLEDGE. They found a bicycle now leaning outside the gate of the policeman's bungalow. Just as they came up to their own drive gate they saw, standing in the road, a wooden grocery box hitched to perambulator wheels and stacked with logs collected from the woods for fuel.

'That belongs to our cook's cousin. The one whom the policeman visited about the baby in the incinerator. I expect her eldest boy, Dan, left it there. He's probably picking hazel nuts up on the bank.'

Ned looked up at the bank. But he only saw a cow looking down at them through the wire fences at the top, with a finely chiselled smile carved on her cream velvet muzzle.

'That's a Guernsey cow,' said Aron.

Seeing them staring at her she whisked her tail and gave a curvette with her rococo haunches, at the same time shifted a cream velvet ankle slightly in the grass. Then she raised her rose-coloured nostrils and blew politely at them once or twice, whilst her eyes, enormous and black, regarded them through their fringe of thick lashes sideways, with a prolonged and bland intentness. She looked out of place in this blowsy field with her fine oriental chic.

'Those legs sticking out of the elder bush – that's Dan.'

They had reached the drive gates. As they turned in towards them, a man on a bicycle came toiling up the hill. When he came closer they saw it was the village policeman himself oddly enough. They waited until he had passed by.

Gwen looked up at Dan's legs again protruding from the foliage.

'I wonder if he knows at all what his mother is going through at the present time.'

'Hardly!'

They followed each other in through the iron gates.

6

IT was after dinner on Sunday that Marina and Violet arrived.

The fire had been lighted at the end of the long drawing-room, and Co-Co sat in the middle of the floor looking at the Indian ivories. All round about him were scattered the small white ivory discs with monkeys and elephant gods upon them. He was looking up at Ned and telling him about Violet.

'Violet is really rather a bore, you know. And what I simply cannot get over is her amazing ignorance. She doesn't know anything at all. Nothing at all. She went for a sort of holiday with us to Mont St Michel before entering the sanatorium last summer. She had never even heard of Wellington! And, do you know, she thought that Buddha was a kind of chocolate?'

'Really?'

'And what was simply incredible was that she didn't know the date of the Battle of Hastings!'

'Pass me another joss stick, will you? For some reason this one won't burn,' said Gwen to Aron. She was kneeling in front of the fireplace and held her hand out towards him where he lay behind *The Times* in the armchair. Aron peered round the edge of the paper.

'Joss sticks! What, in heaven's name!'

'They're in that china shoe on the table just beside you. Behind the lamp-standard.'

Aron handed her the shoe filled with joss sticks.

'Thank you. They should be here by this time. I think we will wait coffee till they arrive.'

'I hope Reamur doesn't drive too fast. A large car always makes Marina feel sick.'

'Is she actually sick when she drives in a large car?' asked Co-Co, staring at Aron.

'Not actually sick. But she has to go upstairs and lie down for a bit. It's tiresome.'

'Visitors who came to Mont St Michel by aeroplane were all quite white in the face. They had dark rings under their eyes, and had paper bags in their hands all puffed out with dampness and with "Sickness" stamped on them, instead of "Oxo" or anything like that, you know.'

'What's that? I thought I heard something.'

Everybody listened. But there was nothing.

The day had been grey with the kind of dull mist that an east wind brings with it, the countryside had looked sad and everyone was reminded of autumn, hence the fire in the drawing-room. Now, however, just as the sun was setting, the garden was lit up; the air was clear again, and an ice-blue glitter with scarlet sparks showered off the magnolia leaves which crowded at the long windows – the reflection of blue sky and indoor firelight together upon their glossy surfaces.

'Put away the ivories now, darling. They'll be here any minute, and you know I only promised you just to stop down and see them for a minute. And put the long ones in alternately with the square. Otherwise they don't fit in.'

'I see they are on about the old channel tunnel again. What a time to pick. Europe is going up in flames and now they want to open up a way to let the Barbarian hordes come flooding in.' Aron folded up his paper and turned to the crossword puzzle.

'Violet doesn't play any games at all,' announced Co-Co. 'She doesn't like any games at all. Except she has a game which is really just like hide-and-seek, which she is always trying to tell us. It's just simply hide-and-seek, really – but she will not admit it. And she won't play anything else at all. And she cannot *bear* hide-and-seek.'

'Co-Co darling, *will* you get those ivories put back. Ah now! There they are!'

And sure enough the car drove past the far windows and came to rest at the front door.

Co-Co sprang up, screaming, and rushed from the room, sawing the air violently with his arms, like a Turk with a scimitar. There was a banging of doors from the car outside, and Reamur's voice. Gwen and Aron got up and went into the hall. Ned walked over to the mantelpiece mirror, smoothing his hair. There was more banging of doors and Violet and Marina could be heard in the hall greeting the family. Co-Co began to scream.

'Stop it, Co-Co.'

'Violet Edith Hasker and Marina Cedar welcome!'

'Will you be quiet, Co-Co!'

Wilkes walked into the drawing-room carrying the coffee things and laid them on the table.

Now they were all in the room wandering round and laying down packages on the arms of chairs. Co-Co carried a string bag in one hand and an umbrella in the other, which he brandished with Gothic gestures – hobbling round the room with his knees turned inwards and touching, and his heels out sideways at right angles, imitating Lewis Carroll's Anglo-Saxon messenger with his bag of hay sandwiches about whom he had lately been reading.

Marina stood by the sofa and made a pile of things on the arm – a rug, a box of chocolates, some magazines, a brown paper parcel, and her hat. She stood folding Violet's white crochet gloves into one another.

'She is going to be sick, sure enough,' thought Ned, looking at her white face inside its carroty locks. The lanky Violet stood silently watching everything with her great languid eyes that always looked as if they were about to cry, and her unkempt hair, not quite red but foxy, reaching nearly to her waist. Ned went to fetch the coffee cup that Gwen had poured, and handed it to Marina. They drank their coffee quietly, exchanging demure remarks about the journey from London, but the rest of the evening passed in utter confusion. The newcomers were kept running out into the garden on different excuses, and there was an unpleasant scene with Co-Co, who refused to go to bed, and in a flood of tears rushed out and sat in the motor car. Finally he was forgiven and allowed to stay up another half-hour. During all this, Violet, on two separate occasions, took out all the ivories from the Indian box again and scattered them over the chairs and everywhere.

At one moment Aron stood talking to his young wife in front of the fire. He seemed to be lecturing Marina about Violet's dentist.

'Yes. But while you were in London, surely it would have been wisest to have her thoroughly examined then? Now we shall have to make an extra journey up there again especially for that in the holidays!'

'There is no need for her to be examined. There's nothing wrong with her teeth. One can tell soon enough at that age, if there's something amiss.'

'Well, but there *was* something amiss.'

'Yes, but I tell you the swelling had completely vanished. When the tooth had come out the pain stopped and there was obviously nothing wrong with her at all.'

'Yes, but all the same one has to report to Mrs Robins about the state of her teeth at the beginning of the term, I thought you told me.'

'No, Violet! – not coffee last thing at night. No, darling! Gwen, she mustn't.'

Ned watched Marina from the window enclosure where he stood. The sun had gone now and the room was filling with the twilight of nine o'clock.

Marina was rather small. After a little she seemed to recover from her sickness, for her face became pink and white and then Ned saw that she was peppered with small freckles.

She chatted without reticence, gushingly. Ned put her down as a progressive type of girl, for she evidently attended many meetings of societies in Red Lion Square and elsewhere, and was, he surmised, an addict of *avant garde* articles. Aron knew how to choose an attractive female, by the way, he noted with a certain surprise.

'What would you say if you saw a man walking down the lane,' said Co-Co to Violet – they were both squatting down at Ned's feet at this time, picking up the ivories – 'and carrying a human head under his arm? And every now and then tossing the head up into the air and catching it again?'

Violet squealed.

'What would *you* say?' she asked.

'I would say, "Well, it's a strange sort of a world where such things as that can happen, and I think that I for one would as soon jump out of a window and have no part in it".'

Who has he heard saying that, Ned wondered.

'Violet! Come on – bed!' Marina held out her hand suddenly to Violet.

Violet and her mother gathered up all their things and, together with Gwen and Co-Co, went off to the upstairs regions, but as they left the room Aron called out to Marina, telling her of some plan he had made to visit some friends the following day in the car, relatives of Marina apparently. Violet, too, turned back in the doorway, calling out to her stepfather something about her going to act in a charity performance with school friends over at Malton.

Ned had hoped to have got in a word with Aron about a queer letter on the subject of housemaid's baths that he had received that afternoon, from the newly engaged matron at Oaklands, but seeing Aron's preoccupied face as he followed along after his family with their rugs and parcels under his arm he refrained.

Things had changed already. The focus had shifted. All this was, as the Russians say, a song out of a different opera. What a difference to the life of a household new arrivals make to be sure!

7

AFTER the arrival of Violet and Marina the old orderly life vanished.

Formerly the long, quiet hours in the silent house, with Reamur like a mouse in his study, and Gwen outside in the garden in her gumboots, left a clear field in which Ned's daydream of the new school could solidify, and in which the future gymnasiums, washrooms, concert halls and class-rooms of Oaklands could blossom in glittering mirages, un-disturbed, in whatever room he happened to be sitting.

Now a scuffling, snuffling, and murmuration filled the stairways, halls and everywhere else. Paper for ever rustled, as if sandwiches and other parcels were being perpetually wrapped up. Small gramophone discs, bathing-caps, gym-shoes, walnuts and opened picture books, strewed the stairs both back and front. People clumped round the verandas all day as if going the rounds of a ship; the old nursery wireless set made itself heard high above the thump, thump, thump of skipping ropes and tricycle bells; whilst roller skating began in the long brick passage outside the flower closet. Worst of all were the cries of '*Coo-eel*' which rang out from every window, and were answered by wails from the shrub-beries, or smothered guffaws from amongst the vegetables, or sometimes by falling slates and flowerpots from the hot-houses at the back.

The tame rabbits and the orchard hens became at this time voluble also.

But more distracting than the noise was the focusing of the indoor-downstairs world upon the 'plans'. Whatever room Ned went into there would be 'grown-ups' making 'plans'.

At what time should the picnic start out? Should they call round and fetch the Robinsons' children on the way down? Should they telephone to the Bellringers and invite them up? Should they accept the invitation to tea at Stock-tons on Friday? Could the Robinsons' Nannie fetch all the children back from the skating rink, or should Gwen go in the car as well? Backs were bowed over shopping lists. When Ned asked if anyone were coming for a walk, the answer though not addressed to him would come back: 'Ten and a half inches – I think size thirteen will be big enough' or, more bluntly, 'She won't be able to eat anything for two hours afterwards, so I should try and make the appointment for ten o'clock,' looking straight through him as if he were a ghost.

One might as well be living in the booking office of some large railway terminus.

So the days went on.

Only in the evenings, after dinner, sanity would descend again upon the house.

During the meal itself, even, things would have begun to settle down, for the children would have been put to bed. And even though the door had to be left open in order to hear what might occur in the nursery regions, and even though Gwen and Marina made frequent pilgrimages between courses to perform 'good nights' and 'settling ins' and 'settling downs', still the tired silence in the dining-room was soothing, and the tinkle of the forks and knives, while the candlelight shone upon rich and adult foods, was an oasis to the soul.

By nine o'clock at night the passage from the dining-room to the drawing-room was as it had been before the visitation. Instead of those disorganized dartings forward and hangings back, with the accompanying stamping clatter of centipede sandals on the wrong parts of the floor, as in the day-time, the pace became majestic, with whiffs of cigar and perfume eddying around rustling skirts.

After coffee, sitting round the drawing-room fireplace, Reamur would take up a book and disappear into the shadows of his winged armchair. Aron would go to the far end of the room and, sitting down at the writing-desk, would write to the Oaklands' carpenter about construction of the proposed squash court; or compare the prices of the local butchers; while Gwen and Marina would sit with piles of monthly magazines and quantities of brand new books on their laps, ruffling their pages and chattering.

Marina, in long silken skirts, with modernistic borzois and sea-gulls printed on them, lolled there against the sofa cushions. Her femininity was not discreet, either by conformation or by the conscious handling of it. Her bosom, which occurred with quite outstanding abruptness, did not arouse aesthetic emotion in the beholder. Nor were her small waist, her flat stomach and elegant hips and bare gold-sandalled foot with red toe-nails, engendered, obviously, by long twilight hours of study in the British Museum. And yet, from the expression of her face, which was deadly solemn, and from the snatches of her talk which Ned overheard in the intervals of his visiting the drawing-room – for he amused himself after dinner by putting records on the gramophone in the music-room next door – he gathered that she was in fact negotiating the most unwieldy materials intellectually speaking, – summing up international intricacies and economic structures, appraising historic catastrophes, castigating moral systems and cultural trends, but not spending much time over it – rather, devoting a few short sentences to each. Much emotion there was to it, however, for she kept on with the apportioning of heavy blame, or feeling praise, by steady turns; while certain key words kept rising to the surface of this rippling after-dinner tide – tins bobbing along downstream, disappearing only to reappear, vanishing always to bob up again. 'Decade' was such a one. 'In the last decade', 'present decade', 'next decade'.

There were also recurring names: 'Hodgeforth', 'Kit Saumerez', and 'Grumble'. These were her prophets, evidently, whose word on things was final. 'Hodgeforth', 'Grumble', 'Kit Saumerez', these were the names too that shone out, green, red and blue, upon the covers of the new books that

Marina had brought down with her, and which every evening strewed the two women's laps, and these names appeared in all the cultural magazines as well.

Ned did not know what was in all these magazines, for in his spare time he gave himself over to music and botany. He had, therefore, no means of evaluating the pronouncements of Hodgeforth, Saumerez and Grumble.

Anyway, it was only the two women who carried on these conversations. Reamur had not read any of the articles in Marina's magazines either. His day's work, whatever it was, tired him out, so that after dinner he preferred to do crossword puzzles or to re-read some familiar old play or other, *Macbeth, Henry IV*, or, on alternate evenings, some story by Agatha Christie.

Aron, on the other hand, did know what was in the cultural magazines, but never openly alluded to their contents.

Marina, Ned judged, had read all the articles in all of them several times. She gave him the impression of sitting simmering in their contents as in a *bain marie* – and a most delectable little *oeuf poché* she looked.

Gwen herself had read from these magazines only an article here and there, and of the books only one or so, but was evidently perturbed and ruffled over the whole question of this literature. She sat at the opposite end of the sofa from Marina, and Ned noticed their conversation tended to repeat itself each night. Early in the evening, with the coffee, Gwen would ask Marina, 'Now tell me about this philosopher X. Y. Z.? We are so provincial and out of things down here, and I'm ashamed to say I haven't read any of his works, although I've heard, of course, a lot of talk *about* him'; or, 'Can you explain Mr A. B. C.'s poetry to me? What do you think of it? I have read only a little, I'm afraid, here and there ...' and in her voice would be a Chinese respect for the person in question. But later in the evening, when Ned would potter back from the music-room and sit down by the fireplace for a rest and a drink, Gwen would be saying with knitted brows, and that kind of hollowness in her voice that betokened deep whirlpools within, '... but there are no such things as "intellectuals"! People talk of "intellectuals" as if they were a separate race of beings! There are no intellectuals! There are only intelligent people, you know – scattered all over England and Scotland and Wales, don't forget that. Radio experts and copra kings, shoe makers and bird watchers ... people whose names we never hear ... all over the world. I really cannot recognize this term "intellectuals".' She would sound exhausted.

Marina, by ten-thirty, would start holding her forehead with both hands and wearing a frown, and by bedtime would be asking for a couple of aspirins or some bromoseltzer. She would complain of headache, or else indigestion, Ned had noticed, after any long discussion, and would lie back apparently exhausted, her head resting on the sofa top with an effect of just having fainted away. Yet he was glad indeed to see that for all her cries for aspirin, her flesh never for a moment lost its wonderful look of having a lighted lamp inside. It was an impression of deep-seated energy, and Ned felt sure that if the drawing-room lights were to be switched off she would be like a glow-worm all over.

One night the couple discussed a book he did happen to have read. It was a popular book dealing with the subject of crime amongst slum children. The work was referred to as a novel – unjustifiably so, it seemed to Ned, it being in his view a mere re-hash of all the most gruesome items that the daily press had been writing of during the last few months.

'Our whole generation has felt the impact of this book,' Marina told Gwen. It was open on her knee.

'One can never be the same again after one has put it

down. We have all been through something – a major experience – in reading it. Really, you may say it marks a turning point for our epoch. The imprint upon the next decade ...'

Ned saw her wide eyes held a baffled stare, uncertain yet intense, like a person stepping off a kerb into a fog.

Gwen's face, at the other end of the sofa, had assumed a look of total assiduity. A Sunday-school look; in which everything else is blanked out except a helpful portentousness. It was early in the evening yet.

'Have *you* read this book, Ned?' asked Marina.

Ned looked round from the drinks, still at the side of the room, his tumbler half full of whisky and soda. Marina was looking over at him questioningly.

He flinched. Marina, mistaking his silence, began to tell him about the book, dwelling hungrily on the bloodthirsty behaviour of the wicked children in it, and with gusto submerging herself in righteous indignation against the parents, and in charitable pity all round.

'It is far the most important book of the decade,' she repeated. 'I agree with Kit Saumerez in his evaluation ... that none of us in this epoch can ever be quite the same again after having put it down. Don't you agree? You have read it, of course?'

Ned was overtaken by embarrassment, and muttering that he had not as yet read the book but would do so at the first opportunity, seized up his glass of whisky and fled back to the music-room.

Half an hour later, when he returned, his glass empty, to the drinks tray, he perceived Gwen humped up inside her brocade jacket on the sofa, somewhat flushed. Several strands of her black hair had fallen out loose over her nose and ear. The 'weekly' that Marina had mentioned as carrying an article on the novel about bad children was open on her knee. She was staring at the name 'Kit Saumerez' with a most peculiar look.

Reamur's wing chair by the fire was empty now.

Aron, in a little circle of lamplight at the far end of the room, sat in a chair with his legs over one arm and his chest resting on the other, his arms dangling over it to the floor, where lay a blue architectural print which he was busy marking with a red pencil.

Scattered round about his chair on the floor were a transparent protractor, four or five pigeon's feathers, a tube of Secotine, and three walnuts.

Marina stood, her red head thrown back, at the drink table, swallowing some kind of a powder out of a packet and washing it down with barley-lemon squash.

Ned put down his own glass quietly on the top of the bookcase by the door, and with a few 'Goodnights' slipped off to bed.

8

AND so confusion continued, it seemed to Ned, to the old background of zizzing flies, bellowing cows, walks, and hot, cloudy weather.

Friends came sometimes for the weekend, and went away again. Sometimes they all drove off to dinner with neighbours.

It was not till a week after Marina's arrival that, one day at lunch-time, just as everyone was rising from the table making for coffee in the drawing-room, the sun suddenly blazed out. White plates and flowers down the centre of the lunch-table glittered and seemed to spin round up in the air without any focus, the effect taking everybody by surprise.

After three weeks of muffled insulation they had forgotten the hidden violences that could be loosed.

They stepped on to the terrace. The sky was a clear blue. In the illuminated garden it was the black shadows – of the yew tree, of the cedars, of the summerhouse – that dazzled.

'Let's have coffee on the lawn. Wilkes, please bring out the rugs and deck-chairs underneath the cedar tree.'

To the shade of the cedar Wilkes brought out coffee and brandy too. Gwen laid out a rug and Marina lay flat upon her stomach on it, and was soon teaching the children how to tell fortunes from the bottoms of their coffee cups.

After a little Gwen remarked, 'If it remains as pleasant as this, we might have our tea out here as well. Children, smarten yourselves up for tea, please. We have visitors coming.'

'Visitors!'

'Visitors!'

Co-Co sprang to his feet as if to ward off a death blow.

'Jiminy whiskers! Whoever is coming?'

'Sit down, Co-Co. Only some very old friends.'

'Yes, but who? Who?'

Marina rolled over on to her back, propping herself up on one elbow.

'Gwen. Who is it?'

'The two great friends.'

Reamur groaned and sank down in his deck-chair with shut eyes.

Gwen poked him with the tip of her shoe. 'Don't try to pull the wool over our eyes with those loud groans, Ray. The woman you love is coming to tea. No use to hide the fact, for by the end of tea everybody will have seen it.'

Reamur failed to rally.

'But what are their names?' asked Marina.

Co-Co shouted, 'Elsie and Lacy!'

'Ssh-sh.'

A screech, loud as an express train, split the air.

'Co-Co! *Please!*'

Co-Co opened his mouth to screech again, but Aron put out his right arm and brought him tumbling to the grass, whilst he placed his left hand over the boy's mouth, though not without a struggle.

'Elsie and Lacy?' asked Aron.

Co-Co knelt down on the rug in front of Aron and looked up at him.

'They are not *really* Elsie and Lacy. But we just call them that.'

'They are our new neighbours from Softon,' said Gwen.

'And which is the one that Reamur loves?' asked Marina, and stretched out and wriggled her fingernail on Reamur's knee.

'Wait and see.'

'They are really Miss Anstruther and Miss Patterson-Taylor,' Gwen explained. 'Ladies of now respectable middle-age. Lacy is a picturesque lady in draperies, a follower of Jung. Elsie is made of sterner stuff – a believer in absolute values. Right and wrong. She wears the trousers and is a social worker.'

'I remember them,' said Ned.

'But shouldn't there be a third? What about Tilly?' asked Aron.

'There was a third, but she lies in the churchyard now,' said Gwen.

'Once upon a time there were three sisters, Elsie, Lacy, and Tilly, and they lived at the bottom of a well!' bawled Co-Co, turning a somersault. 'Don't you know *that*!'

Gwen got up and, collecting the papers and the coffee things, walked into the house.

The children raced off into the shrubberies. Aron followed

Gwen indoors more slowly, back to his blueprints and sylla-buses. Reamur opened up his heaviest London Library book.

Marina suddenly jumped up and decided to change into her sunbathing suit.

Ned lay back in his chair and went to sleep.

He woke again suddenly. In front of him, at his feet upon the rug, lay a young woman in a sunbathing suit. She was propped up upon one elbow smiling at him, and was saying something. He was dazed from his dream and understood nothing, not even who this girl was, naked, but with the cherry red handkerchief round her breasts, and cherry shorts. In her freckled face, in the shadow of her hat, her brilliant blue eyes were smiling at him. There was a wild look in her eyes, quick feelings all alight seemed scuttering and whisking through them as they gleamed at him, and all the time she wore an expectant air – she must have asked him a question.

'Sorry to have woken you,' he heard, 'but here are the visitors, don't you see? Just arrived.'

She slightly bent her head towards the drive, and Ned, fol-lowing her look, saw a grey car drawn up in front of the house. Its door was open, and women in summer frocks were stepping out of it. Then it came back to him, percolating his sleepy sun-baked brain, that this was Elsie and Lacy; and that this naked girl on the rug was the person Aron had married; that this sunlit lawn with the blinding ink-shadows under the trees, and all the flattened dandelions and daisies in the mown grass round about his chair, was a place very familiar – belonged to his friends Gwen and Reamur, and was called Flitchcombe Manor. In this way he knew he was awake. But it had all happened in a second.

The next moment he found himself walking towards the back of the house, the idea in his mind being to escape.

What he was to escape he couldn't think. Yet he succeeded! Was upstairs in his bedroom barely before you could say 'knife'.

Finding himself there, at a loose end, he changed his tie. He put on a red Paisley one in place of the yellow.

He could see from his window the cedar tree with the rug beneath it, and Marina standing there in a red-patterned cotton skirt now, which covered her bare legs, smiling greetings to the visitors as they strolled across the lawn. Then the two children, Violet and Co-Co, broke out from the shrubs by the drive and started to wheel, capering, round the visitors in wide encircling arcs.

Behind the cedar tree, with the rug at its roots and the personages assembling in its shadow, heaved an ocean of parrot-green leafage in the windy sunlight. Beech, ash and wych elm. Through a gap were fields stiff with barley, and behind them the village with its church and barns, its new water tower, and all the pylons roundabout, and low hills powdery with the grape-bloom of distance.

The coloured splendour and the shimmer of the scene outside the window, with its meticulous perfection of rainbow enamelling, Ned greeted coldly, merely as a provincial pantomime backcloth. It stayed flat, behind the proscenium arch as it were, for Ned. It got stuck upon the outside of Ned's retina and would not enter him. Its gala beauty was registered, it is true, violently, but yet was not to be digested. There stood the champagne, but not for him.

He decided to change his jacket. This didn't take up much time. Then he refilled his fountain-pen. Afterwards he re-read a letter from a young doctor who had been asked to work as a regular visitor to the boys at Oaklands, and this letter he pondered over for some time. Letter in hand, he glanced absent-mindedly again out of the window. The party were now sitting down on the grass round the tea things which were spread out upon the rug.

Reamur, however, was in his own deck-chair with the hood on it, his face lost in shadow.

Co-Co was kneeling up, slashing round in the air at wasps with his knife. Violet sat beside him, motionless, cross-legged; a thin white Buddha staring ahead, lost in a dark dream, but steadily munching. Aron, too, was kneeling, but, instead of eating, gesticulating largely with his right hand as he expounded something to the visitors which made them laugh.

With a kind of runcible panama hat perched on his long black curly hair and a fancy linen jacket which had belonged to a great-uncle, Aron looked ebullient. He struck Ned as the perfect focus for all that summery frame, with Marina sitting beside him in her Tahiti red.

Gwen, in an alarming coat and skirt of a white cartridge paper (so it looked), bent busily over her teapot.

Good heavens! He should be down there with them all. What would they think had happened to him? He should go down at once. He wheeled round and strode away from the window, but instead of going to the door he went to the back of his bedroom and sat down upon a rickety cane chair beside the slop pail. From here he could see only the top of the yew tree against the blue sky. How low his spirits had sunk! Why? It was all such a pity; all this sunlight and the visitors – this festive scene descending like a thunderbolt.

If only he had some sun glasses it would be better.

An idea struck him. Could he not slip out unobserved through the farm gate at the back and go off for a walk by himself somewhere? Nobody would see him go.

But of course such a rudeness was unthinkable.

A bee sailed in at the open window. It began swooping and looping everywhere; enjoying the dank coolness of the bedroom, no doubt, after the heat outside. Or perhaps drawn in by the toothwash or something in here. He followed it with his eyes everywhere, mind blank. In the end it turned out to be the roses on the dressing-table that were the attraction, dropping apart though they were.

There was nothing for it but to go down and plunge into the tea-party, God help him.

He got up, heavily left the room, and dragged off down the stairs.

When he reached the tea rug he was vociferously greeted by the visiting ladies.

At once Ned's nerves were engaged in full battle.

'We have been hearing about your school!' called out the eldest Miss Anstruther across the rug. She was obviously the one who wore the trousers, with her crab-apple face, short hair, and the fact that she actually did wear trousers – blue linen.

'Reamur is being very perverse, and agreeing with me – for once in his life – that the old-fashioned public school is the best form of education,' said Lacy, in her slow, demure voice. She darted a blue glance in Reamur's direction. Forty-ish, she was still pretty and flower-like. Still with the complexion of a pink and white girl under her dowdy old hat. In her full-folded flowered garments and her lacy shawl, she had obviously aligned herself with some previous epoch. She was strangely shy, and often completely silent.

'Yes! He says the more conventional they are the better! And his friend agrees! Really!' called Elsie over the rug again. 'We've come over all this way to tea – hearing rumours of the distinguished new pioneer educationalists who would be present, and expecting to be deliciously shocked with all the improper theories bandied about – and what a let down!'

'Gwen, we haven't heard yet what you've got to say,' said Lacy.

Gwen was looking across the tea-things from under her

white sun-hat, staring unwaveringly with a masked face, at the ideas presented to her. Now her voice sounded out, muted and hollow: 'I'm afraid you won't get much fun out of me, either. It seems to me that what children need is simply a lot of ruts or grooves to be chivvied along. So that they need bear no burden of responsibility on their shoulders for choosing their way of life at all. Also, and equally important, is that they should have something rigid to react against. The public schools give them this.'

'I must admit that there's a great deal to be said for Gwen's point of view,' said Aron.

The two visitors looked at Aron reproachfully.

'And you a pioneer educationalist!'

'Yes. They need a rigid programme against which they can – at any rate emotionally – rebel,' repeated Gwen.

Everyone knew that the year before Gwen had held a theory about schools which was diametrically opposite. And the closer friends, at least, remembered how before that she had created a theory of her own: education through drama. In which every classroom must have a stage. And before that, again, it had been education through high jumping and educative muscular co-ordination.

In the reflective silence that followed Ned felt it was about his turn.

'Aron, we must construct a syllabus especially designed for the children to repudiate. It will be quite interesting,' he said.

Aron smiled, and suggested, 'How about three days a week of that at the school, Ned? Say Mondays, Wednesdays and Fridays. Then on Tuesdays and Saturdays "Pioneer" again to restore the balance.'

Ned stretched out his hand for a cucumber sandwich. Seeing him unable to reach, Co-Co plunged forward across the tablecloth on his bare knees, grasped the cucumber sandwich plate and lashed it forwards close beneath Ned's nostrils.

'Oh, gracious! ... Thank you, Co-Co.'

These words, accompanied by a friendly glance from his tutor, caused Co-Co for some reason to spring up in the air like a jack-in-the-box and to shout, '*Edward Thorncroft Moon!*' at the top of his lungs. (He had formed a habit this holiday, when in a large gathering, of shouting out aloud some one member's name in full length, imitating a station megaphone.)

'Co-Co! I have asked you *not to do that*!'

Gwen turned her concentrated face round to her son; seeing which, he gave a further shriek, bounded into the air, scrabbled off across the lawn, and came wheeling round sideways, hand over hand, to his former position by the rug. Violet went into a paroxysm of giggles, got pink, and mouse-tails fell down over her eyes.

'No, but what do you really think about this public-school business, Mr Moon?' pressed Elsie. 'Surely it is a very dangerous thing to inculcate false ideals, as Gwen suggests, into a lot of little mites, just in the hope that they may refuse to take them in?'

Reamur laughed. It had a demoniac ring. Elsie looked round at him and he stopped at once and fell courteously silent. After a moment, however, he said in his impersonal drawl: 'Children are not influenced by ideas in any case. Manner ... mood ... that's what counts with them surely ... I mean, the atmosphere. The school atmosphere will certainly affect them for life, whether they consciously repudiate it or accept it.'

'Oh, but surely it is the *personality* of the individual teacher that counts!' murmured Marina, her head bent down over her plate, so that only the parting in her red curls was visible. 'At least for girls. I can only speak for females.'

She looked up and round the table, her eyelashes fluttering as if to veil something. 'Woman's life is so bound up by personalities. To love a man. To bear his children. To look after the family – or, if not the family, then to look after somebody of some sort, to be concerned and wrapped up with human personality, I mean ... is surely everything, fundamentally, for a female. So that for us at any rate, when we are young, it is surely the personality of the teacher that counts.'

The faces round the rug turned towards her, taking in her female charms, the naked limbs above and below the red cotton sunbathing suit, which seemed part of the argument somehow.

'And for boys, too – surely – the personality of the teacher is what counts,' said Miss Anstruther, in an almost gallant tone. 'Hero worship, y'know! It's a great thing! The boy who worships the history master ... do anything for him! A boy will do anything for a man he admires! He'll go to the ends of the earth.'

'Do anything except learn history,' said Aron, staring at her through his great horn specs. 'A boy can certainly get very worked up, hero-worship a master, and be led by the nose by his hero to the ends of the earth I don't doubt, but not a single name of a king of England will remain in his head.'

'Quite so,' said Ned. 'It's not charm of personality. It's the quality of the teaching that counts. Have you good teachers at your school, that's the question. If you have, the boys will get educated; if not, not.'

'Well!' Marina's large eyes looked over at him, hurt. 'Surely cramming a child is quite out-dated! Really! ... for someone who is starting a new, modern – presumably modern – school ...! That is what *was* thought two or three decades ago I know, but we've learnt something since then, surely? This generation has pressed along the highway in the steps of Lawrence, James Joyce, Bertrand Russell, Ouspensky, not to mention Picasso and Auden and countless other apostles of freedom. There can be no turning back, surely, to the old cramped, cramming days. Fred Dysart was saying the same thing only last week.'

'I said teaching. Not cramming.'

'What does Fred Dysart know about it?' demanded Aron.

'Who *is* Fred Dysart?' asked Ned.

'Fred is simply an old owl in an ivy bush. Understands nothing,' said Aron. 'He is a half-crazed biologist that Marina and Violet made friends with at the Zoo,' he added, for Ned's information.

There was a silence. Co-Co took advantage of it.

'*Lacy Patterson Taylor!*' he bawled out. He had been getting bored, and now placed himself at Lacy's elbow, just behind her left ear, with an attracted look. She turned round on hearing her name shouted, and he smiled excitedly, and with a yelping whoop spun backwards at an angle, veering round arc-wise, staggering on his heels somehow past the shrubberies and round again like a boomerang.

'Co-Co! If you're going to be a nuisance, you and Violet will have to go and take your tea in the nursery. I mean it,' said Gwen.

The conversation continued.

Ned didn't listen to the talk. He merely received the impression of the summer evening all around. In the field at the end of the garden some cows were munching grass. The cows kept shifting their feet and flicking their tails, and they all moved slowly off across the grass, walking away from the house. The motor reaper was cutting the corn in the field beyond again. It was out of sight. Rabbits began to appear in the nearby portion of the cows' field, occasionally loping across diagonally, but mostly sitting up, quiet in the evening sun. He kept wondering how long the tea-party round the rug was going on. He could still escape. Aron could well hold the fort. Aron had that mysterious thing, Presence. It made him the centre of attention everywhere. He was now well in his stride, telling story after story about the schools he had taught in one time and another.

The sky had impressed itself everywhere about in a blue network of reflection cast wide, liberating leaves, grass fronds, the backs and fronts of the china and cutlery.

Then there were the people round the rug: Aron holding forth with arms upraised like a dancing bear; Reamur limp in his deck-chair; Elsie and Lacy attentively listening; Gwen, convoluted, behind the teapot; and lastly himself. There was something closed up and come to a standstill in this group. One felt in them the shut-off engine and the passive gliding down again to earth. This was the universe of the middle-aged.

Then there was Marina. At first glance she seemed to belong to the group around the rug. Yet one had only to look at her luminous eyes to see the wild capriciousness, the liquefaction, and the rage of the thing not yet netted by the shade.

Again, there were all the things taken by the sun.

And the vegetable world, rippling and wriggling with an insensate metabolism of its own.

Ned's thoughts were admittedly confused, but it seemed to him to be a truth, and not an insignificant one, that he was beholding many quite separate universes, a crowd of systems which interlocked but which could never fuse, each with a meaning and silent language of its own, each cut off from the rest. His depression returned to him.

He stood upright beside the rug and, making the excuse of having to telephone, left the tea party and disappeared indoors.

9

It was the morning after Elsie and Lacy had been over to tea.

Daylight crept into the 'yellow room' where Ned lay asleep, and was greeted with indifference. Hour by hour it expanded, leisurely and in silence, patronizing the sponges and the tube of toothpaste without a top on the washstand, flattering the roses on the dressing-table, staring upon the socks in the armchair. Even much later on, a little before Doreen came in with the tea, when a chip of sunlight lay across Ned's face upon the pillow, dazzling his eyelids, from between the cedar branches, he still did not stir.

He was dreaming. He thought that he lay in bed with Marina, embraced and embracing together in an intimacy that was absolute.

He only understood this and realized what was happening, as he began to wake, for as his conscious mind came forward through the mists to greet him it saw her there, beneath him, her naked throat and breast, and the collar-bones of satin, sunburnt flesh with the small dark mark just above that he knew the look of so well from her sunbathing suit. As he swam back up into morning consciousness he was in the last throes of erotic excitement, actually in the final thrill; and she also.

Dimly it percolated to his mind what the surroundings were that lay outside their pleasure. From far away it came to him: they were in Flitchcombe Manor spare bedroom. And the spare bedroom was in the house of his friend, Reamur Cedar. And gradually, as he lazily floated in again to Flitchcombe, he knocked into a number of other mun-

dane things, such as that he was visiting this house during
the summer holidays, preparing Co-Co for his exams, and
that also staying in the house was the little girl Violet, who
was the daughter of Aron's wife Marina.

All this was mere factual information, like a boring signpost on a road, something for the brain. His feelings were
occupied solely in savouring the pure happiness of the intimacy with her who was lying in his arms. Suddenly the
door burst open and Doreen entered with the morning tea.

Ned turned away from Doreen unthinkingly on to his
side, and still the only reality for him was his happiness. In
his dream there had been sexual ecstasy, and the memory
was on him in all its strength.

Then like a dam breaking the Flitchcombe spare bedroom
burst all over him, with all its sponges and hairbrushes and
chests of drawers; also with Doreen and the tea. He had
been mistaken in imagining himself in company; he was
alone in the bed.

Following upon that, at once, came a convulsive shock.
He suddenly knew with his daylight self that he had just
done this astounding thing with Aron's wife.

Doreen withdrew.

Ned was now wide awake. He lay suffering from acute
shock at the recollection of all he had done a few moments
before with Aron's wife, and of what she, Marina, had done
with him. How on earth could he have got into such stupefy-
ing intimacy with this person?

He was amazed at what had taken place, and horrified.
And thinking it over, it struck him as eerie that what now
seemed to be in such bad taste had been only five minutes
earlier so perfectly correct.

But what he felt now! Aron's wife of all people!

He sat up and, taking the tray with its wickerwork edging
on his knees, he poured himself out tea. He looked at his

letters. There were three letters, one again from the matron recently engaged for Oaklands, who now seemed to be trying to get out of it, the other two were circulars.

But for some reason he was unable to shake his dream out of his mind. As he munched the ginger biscuits, taking them one by one off the plate with the painted violets, here was something that worried him: the whole thing seemed not a dream at all, but *real*.

He poured out some more tea.

Another shock, as great as the first, was in store for him over his second cup of tea. Namely: the realization, coming to him as he drank, that his feelings for Marina were indeed, had actually been, during the last few days, those of his dream. His eyes happened to be only at this moment opened to what he had in fact been feeling for her all along.

This was a revelation.

As he ate the last of the ginger biscuits, by this time totally restored to his ordinary waking self, his mind stepped in and took over the situation. It began telling him that a man is not responsible for his dreams.

Other comforting generalizations followed: it would be a queer thing in general if men were obliged to blame themselves for such dreams! Such dreams were the merest commonplaces. They had a special name and all the rest of it, and they were just a joke, really – in a smutty sort of way. All the world over! And people forgot about such dreams immediately, in any case.

All right.

He got out of bed and made for the washstand, where he collected up his washing things, and went off to the bathroom.

Back again in his room later, affairs did not go altogether smoothly. He mislaid his wallet, and in counting his small change, left overnight on the mantelpiece, half a crown rolled into the fireplace, and he got smeared in sooty fluff getting it out. He also upset his half-drunk cup of tea over the embroidered tray-cloth at one point. So, although he had risen early, his dressing had taken an unusually long time.

'Well! So I have committed adultery with my best friend's new wife. A stranger. Someone I hardly know. That's nice,' he kept telling himself; adding each time, 'Why not stop thinking about it?'

He ought to hurry down to breakfast. In the crowd round the breakfast-table, everything would be as it always had been.

He glanced down at his wrist-watch. It was certainly not early; the family would be well into their breakfast.

As he ran down the stairs he felt excited. And outside the dining-room door he stopped dead. He couldn't go in.

The other side of the door he heard all their voices. All were there. All! He put his hand on the handle quickly and broke into the room.

There she was.

In spite of the green linen slacks which he had not seen before, she was identical with his dream. And on seeing in public – amongst his friends – the full throat with the small dark mark above the satiny collar bones, and the rest, which he had left in his bedroom only a matter of minutes before, he felt embarrassed. There, sitting in front of an empty bowl of grapenuts, was sitting a private, a very private piece of his interior life.

He dared not give her more than a glance before going over to the sideboard to help himself to cereal.

Reamur was talking.

'Ah no, Marina, that is what *Lacy* thought! Not what *I* thought. *She* is in favour of this go-as-you-please pioneer school. My point about all those places was, that for a child, no less than for a grown-up, the obligation to choose and to *decide* what you should do is the heaviest punishment that can be given.'

Marina was surprised. 'Oh, but surely! Freedom of choice . . .'

'Diabolical,' said Reamur. 'In fact, I have always suggested it as an alternative to hanging for criminals.'

There was laughter which, as it faded, uncovered Marina's troubled words, '. . . training for a democracy. We all of us feel . . . *surely* . . . this decade . . .'

Gwen put aside her bacon plate. Aron getting up quickly and removing it to the sideboard. She stretched forward her hand to a rounded china pot, painted to represent a beehive, and with a modelled, striped bee perching on top.

She looked in. 'Marmalade into the honey jar, I know . . . they *will* do it. Here is quince jam however. It really *is* stupid. I'll have some, I think.' She helped herself to quince, adding, 'and what do you feel about what I said yesterday, Ray – that a conventional school gives a child something to rebel against?'

Marina looked uncertainly at Gwen, but couldn't tell much from her mask. 'But surely, surely, *surely*! to give a small child poison merely so that it can spew it up! You're a mother, Gwen! How can you suggest such a thing?'

Aron came back from the sideboard and sat down again, smiling slightly. Reamur put out a long thin finger and rested it lightly on the rim of the butter dish, and said, looking at Marina :

'The brighter spirits of the school will spew up a lot of the doctrine, whatever it is. That is, they will think for themselves, no matter what you teach them. The rank and file will swallow up whatever diet they're given, as usual. But then, the diet they're given is what the brighter souls of a former age have decreed, thought out for themselves. It's not a question of giving them poison, it's just a question of time lag. The rank and file are doomed always to swallow down what some bright spark has decreed for them in a former age under circumstances which no longer apply. That can't be helped. It'll always be so.' He laughed gaily, took up the *Manchester Guardian*, and began to read it.

Marina was shocked. By the demoniac note in his laugh and by the speech itself, and by the expression 'rank and file'. At last she said, 'But that's a *defeatist* point of view!'

Aron, speaking almost at the same moment, said, 'Let's see now – what's all the fuss about? What is so very wrong about a public school anyway, after all?'

'Why!' cried Marina, as she stubbed her cigarette out on her plate, 'the dreadful thing about the public schools is that they mass-produce the children and make everyone run in grooves. They cut all the corners off and make everybody the same. Fred Dysart was saying that very thing only the other day!' She looked deeply pained.

'*I* haven't noticed that everybody is the same,' said Aron.

Marina looked as if her husband had struck her.

'But one does not want mass production of human beings! I thought that in this decade enlightened people had realized that. And, Aron; why, we have both often agreed that the old-fashioned schools rub all the corners off!'

'Oh? Have we?'

With his dark, olive-pale face quite casual, he began flashing his spectacles here, there and everywhere all around the breakfast table, looking for the marmalade.

In the silence that followed Marina took out a fresh cigarette from her case and tapped it, brows knitted, on the table-cloth.

Gwen was glancing through a London catalogue, and murmured, 'Some people can tell what school a young man has been to at once, as soon as he is introduced.' She put down the catalogue and began buttering herself another piece of toast.

'School diviners,' murmured Reamur, behind the *Guardian*.

'Yes,' said Gwen. She applied quince jam again to her toast. 'I *have* had it explained to me what are the different characters of Winchester, Rugby, Harrow and the rest, but I can't remember what they are at the moment...'

'Yes. Now what is it again?' said Aron briskly. 'Hard-working prigs come from Rugby. From Winchester: swindlers and lunatics. From Uppingham: dark horses. From Harrow: tough eggs and business tycoons. From Eton: *l'homme moyen sensuel*. Or is it the other way round?'

Marina looked round the table, finding only casual expressions on the faces there. She looked down again at her plate. Here were a group of people she had taken for progressives, and look at what they were saying. Furthermore, they were being hard and callous again – didn't seem really to care one way or another. How terrible to feel so flippant about helpless children. What dried-up creatures they all were!

Ned read her expression.

It was uncomfortable, he thought, to see this group surrounding this young woman, who imagined herself to be the same as the rest but who nevertheless misinterpreted all that was happening.

Like those muscular cowboys who throw out dancing lassoes over the galloping buffaloes of the prairie without themselves for a moment quitting the saddle, Gwen, Reamur and Aron habitually left their personal emotions and passions securely enthroned and undisturbed while they threw out, unhampered, variegated theories, explanations and hypotheses (none intended for absolute or final) – threw them out as so many circling whirls and loops, hopeful of trapping something of the truth that galloped in a million shapes furiously away over the prairies in every direction. Half the time they were joking, anyhow, as this morning. Watching Marina the last few days, Ned had seen that she herself lacked the spiritual muscles needed to divide her opinions from her feelings. In conversation, and at all times, her feelings bowled her off her feet and she gloried in it. Nor did she stop to see what manner of object it was that had hit her; the fact that she *had* been hit was good enough. Or, to put it differently, emotion in itself – to the others a source of danger – to her was always a positive goal. And so arose the misunderstanding: that when she heard the people, as here all the time at Flitchcombe, saying things of dread and horror yet without emotion suffusing their voice or face, she concluded that they were dried-up old fossils and had no emotion to feel, hard, horrid, smug, and cold.

'Do you know, Aron, you have never really committed yourself,' said Gwen suddenly to her cousin, as she watched him scrape out his pipe with a gadget which he had designed himself, 'as regards the policy of *your own* school!'

'Oh?'

'Exactly. It is always "oh" or "ah" or some evasive joke or other. Can you give us *no* idea as to what your particular brand of upbringing is to hinge on? You are afraid to commit yourself.'

'I refuse to commit myself to naming any magical formula for running a decent school, if that's what you're after, because I don't believe there is any. All that's needed is a little common sense, that's all.' He frowned and turned his pipe upside down and banged it on his plate. 'Common sense in matters of health, and in chivvying the children into doing their lessons. One thing I do feel – yes! I want to make sure that the children are surrounded by people who themselves really enjoy life, and find it a worthwhile occupation spontaneously – not simply on principle. Damn this!' The gadget had flown out of his hand across the room and he went over to pick it up. 'I don't want any hint of bitterness towards things in my staff,' he said, as he returned to his seat. 'But why? Did you think I believed in education by telepathy, or something?' He started knocking his pipe on to his plate again. Then he put away the gadget and took a pigeon's feather out of his pocket.

'I see,' said Gwen.

She thought it over; whilst Aron carried on with the feather.

'But then,' she said after a moment, 'you must let me tell you the sad story about a master at my own school who was a very sincere well-wisher.' She paused and added hollowly, 'A joyous soul, without a hint of bitterness. You've heard me speak of old Ma Bracegirdle?'

And Gwen went off into the tragic tale of Miss Bracegirdle, the hardest ragged mistress in school history, which Ned had heard already and did not bother to attend to.

When Gwen had started her story, Ned had risen from his seat and, walking round the table behind the others carrying his silver lighter, lit the cigarette with which Marina had for some time been playing. She leant forward, cigarette in mouth, towards his hand as it held the lighter, so that his low bending head came close and rested in propinquity with hers for several silent moments, whilst she was pulling at her cigarette.

During those moments, total happiness came down upon Ned, surrounding and insulating him as might a thick glass bell. He had a sense too of being made suddenly whole again; as if one of his own feet, or one of his ears, or eyes, having long been severed from the main body was now unexpectedly handed back to him in excellent working order. That was the order of the relief he felt.

'She is part of me,' he thought, surprised. He returned to his seat at the far end of the table.

There was a jar of potted shrimps on the breakfast-table again today. Although he had finished his breakfast, he now helped himself to the shrimps with the long-handled spoon. He piled them as usual on to a slice of Ryvita biscuit. And, as usual, they all tumbled clumsily off again in all directions over the red and gold pattern of his plate.

'Do male and female together then form part of only one organism?' he wondered as he munched his shrimps. 'That would account for the vividness of the bible story of Adam and his rib ... Yes. One creature, perhaps. Not visible as such to the physical eye but apprehensible in other ways.' The story of Adam and Eve had appeared fanciful, he remembered, when he was a schoolboy. Had had to be taken on trust. Now he felt the full import of it.

The talk at the table rumbled on. Ned kept his eye on the others, munched his shrimps, and heard Marina punctuating the conversation with such remarks as: 'I cannot bear seeing children unkindly treated'; 'To be good at class work is not everything'; and, 'One must guard against giving them an inferiority complex.'

Her remarks seemed to him to show good nature and simplicity of soul. And looking at her femininity, which gave him a vertiginous feeling and kept his nerves ruffled so that he seemed to be leaving the ground whenever she looked directly at him, looking at her perfection of health and sex, he meditated on what a small place really a human being's powers of conversation take, in the aspect of him, or her, as a whole. In fact what matter if a goddess's remarks should fall short of the precise degree of sophistication of the Flitchcombe set? One would feel her to be descending from the celestial to the provincial, no doubt, if they were so to do.

He couldn't afford to look at Marina much, he was in such

dread that the others would notice something. So he lit a cigarette as soon as the shrimps were despatched, and sat, eyes cast down, sagely regarding the burning end of it.

But out of the blue, a horrid thought.

All very good to sit picturing himself and Marina as being one creature, one mystic organism (in the eye of God perhaps – so he had started to amuse himself by picturing – something like a magnificent moth with quantities of wings, legs, and bunches of eyes and only one back) – but what of Aron? Marina was assuredly a part of that organism too! Heavens! Apart from getting harder to picture (this three-in-one moth with some sort of, perhaps, triangular arrangement of legs and wings grouped round the single back), it was a disturbing thought.

In fact it brought back his early-morning's load of guilt to him in fullest strength.

10

AFTER that first shock – that first early morning thunderclap of his dream – during the days and nights that followed, her voice sounded in him perpetually, and her movements, her gesturing limbs, her form, her glances, her withdrawals, her laughter, twisted and wreathed through his geometry classes, through his long, solitary afternoon walks, through the music he played, and between the leaves of the books he read. Her image invaded him without respite, infiltrating everywhere and into everything.

What was he to do? His position was now impossible. Even if Marina had wanted him, and he knew of course she did not, even so *he*, Ned, would not take her – would of course not touch Aron's wife. Yet her attraction persisted, violently.

With one great heave he twisted himself round and contrived to rid himself of his guilt, in arguing thus: in reality he would never have her. It was plain: on the one hand there was reality, on the other merely a dream. He had cut himself neatly in two, the erotic dreamer and the innocent, loyal friend. And so certain was he that he truly did not wish this thing upon Aron that then and there all his guilt shrivelled away. So much for that!

Meanwhile, her attraction for him still violently held.

He found a way to negotiate it: he became 'amused' at what was happening to him, 'entertained' by his 'double self' in an analytical, intellectual sort of way. And in this manner everything, all round, was kept in good practicable order.

The days passed on.

Meanwhile his desire benefited by that rule which decrees that things become invisible in ratio to their dreadfulness.

Something too dreadful to behold, if it cannot melt away, at least turns conveniently transparent, enabling a more acceptable landscape to show through.

Thus, Ned's desire, dreadful as it was, so *hopeless* as to seem innocent, was free to dog Marina invisibly everywhere around. Around and about all over the house, up the stairs, down the passages, in and out of the gardens, wriggling into her plans for picnics and for visits to friends, shadowing her in her trips to the shops, or her bus rides, ensconced in the Malton cinema on her visits there, and lurking in the shadows of the pier at Spatchampton when she went with Violet to watch Co-Co practising his steps on the rink.

Ned, letting his desire streak on ahead, remained himself behind in ambush – scouting things out. He must always know where she was likely to be; what she was doing with her time.

He would linger by the foot of the stairs to catch the rumour of afternoon schemes, as he heard them discussed in snatches of conversation through half-open doors:

'Well, then, Marina, you and I will bicycle over to Softon this afternoon and meet the children at the Macnaughtons' after tea . . .' in Gwen's voice. (Softon.)

Or, in Marina's, 'Gwen, I think I must stay at home this morning. I have some letters to write . . .' (Home.)

After lunch one day, coming down the front stairs with his camera, he had heard voices below from the kitchen quarters, women's voices that were not the maids'. He stopped and listened; it was Gwen and Marina. That was what he had hoped. But what were they saying? He couldn't catch it.

He ran downstairs, stopped at the bottom and listened again. This time he heard more, something about a cake from Sandymans, the baker in the village. Feet were coming his way; he turned aside into the drawing-room, leaving the door ajar. On the little mother-of-pearl table in there, on top of some American magazines, was a child's coloured 'comic' opened out, something that Co-Co must have been reading. Ned bent over this breathless, rigid, and supported on one elbow, studying with ferocious stare the pictures of frisking elephants in spotted party frocks and small tigers gleeful upon roller skates. He noticed, in actual fact, nothing of what lay before him, so avid was he to pick up the thread of the women's conversation in the passage outside.

'No, don't bother,' he heard in Gwen's voice. 'I'll pick it up on my way back from the meeting in the car; he stays open late on Wednesday night.'

'Well, if you're quite sure . . .' from Marina. 'I'll just go off to the woods then, I think. Don't wait tea, in case I lose my way.'

The footsteps parted outside the door, one lot going into the dining-room, the other tripping up the stairs. The latter would be Marina going to her bedroom for her gloves and coat.

He would join Marina in her walk! Would wait to hear her footsteps coming down the stairs again, then sauntering out into the hall would be just in time to be observed casually tapping the barometer with his fingernail with a dreamy air: 'Dare one venture out?' Or 'Is the storm going to break?' Or 'Would it be nice to take a stroll?' No, that would hardly do. Try something else ... In any case, once they got down into the wood everything would go of its own accord. They would stop by the gate that led to Miss Viller's farm. There they'd be, side by side. Little by little they would come closer and closer together, he imagined a long sequence, link by link, until at last they would turn from two to one, totally fused. He got drowned in this thought, but suddenly he heard her feet coming down the stairs again. His heart thumped and he couldn't get his breath – for she had stopped at the door. Then slowly she pushed it open. *He must say his casual words now.* Must, even though he felt he had been struck in the stomach by a horse's hoof. She stepped into the room. But why was Gwen standing there? It was Gwen! Gwen did not notice his amazement, because she was looking down at the shopping-list in her hand, whilst at the same time she endeavoured to wriggle her free arm into her green woollen cardigan. After a few moments she glanced abstractedly up and saw him. Looking through him abstractedly she made a reflective grimace.

'You can't lend me a few shillings, I suppose? I only want about five or six shillings ...'

But she was already fumbling in her cardigan pocket, and at once: 'Oh no, there we are! That's all right! Don't bother,' and she turned vaguely away and wandered out again.

What had happened? Where was Marina? Glancing out

of the window as he followed Gwen out into the hall he spotted Marina half-way across the field among the cows. So now it was too late. What a mix-up!

The next afternoon he had been standing on the terrace, mending one of Co-Co's stilts. Marina appeared round the corner of the house and, walking towards him, stood and watched him adjust the little wooden step.

They exchanged some words.

He felt as if an invading army had suddenly jumped out of ambush and surrounded him, and while he stood terror-struck at the cohorts, was still obliged to negotiate single-handed with the Commander-in-Chief.

All the same, he was not slow to seize what opportunity offered.

In the conversation that followed he managed to steer them both into regions erotic. It had to be done quickly, as best he could – she was on her way round the house to some-where else. He rapidly recounted two stories – the first that came to mind (dragging them in by the tail somehow) – gos-sip, of a smutty variety, that he had heard and that was too suspiciously outrageous to be true; expressing facts (which he recounted in a fashion most indecently vivid) calculated to excite her.

His need was for sexuality with her. More active measures being barred, this kind of thing seemed the only outlet. He was, in fact, courting her; trying to disturb, excite, and tempt. He knew he ought not, and succeeded in feeling both shocked and surprised. As for the latter – his own surprise – that he could achieve it was the measure of his political triumph in cutting himself into two halves.

This conversation on the terrace was the pattern, in essence, of their communion during the following period. And he found other surreptitious methods of courtship:

meaningful lingerings; remarkable methods of handing cups and things; peculiar efforts with cigarettes.

But heaven knew whether his message got through to her. It was impossible for him to make sure whether her own responses were correspondingly impure; and the reason for that was simply that his need for that was so imperative.

11

A WEEK after his dream, in the afternoon, after lunch, Ned walked into the schoolroom, but instead of stopping at the central table he turned and stepped round the L-shaped corner. Round here was a deep window embrasure filled by a red seat, upon which he sat down. Littered over the cushions were the contents of his writing-case. He had left them there earlier in a hurry, on hearing the luncheon bell.

But instead of taking up his pen and dealing with the letters he leant back against the wall of the embrasure and, turning his head sideways, looked through the little leaded panes. There he remained for two hours until the tea bell rang.

This window looked on to a stretch of grass bordered by a row of severely pollarded little trees, so cut and stunted that they resembled green, open umbrellas. This row of umbrella trees started close to the window and ran away across the grass, ending by a compost heap and a small shed under which stood wheelbarrows and a lawn mower.

Co-Co had been given the day off in order to practise his roller-skating, for the Kursaal competition was not far off. He had gone off by the early bus to Spatchampton, taking Violet and Marina with him, and in their absence quiet weighed on the house – a stillness rather weird.

Out of doors there was a softness and scented freshness in the pallid atmosphere, with the sun almost through all the while but never quite. It was a palpitancy of warm sunlight, which kept melting through the cloudy greyness in spasms, fitfully illuminating the pollarded trees and the garden with a kind of honey-coloured blushing in which everything seemed mellow and full of summer life. Then the blush would fade, and the big leaves on these little trees would pale, their forlorn greenness once more a prey to the stern, steely sobriety of the clouds. Then would come, from the jutting roof of the window embrasure over Ned's head, an all-pervasive creaking, as of some elephant turning around and around, cautiously and methodically, in a great wicker basket up there over his head. And, warned by this signal, Ned knew it to be raining once again.

Then he would see the pollarded limes receive the gushing wetness on their big leaves, which began to shiver and to whirl forward and back on their branches in a kind of delicious hysteria of excitement under the downpour's ardour, and would hear, after a moment or two, how they hissed with pleasure as they streamed. All the while a loose stem of climbing rose scratched viciously at the window-pane, its thorns slipping and squeaking in the sudden irritation of the wind.

Afterwards the honey light would melt through again, the elephant overhead lie still, the rain would be over; and Ned would be left staring down at the image of the loosened rose-spray clearly limned in the rain pool left on the sill, over which the living rose, yellow, of the scrumpled, bunchy kind, drooped forward in meek meditation, red and green prismatic water sparks among its leaves.

After each shower of rain the birds – that is to say, a number of thrushes, one robin and one wagtail – would, in a quick-fire, hopping-rushing motion, sweep all together across the lawn past the feet of the pollarded trees as if from the wings of a theatre on to the stage, to capture the after-shower worms.

Ned noticed the changes from rain to sun and back again when they first occurred; but after a little he left the window-seat and the room – though not in body.

Ned during these weeks was at any rate still sitting physic-ally on visible chairs, touching the communal fire-irons, taking up an ash-tray available to everyone, tripping, for all eyes to see, over a palpable hearthrug, and it did not perturb him that his private self was out of the room doing some-thing totally else all of the time. There is no man, he felt, whose 'reality' is in the same room, at least for very many consecutive moments. Even the least imaginative of beings is forced, willy-nilly, to flicker, a spectral butterfly, in and out, in and out, amongst the furniture where he is cor-poreally anchored.

Ned had been for years inured to the idea that things physical are anyway only a kind of knitting needles, which a man holds up in front of his eyes in order to knit with them the garments that he wants or must have. He was now, however, particularly thankful for the fact that though these knitting needles are visible to the bodily eye, *the pattern for the current pair of socks is not.*

Ned did not see that the schoolroom door had blown open. Nor that a draught was fluttering the yellow corner of a typed letter lying open on the pile of correspondence beside him; nor hear that it made a cracking noise as it flicked in the current of air. He was staring at the letter heading: Davis & Son, High Class Stationers, 26a High Street, Fur-minster. But though he had entered the schoolroom with the express purpose of answering the question this letter had put to him (as to what type of exercise books would be required for the school store-cupboard), still, at this moment, he was no more aware of Davis & Son of Furminster than of the Dalai Lama of Tibet.

In imagination he stood by a round, cement-edged pool. Big rocks carried on their ledges fat black seals with bushy whiskers, who lay hunched and bending over, peeping down at their companions swimming below, or suddenly jerking back their throats to catch the herrings as they shot through the air from the keeper's hand.

A barren winter light, a cold emptiness of air surrounded the muffled-up visitors at the circular railings watching the sea-lions' feeding time.

All over the zoo Ned led Marina and her small daughter round, from seals to reptile house, from camel to giraffe. It was actually rounding the wire cage where the king of beasts, mangy-looking and bored, lay seedily blinking his eyes whilst his mate fumbled over a bone in the far corner, that they came face to face with Marina's friend the biologist. Mr Dysart – Fred Dysart.

There he was, in his checked overcoat, with the face long, clever and handsome, 'like a seventeenth-century Spanish grandee' as Marina had expressed it.

Didn't he look disappointed to find a distinguished stranger, Ned, who was obviously an intimate, taking Marina and her child round the zoo like this! Ned tried to see himself in his own grey swing-back overcoat through Dysart's envious eyes.

Fred Dysart, according to Marina, who had let fall a few words about him the previous day, and again referred to him at breakfast that very morning – Fred Dysart was a biologist who worked at the zoo. He had apparently formed a friendship with Marina, and was in the habit of meeting her and Violet there almost every Tuesday.

Ned, on hearing this, and about how Dysart looked like a romantic Spanish grandee, was instantly hot upon the scent.

What was there 'between' Dysart and Marina? Undoubtedly the biologist must yearn to be her lover. But had he yet succeeded? What did Marina feel for *him*? This weekly tryst at the zoological gardens was a most unfortunate affair.

Since hearing mention, and not only once, of Fred Dysart and his long, clever face, Ned had been driven by a fiend's fixed determination to oust Dysart at all costs, both at the zoo and everywhere else.

And since that moment many and vivid were the visions of Mr Dysart that Ned had conjured up. In every daydream on the subject he met Dysart face to face somewhere, whilst Marina and Violet hung lovingly on to *his* (Ned's) either arm – at which *tableau* Dysart's clever face would fall a mile. But there were also other places for the great confrontation.

The best daydream meeting had occurred at Marina's London flat, at cocktail time. There were a group of friends, Dysart included, in front of a blazing fire. Marina had taken Ned round the corner of the L-shaped drawing-room where stood the piano. There they had remained together, playing duets, whilst Dysart's Spanish face through the cigarette smoke on the hearthrug loomed dismal with the knowledge of having been villainously superseded.

Aron himself never appeared in these dreams. Ned kept him in a separate dimension. Aron was 'real' in a way that Ned's dreams of Marina were not. So why bring him in?

There had been several people in the schoolroom where Ned sat for the last half-hour, talking, fiddling with the wireless set, struggling with the kite and, it seemed, making plans for the roller-skating competition. Ned, accompanied by Dysart and the Penguins, had joined in and played a part with the others. First Gwen had come in, then, later, Aron.

Gwen had rung for Wilkes, for he had mended the wireless once or twice before. Wilkes confessed himself nonplussed. He had called in the gardener's boy, with mauve felt cap, for he too was considered a dab at the game. Later Reamur had looked in, quite by chance, in search of a lost paper-knife, and had stayed on, telling the others that the Malton pier boards were rotten and that the roller skaters would fall through on a day when a crowd was gathered to watch the Kursaal competition.

Ned was anxious if anyone was aware – if there was any means by which anyone *could* be aware – of his alteration towards his Flitchcombe friends.

Only a week or two ago, if he had been standing with these friends round the wireless set and taking off its cover, as now, he would have found himself confronting the same situation as they.

But since then something had happened. And now a universe was in the place for him that was not there for them; and its hot circulation had melted the others quite away. They had become insubstantial wraiths, bombinating meaninglessly, in a medium that was to him untranslatable.

It was a quarter to twelve, and these wraiths were still all fiddling with the wireless knobs! They were still all chattering about the wireless. It would be so much better if they would all pack up and go. There really was no mutual context, at the moment, in which he and they could co-exist.

He knew that an immense commotion had in full surge swung him forth from their little mundane landscape to some other.

Swung him to where?

To a place obscurely felt but not reachable by words or even by thought, of a rational order. Like the moon, his namesake, he was shining at them from echoing spaces; from the past; from a new constellation. They would have to evolve clever instruments indeed to get into touch with him there.

12

NEVERTHELESS there were also times when the amorous afflatus, which fawned on Ned so unwieldily day and night, battering him without reserve, quite unexpectedly fell to the ground and treacherously unmasked a nothingness in the air.

On Tuesday night, for instance, Reamur returned from London with a picture he had bought.

Quite unpremeditatedly, Reamur had bought a picture at a dealer in Bond Street at three o'clock that day. He had already paid several visits to this dealer, though, for he had fallen in love with the Vuillard. For such it was. It represented a lady in white sitting at a long tea table, beside open french windows, through which showed evening summer trees with something glimmering in their shadow. But although returning frequently to look at the picture, Reamur had not guessed that he would find himself writing out a very large cheque on that particular afternoon.

While coffee was being poured in the drawing-room, Ned hung up the picture over the mantelpiece, standing on a chair. Reamur and Gwen sat opposite each other on either side of the hearth in large wing armchairs, from which they leant out sideways to get a view of the chimney breast. On the sofa, opposite the picture, Aron and his wife sat side by side. Only the sound of spoons grating round sugary coffee cups and the far, laughing cry of an owl hunting the Flitchcombe meadow in the dusk broke the silence. Ned was busy shortening the cord and setting the picture up.

At last he got down from his chair and laid the hammer on the mantelpiece, so that the picture could be seen.

Everyone began to drink in the spectacle on the canvas,

the mysterious bundled-up white lady sitting alone at the table in the twilight, facing the used plates and the coffee urn, while the last of the sun's rays touched the top of the green trees outside; and everyone began to praise.

Only Marina sat silent.

'Not that it matters in the least,' said Gwen, 'but out of sheer curiosity ... that little thing ... out there under the trees ... a sort of pavilion?'

'A summerhouse, obviously,' said Aron.

'I don't think it's a building at all,' said Reamur. He had relapsed languidly back into the wing shadows of his armchair.

'What is it, then?'

'A figure of Chopin. Composing a nocturne under a tree.' His own thin white fingers were poised on the top rim of his coffee-cup cautiously, as if to restrain it from flying boisterously away into the air. 'Or the ghost of Alfred de Musset,' suggested Aron.

'Whatever it is,' said Gwen, 'and I think it is an arbour, it gives a feeling of secret excitement to the twilit wood.'

Everyone still sat drinking in the new picture, and exploring in silence those things about the artist's execution for which only professionals can find satisfactory expression.

Marina puffed out clouds of cigarette smoke and looked a good deal at her toes.

At last Gwen turned to Marina on the sofa beside her.

'And what do you think of it, Marina?'

'Oh, I'm afraid I'm very bad at that sort of picture ... It's too easy!'

'How do you mean, too easy?'

'Too "precious" for me. All these nineteenth-century drawing-rooms draped in muslin ...! Vuillard and those sort of painters spent their whole lives glorifying expensive boudoirs and ladies, together with those husbands, maidservants and rich viands that the dear creatures considered necessary to sustain their *amour propre*.'

There was silence. Marina added,

'If it had been by Renoir there would have been pink-and-white sugar-cake misses sitting about on poufs, thinking of all the chocolate creams they had eaten. Or else resting from having arranged the flowers in the morning-room!'

Marina's own pink-and-white sugar-cake face wore an expression of barely veiled triumph, as she sat back as if enjoying an inaudible chorus from all round of '*Touché!*'

The company did not attempt to answer her; and presently she added:

'But that *princesse* or *duchesse* – whatever the old trout is – from the Faubourg St Germain, she's more probably wondering how, at her next salon, she can score off her husband's *belle amie*. Or possibly suffering from indigestion after all that *pain d'épice* and coffee.'

'Indigestion, perhaps,' said Aron. 'But a *princesse* – I think not. I think you'll find, dear, that that is a small pension ... some provincial *jardin publique*. And that lady is the widow of the local ironmonger, sitting on there after the other *pensionnaires* have gone.'

'Her own neat villa and goods have been sold up,' said Ned, 'that's why she looks so pensive and hunched up.'

'Outside you can see,' added Gwen, 'under the trees there, the tram-operative waiting to go on duty when the six-fifteen arrives at the *terminus*. I can see more plainly what he is now.'

'*I don't believe it.*'

There was laughter.

'However,' said Reamur, as if apologizing, 'I expect we are both – all – really agreed that it is the treatment of the subject by the painter, rather than the choice of the subject itself, which is important?'

'Oh yes, I realize quite well that it is the artist's *approach* that matters!' said Marina.

'Quite,' murmured Reamur; he sank back into the depths of his armchair.

'And don't you like the way it is painted?' asked Gwen.

'No,' said Marina forcefully, 'I do not.'

Gwen said, 'Well ... but ... surely it is not only in his very individual vision that Vuillard excels, is it? The pattern on the curtains, and on the wall – there – how he has manipulated them to express depth? I'm no art critic, but any – anyone can see ... in short – but do you not feel any admiration for even the bare technique of Vuillard?'

'I should feel more admiration,' said Marina deliberately, holding her hands against her temples and staring with bowed head down at the carpet, almost with the air of repeating some homework she had got by heart, 'I should feel more admiration if the painter, by his technique, had addressed a less *select* and *privileged* audience. The ordinary man and woman in the street did not – at the time that picture was painted, and still does not – understand the language that this artist has elected to speak. The "vision", as you call it, is indeed "individual". Extremely so! Seeing that it comes out of an ivory-tower window! But some of us believe that Art should be universal,' Marina was saying. 'I think that most people of good will – I mean of the present decade – are agreed that in art, *as in everything else*, *everyone* should benefit, and not only a mere handful of the elect.'

A faint click sounded from the shadows of Reamur's chair. In the silence that again followed, Ned looking chilly and depressed, said: 'Must the artist then do everything? Not only receive the inspiration, perform the labour of the construction of the work, but also take time off to try and forget all he has ever observed in life, and try to learn a language of one-syllable words, so that he may force his vision, as into a Chinese shoe, and address the barbarian in his own limited code of things with "The cat sat on the mat" for evermore?'

'But that is exactly what we say – the people of my generation – to these painters of privileged ladies in beautiful boudoirs amid beautiful flowers! Fred Dysart used those very words only the other day "We're sick of being told 'The cat sat on the mat' for evermore" he said.'

'Fred Dysart!' cried Aron. 'What does he know about painting!'

But Marina went straight on. 'Today, in the age of the machine, and of the inheritance of the ordinary man, these harmonious sweet nothings are an anachronism! Picasso was the first to break through all of that! ... Oh, you have got some fine pictures on your walls, Gwen ... but forgive me if I say that most of this house is rotted away by your bourgeois outlook. I don't mean anything personal – you were all brought up that way.'

There was a moment's silence. Gwen, who had now got on spectacles, for she was doing some embroidery, looked out over the top of them with an owlish benignity.

'Well, that is certainly a point of view, and I'm very grateful for it. One gets so buried in one's own little world, and it is hard to assess it in the light of ... in other lights,' she finished off vaguely.

Sitting in a small armchair facing the windows, Ned looked out towards the garden.

The curtains had not been drawn and on the other side of the panes a tall wall of green fire-flakes hung, staring in at the window and curtaining the black night sky.

Amid the torrent of illumined green leaves with the white magnolia cups spangling them a woman's face floated with fiery hair and a stony expression.

A great, broad, swinging arc of creeper leaves outside had

caught up the lamplit sitting-room in its arms, and so inter-
fused that it was hard to tell which things were showing
through the others and whether there were really a forest
of leaves growing between sofas and chairs in the sitting-
room.

Marina's words 'the woman in the street' echoed in Ned's
head. And who *is* this 'woman in the street'? he wondered,
as he looked again out at the night sky where was imprisoned in her green vegetable cage the baffled, angry girl.
It could not be *her*, with all her cultured reading and her
pioneer-philosophy?

Gwen got up and started fussing round the coffee-tray,
helping energetic second cups. As she poured she murmured,
'These are large and difficult subjects ... The divorce between the educated and the uneducated public certainly is
distressingly wide ... It is difficult to see exactly how one can
set about remedying it. Two lumps, Marina? It is all most
unfortunate. Ned ... a little more? Perhaps tragic is not too
strong a word for the situation. And in the last analysis ...
anyway it's a difficult question ...'

'Intellectuals always retire into their towers with that
graceful phrase "it's a difficult question",' said Marina. 'Then
up goes a smoke screen, clouds of words – "analysis", "sub-
conscious", "inferiority complex". And the rest of the world
can go up in flames for all they care! And *is* going up. Why
don't they wake up and *do* something for a change? Why
are we all sitting here for instance pi-jawing and sipping
coffee out of gilded cups whilst men are risking their lives in
Spain at this very moment really dealing with the basic
issues? Why?'

Silence.

'Do you mean that you feel we ought to shut up the house
and go off in a body to the Spanish battle-fields tomorrow?'
asked Ned.

'Why not?'

'What about Co-Co? Will he be much use firing a cannon? And in general the education of the young of this country – who's going to carry on with *that* if Aron and I join up?'

'It's no good going on turning out little gentlemen in your privileged schools as if nothing out of the way was happening anywhere! And that can wait. Now's the time to stop writing essays and to put our shoulders to the wheel and shove for dear life. Teach Co-Co how to use a gun! He's going to need it!'

'When the country goes to war we shall all learn to handle guns,' said Reamur.

'I should be sorry to put a gun into Co-Co's hands, at any rate these holidays I must admit, from any point of view,' said Ned. 'But until that moment it will be wiser for us all to learn how to create a climate of good will, and an enjoyment of the things of the spirit, as Vuillard did. And the two states of mind go together.'

'It's too late for that!' said Marina. 'It's no good indulging in fine states of mind as the ship is going down!'

'I think this is where I come in,' said Aron, and leaning towards his wife on the sofa he pointed to a photograph in the magazine he was looking at.

Reamur got up and wandered towards the door.

'Ah well ... I think I must go and do some work now. Good night.'

'Good night, Reamur.'

'Who's going to have a bath tonight?' asked Gwen. The hot-water system had to be dealt with every evening with relation to the baths desired or not desired by the visitors. 'Only three baths can be drawn at a time, I'm afraid, with the wretched water tank, as you know.'

After this matter had been settled, Ned turned to find Aron, who had remained during the entire conversation half lost in his own thoughts and half immersed in the *Country-man* on his knee, holding his wife's hand on the sofa with a beneficent smile.

As Aron stroked her hand her face began to lose its angry aggrievement. She laid her carroty head against his shoulder on the sofa as she stared down at a photograph of a tame family of hedgehogs feeding out of a hat.

Ned wandered off into the music-room instead of going to bed. He felt depressed and chilled after the evening's conversation. For some reason that evening he had been aware of Marina, not as the adored one, but had seen her, he felt, through the eyes of the others. He had not liked her crossness at the fact that the others in the room had not shared her philosophy. He disagreed with her summing up of matters, and had felt suddenly that a mountain of thought processes intervened between them which nothing could bridge. But most of all it hurt the image of her that he treasured. This image had had a perfection. He had seen her as a creature exquisitely skilled in her own line – that of perfect femaleness. Tonight he had witnessed her in an alien territory, a territory where perfection of femininity could not enter, and in this territory – that he shared so happily with his friends – Marina had seemed not skilled and perfect but clumsy and of a somehow ludicrous gait, and he found his own coldness in the face of it most painful.

13

PAINFUL impressions, however, Ned realized, were to be received sometimes of everyone. They proved, in this case, that the girl was flesh and blood to him and not a myth; they certainly failed to stem the general tide of things.

And meanwhile August had passed away.

It had been a strain, for he was walking on a tight-rope all the while.

For instance, he had been obliged, during the whole month always, to look upon Marina with eyes closely guarded, eyes that showed nothing; because glances too easily communicate, and his situation required a thick packing of ambiguity, and this only words could provide. So that through all occasions and all meetings in those last weeks he could hardly think for the life of him what had really been happening between them.

Running with the hare and hunting with the hounds he remained successfully circular inside the maze.

Sometimes, passing her close in the passage, or leaning towards her with a plate or cup, he was overcome by her fragrance – her personal smell – and fell to marvelling at the supreme power to subjugate of an odour that, after all, seemed only to be, on analysis, like a combination of honeysuckle, cottage pie, and hay. Analysis on these kinds of lines was the only type of analysis that he could at the moment afford.

September came. And still Ned failed to see his danger. None of the symptoms of his undoing had he yet recognized as such.

Private pleasure. Simply pleasure of a private kind. That was what he took the fabulous bird for, that had been busy weaving its fire-nest with his nerves, all through that time.

The bird had weighed light in him at first, but he had felt it grow daily heavier and more vociferous. Most of the time it lay low, on its bed of suffocating, sulphurous ember. But when Marina appeared in the doorway it instantly unfurled top-heavy wings, beat them about inside him like giant flails, regardless of the agony to his cramped system, and, if she talked directly to him, screeched loudly, so that he shrank back in dismay. When Marina sat close beside him, it began by humming sweet nothings, softly delectable oriental things, but finished off by growling and squawking barbarously. At night it had always sung an unhallowed song of its own.

Even so, he felt no real fear; never noticed that his enjoyment was by far too great; merely rejoiced in his flashy parasite; did not perceive that the sharp-clawed thing was using him for a purpose of its own.

14

ALL the same, the moment did come, at last, when Ned woke up to the fact that disaster was near.

It happened in the walnut-tree yard at the back of the house.

One morning after breakfast Ned went into the schoolroom and found Violet. She was standing up on top of the covered-in cistern in the corner and peering out of the small ventilator in the frosted-glass panes that ran along that side of the room.

'Hello, Violet! What are you up to?'

'I was endeavouring to get a good look at the wild cat family,' she replied, in her mincing little voice. 'They have their home in the woodpile out there, you know. And if you open the window properly below and stare out at them they get frightened and hide.'

'Yes, I know. Really, the best place to see them from is the upstairs bathroom.'

'Oh yes, I know,' piped Violet, 'but there is somebody there at the present moment. After all, it's not only just a bathroom, is it? And that makes it rather difficult.'

'Well, yes, it does.'

'And if you go outside and stand in front of the woodpile, it's all right if you stand there for about twenty minutes in frightful isolation; then they *do* begin to come out again, but I haven't the time to spare.'

Violet looked down at him primly, her feet in their white socks on the ledge of the covered-in tank on a level with his nose. She had put up the nursery ladder, especially kept there for the purpose of opening the ventilator which had no cords for adjusting it from the ground. Even from that height, so near the ceiling, Violet's strange, hypnotic gaze caught and held his. The little girl's gaze was quite unusual. Her large, thickly lashed eyes, apparently so languorously half-closed, from a distance gave the impression of swimming in tears and sleepiness, but Ned had noticed, from watching them close to, that she was observing one's face with absolute attention, reading it meticulously and coolly as if it were a book. She did so now, looking down at him, and such a mature consciousness was in her gaze that he looked away hastily as if she had struck him. He leant forward to the window-sill and brushed a dead fly off on to the floor.

'Well, what are they doing, Violet? Are they out there? The mother usually comes out and sports about in the sun at this hour.'

Violet peered out of the ventilator again.

'Yes. She *is* there.'

Ned turned away and began hunting for the atlas.

'What a pity,' said Violet, 'that her leg never seems to get any better! She still limps about on three, and never puts it to the ground at all. Poor thing. And I wonder if that funny rusty red colour that leg has gone is something to do with it ... She's really a black cat, isn't she? I think that brackish-red must be part of a disease. But she won't ever stay still enough to let you look at it.'

'And yet she doesn't seem really frightened of any of us,' murmured Ned, hunting about amongst the paste-pots on the shelf. 'She and her husband have been living in that woodpile for six years to my certain knowledge. That's a long time, you know, for married cats to be faithful to one another. Goodness knows how many families they have reared up in that woodpile – scores of them. Do you happen to know where the drawing-pins are?'

'In the compass-box. But they are all wound round with white cotton, I'm afraid, because we used them . . . for something. Ah, there goes Doreen. Off on her bicycle attired in regal splendour. I wonder where she is going?'

Ned opened the compass-box and was horrified to see the drawing-pins tangled up in a network of white cotton threads.

'Oh *no*! What on earth have you two been doing with these pins?'

'Oh, nothing . . . only something.'

'Yes, but look here, Violet–'

'Oh look, look – there's the father coming up over the farmyard wall! Perhaps he's brought them a rabbit! But he doesn't seem to have anything in his mouth . . .'

Ned stood staring at all the little points of the drawing-pins standing out from the white frothy nework.

'Now he's jumped down and run over to his wife. Well! So he is licking her. They always seem to be rubbing up against each other. They are a very loving pair, I must say.'

Ned shut the lid of the compass-box down and sighed.

'You really must get me some more drawing-pins, Violet. Today. In the village. Will you, please? We can't get on without them. Or else you could disentangle these, if you prefer it.'

'Oh, certainly. I dare say we can disentangle those. If we really go at it. Something, I expect, can be done. But there's absolutely no sign of the kittens!'

'Oh, they're inside the pile there. They never do come outside.'

A sizzling sound came from deep within the cistern. Violet's head was almost outside the ventilator as she stood straining there on tiptoe.

Gollop ... gollop ... gollop, from the cistern.

Violet drew her head in again.

'Yes ... but they frequently come out along the boughs. Especially when the mother is out on the ground outside.'

Ned slid open the long satinwood lid of the pencil-box and inspected the blue and red chalk pencils within. He frowned. Then slid the long lid back again.

'Shall we go out and look at the family?' inquired Violet.

Ned stared in her direction without answering. He was thinking that, because of the lack of drawing-pins, it would be difficult for Co-Co to make a tracing-paper map of America that day. It would be better to get him to write something about it instead.

'Yes. I'd like to see them.'

There was still ten minutes before Co-Co's lessons were due to begin. Violet jumped down from the tank ledge. Together they left the schoolroom.

They passed through the garden-room, an elegant room with an Adam fireplace. This room was unfurnished – against the walls were stacked garden chairs, rusting flower-pot holders and the like, whilst in the panelled window embrasures stood half-opened crates, garden shears, and so on. An old roll of tarpaulin supported a great pile of seed and bulb catalogues, and beside it on the floor stood a crowd of china jugs and flower bowls. Threading their way through these they opened the garden-room door and made their way along the gravelled path outside to the low doorway with its pointed stone arch into the gravelled kitchen yard beyond.

This kitchen yard was enormous, for it had once been a farmyard. Now the farm had retreated on to the other side of the far wall. The top half of a small stack of hay stood up behind the wall, and though the farmyard could not be seen it could undoubtedly be smelt, and one could hear the young heifers thundering to and fro across the straw and cobbles. Up against the near wall, where the pointed doorway was, a mountain of firewood had been stacked, within a few yards of the schoolroom window.

This was rather an unusual yard for two reasons. The ground was covered thickly with small round pebbles such as you only see on the seashore, over which it was hard to walk, for they got into the shoes as one's feet sank in amongst them, and the clattering noise they made was bewildering. Also in this yard there were three ancient walnut trees of titanic proportions – measuring both up into the air and outwards into the branches. The yard was entirely shadowed over by these trees, which cast a lacy carpet of little gold flecks of sunshine dizzily over the pebbles, and whose topmost leaves positively looked down upon the leads and the pointed gables of the house itself.

Violet led Ned in front of the woodpile. They stood side by side bending over with their hands on their knees trying to pierce the darkness within. The branches of the boughs of which the pile was composed were like so many tangled antlers, and if this were really a dwelling place it was certainly a very rococo one, Ned thought.

He looked for some time this way and that amongst the straggling awkwardness of the crowded boughs and branches.

Near the top of the pile, deep within, part of the shadow seemed to be blinking and vibrating in perpetual motion. He looked closer, and saw, balanced on one of the branches, a kind of squirming muff, from which short tails were protruding and thrashing the air. In the middle of this muff he saw minuscule paws upraised and tapping on the empty air repeatedly, like little leaves fluttering and drumming in a breeze. It must be the kittens.

He didn't dare to pass a remark for fear of frightening the kittens. But when he turned his head to Violet he found her pointing with her finger towards the nest. He nodded his head.

For a while this strange winking and blinking of the black shadowy muff in the heart of the pile continued. The short tails flicked the air with smart regularity, like metronome needles clicking. After a bit one of the kittens turned around tremblingly and crept out along the branch towards him. It came out into the light and sat down primly on the tapering tip of the branch, looking at him, revealing itself a small tabby with a white chest and a tiny, smug face topped by small attentive ears.

Behind it one of its brothers came tremblingly forward along the branch also. A third came hurriedly afterwards, but these two became distracted by each other half-way along and started batting at each other's faces with upraised paws, alternately shrinking into the crooks of the branches and lunging forward over the twigs upon each other.

They stood for a time watching the kittens. The white-chested one, who would have fitted comfortably into a teacup, sat quietly looking back at them with equal attentiveness. Once or twice she stood up and placed a white paw falteringly at the side of the branch, feeling uncertainly below it as if ready to jump on to the ground and join them. But she immediately sat down again and continued quietly staring. The two others behind her fell at last into a battle. One had tumbled on to the branch below and lay on his back with all four legs threshing together, whilst his brother overhead kept perpetually rushing forward with upraised paw, scrimmaging backwards on his belly into his forked retreat again, then pouncing out once more upreared into the air and with straight front paws beating the air like a windmill.

Women's voices sounded on the other side of the door in the wall and footsteps on the flagstones. There was laughter, and the little door under its pointed arch was wrenched open from the other side and, bending their heads, Marina and Gwen stepped into the yard. The two women saw Ned and Violet at the same moment. Marina's face lighted up as she spotted the white-chested kitten sitting on the bough, and she came towards them, scrunching across the pebbles with her high heels. Gwen, however, smiled at them only and scrunched off across the yard diagonally towards the disused stables, in which coke and such things were kept.

'You must come and see these kittens!' shouted Violet to Gwen. 'They are all three out together this morning. We ought to name them!'

Gwen half turned on her passage across the yard and smiled vaguely back at Violet.

Violet started to run after her.

'Come and see them! They are all three out together! It's a good chance to name them,' she yelled.

'What?' cried Gwen, and called out something which they could not hear as she went on her way to the stables.

Violet followed after her.

Marina came and stood by Ned in front of the woodpile. The weather, though grey, was sultry, and she wore a cotton frock. There were pictures of dogs drawn all over Marina's frock, to Ned's discomfiture, who, though recognizing that the dogs were fashionable dogs drawn in a somewhat fashionable manner, still felt strongly that the effect was vulgar, and that her get-up was surely noticeably second rate.

All the same, the frock's colour, an ephemeral, wishy-washy and frigid lavender, showed off the darkly living richness of her mica-gold skin with its light veiling of freckles, at once dusty and sparkling, over the cheekbones and nose, which always so delighted him. With her small head and sleeked-down red-gold hair, her narrow hands and flexible body, she reminded him of a golden lizard in some hot climate where the dusty earth was freckled over with vine-leaf shadows and pinpoints of sun, and he had the desire to grab hold of her flexible waist and to feel her, lithe, struggling and wriggling, lizard-like, away from between his hands.

The kittens were now all three poised in a line along the twisting elm branch, staring down at the pebbles below and raising and lowering their furred faces and bearded chins with a questioning look, apparently getting ready to jump down on to the ground.

They had seen their black mother come round the corner of an old zinc tank that stood by the wall, between the woodpile and the house.

The black mother loped stiltedly forward upon three legs, not touching her injured foot to the ground. When she reached the woodpile she sat down on the pebbly ground in front and, stretching up her injured leg, which was an odd rust colour and looked moth-eaten, into the air in front of her, she started cleaning along it with her tongue.

The cats seemed to have forgotten Ned and Marina, doubtless because they had kept so still, and as all the family were now happily outside the woodpile in the open, it was unnecessary for Marina to edge along so close to Ned and, indeed, to stand leaning and pressing herself against him as in the end she did.

As if it was only fair to the cats to remain somehow glued together without stirring or drawing breath, Ned and Marina remained there, apparently regarding the wild cats for some time. During which Ned saw nothing; every drop of his blood concentrated on the feel of Marina's body against his own from the knee to the top of the shoulder – for she was leaning back against him from slightly in front where she stood. He felt the heat of her body come through the cotton frock and through his own shirt, for he wore no jacket at this time, having left it hanging on the back of the chair in the schoolroom.

The reality of their having come together so closely at last in the very way he had so intensely imagined and hungered for during almost every second of the last four weeks was overpowering for Ned, and what provided the heart of the excitement was the fact that she deliberately willed it so.

It was only a few moments that she stood against him in this way, but it was long enough for her body to give him the message, in full measure, that he had this long time been waiting for.

Like something frail violently uplifted in the plunging wake of a monster as it cuts swiftly and forcibly by, Ned found himself so tumultuously rocked around out of his orbit that when Marina turned and called out 'In a minute!' to somebody behind his shoulder he felt so dizzy that he was obliged to put out his hand and, in order to support himself from falling, clasp the branches of the woodpile, which he found for some reason was directly behind him at that moment.

How he had changed his position from facing the woodpile to standing right at the end of it, while Marina conducted a conversation with Gwen and Violet, who had somehow returned and were now bending over the cats, he could not remember. Nor what had happened in the interval. He felt only that he was no match for the radiant, raging bird, whose fiery wing still beat him backward, into the house, vertiginously reeling back, out of sight.

Once up in his bedroom he threw himself down on the bed. He had only one thought: he could have her. She wanted it.

Everything was changed.

And so the Phoenix on her bonfire in his veins raged triumphantly, revealed as the bird of generation that she was; potent and businesslike, she began urging him, with her fanatic's determination, to make haste and get down to work; pressing him to settle without further loss of time exactly how, when, and where.

15

THE practical issue was delayed, however, for the time being.

For a day or two after the incident in the yard Marina went away.

She went for three days to London, taking Violet with her to the flat, to the dentist and to buy and fit some school clothes before the term should begin.

He knew after they had come back, on 18 September, there would be only three days before the house-party would break up. Everyone would go on the 21st, leaving the family alone again.

There was much talk at this time about the Malton Regatta, which fell by chance on the same day, too, the 21st. Co-Co had been entered for the skating competition on the pier, and had wanted everyone to watch. Finally it had been decided for all to motor together into the regatta, watch Co-Co's performance at the skating competition in the afternoon, and separate only after that, suitcases in hand, at the Malton railway station.

So now, before Marina's last days down here began, Ned

was left alone with the others at Flitchcombe for a space, just as he had been before her advent.

After the sound of her station taxi had faded on the air, Ned, sitting in the schoolroom window-seat, thinking of this, suddenly noticed the fact: that in his thoughts, his friend Aron had indeed become 'the others'! And from that one fact alone could be seen that it was not at all the same for him at Flitchcombe now as before her advent.

He no longer indulged in long philosophical conversations with Reamur in which he boasted of his happiness, his serenity, and new-won power over life. Instead he spent the hours restlessly roaming about the house, ten minutes here, twenty minutes there, a gramophone record in one room, a look at the newspaper in another, on tenterhooks. And all the while letters addressed to him by carpenters and tradesmen at Oaklands piled up unanswered on the bedroom chest of drawers.

All his share of the arrangements for the school had fallen into a confusion of which he was ashamed, and which he had so far managed to hide from Aron.

On the Thursday (Marina having been away since Tuesday) Ned, stirring his coffee by the drawing-room fireplace after lunch, stood looking down at the others as they sat round the hearth.

He felt queer. Oppressed. The morning had been, for him, interminable, with its long hours of silent, sultry heat; a mockery, with its buzzing flies and miserable, trumpeting cows.

'Aristocrats are to grace our middle-class abode on Saturday,' said Gwen.

She was sitting upright on the small brocade armchair, with her horn spectacles on, doing embroidery.

'Aristocrats?'

Reamur murmured the word without stirring from his

supine position – horizontal almost – in the deepness of his armchair.

'What aristocrats?' asked Aron. He did not look up from winding the black twine round one of Co-Co's blue-painted stilts, which had a crack in it. 'Or, rather, which aristocrats?'

'An ambassador. An earl. A princess or so.'

Reamur threw up his hands in an exaggerated motion and let them sink slowly down again, drooping as before.

Gwen sat bolt upright with an expression of being amused at the issues raised.

'Well, what are their names?' demanded Aron.

'It's just that picture-collecting earl who wants to see my Vuillard, I suppose,' murmured Reamur in a weak voice.

'Yes.'

'He hardly counts.'

'Why does he hardly count?' asked Aron, giving a jerk at his twine and staring fixedly down at it with a stern look through his specs.

'We know him too well, somehow.'

'And he owns that place – what's it called?'

'Shandenleigh.'

'Ah yes, Shandenleigh,' said Aron. 'But however well you know him that doesn't alter the fact that he is coming slumming here from a privileged sphere, where the codes are as different from ours, I suppose, as ours are from the Mile End Road.'

'The customs are different. The manners, perhaps, too. I don't know if the codes are ...'

Gwen turned to her husband and transfixed him over her spectacles.

'How can you say the manners are different, Ray? I've never noticed any differences between Charles's manners and ours. His manners are good, and so, I hope, are ours.'

'Oh, good manners are the same all the world over, of

course. An earl may or may not have them. By and large Charles has – when he remembers. But is there not surely a kind of hardened – though graceful – showmanship always about a man brought up from birth in administrative convolutions that–'

'What – what – what?' cried Aron. 'Say that again and illustrate your answer with a map, as the boys of the school say.'

There was some vague after-lunch laughter.

Gwen's neck was flushed, beneath the ear, and she gripped her darning wools. Before the others could press on with the subject she said quickly,

'Then there's this Indian prince he's bringing with him.'

'Ah. An *Indian* prince. I see. What's *he* like?'

'I don't know. Never had the pleasure of meeting him.'

'Well ... carry on.'

'How d'you mean?'

'This ambassador. What ambassador is it? I mean, what country does he represent?'

Gwen told them, or, rather, told Aron, for Reamur was keeping out of this adding, 'His name is Tret.'

'But that's an English fish!'

'*Tret*.'

'*Tret*? It's not possible.'

'Well it sounded like Tret on the telephone. Charles wants to bring them all over. I warned him we were giving a children's party on that day, and said we should all be quite distracted and de-humanized, but he said he enjoyed children's parties and refused to be put off.'

Ned had gone over to the window during the conversation, taking his coffee with him.

Outside the steady sunlight on the garden made one blink.

He stood there in the window and heard the light chat about earls and princes going on round the hearth. As it ran on he felt more and more oppressed. In fact he felt clearly that, labouring under pressures that he could not easily define, he was being overcome with a horror and even a fear of his friends.

They were merely talking as usual upon this and that. And it was not at all the particular subject chosen that offended. Today that happened to be the dazzlement, or otherwise, of a gilded and privileged class. Any other subject upon which they had been joking, but on which they nevertheless held serious views, would have had on him today the same effect.

It had been coming upon him for some time, but now it struck him afresh: that there were distances between the creatures in this room that were far too unhealthily great.

Whatever these people might be saying, what they felt was all too separate. Here was Reamur: languid Ophelia, silent, drowned, floating as usual far away on unreachable currents out of sight. And Gwen: he knew what that flush meant in spite of her impartial tones. He knew she was very much excited that these grand folk were coming to tea. Sniffing the breeze as usual for Messianic news, she was wondering, in her incorrigible way, whether perhaps this new and gilded band, due to heave over the horizon on the Saturday, were perhaps those ones she had long awaited, coming, at last, to save the day. Yes, she was capable of that, poor old Gwen; though she wouldn't, of course, let on at any price. Not even to Reamur.

And Reamur? What did he feel about Gwen's golden calves, a new one set up daily?

Ned had never understood, quite, this marriage, and what the couple meant, finally, to each other. He made his guess, though, all the same: that, whether Gwen knew it or not, each one travelled alone.

Aron, too, sat there in his chair, millions of light years apart from all the others, rotating away altogether on a different axis with his beautiful wife – the luckiest man in all the dusty, gaseous, disc-like system of the universe.

Certainly it was the mighty distances between chair and chair in here that were crushing Ned. And it was these people's false assumption of ease, their counterfeit serenity, their farcical prostration to the courtesies, and the decencies, and the veils, that frightened him on their behalf – on the behalf of all men – and that gave him a panic nausea. He seemed to be smelling the stench of a corruption too deep here in the drawing-room even to be noticeable any more. Neither did it assuage his anxiety to mark with what naïve placidity, sitting round the chimney-place, they wore their twentieth-century coffin cerements.

He must escape! Quietly he put his empty cup on the mantelshelf and walked out of the room. Outside in the passage he fled along to the front hall, pierced the front door and escaped on to the drive.

He must go off, walk and get as far off as possible.

16

IN the drive, walking up the gravelly hill between the rhododendrons, he gaspingly breathed in the fresh sunlit air. Like a motorist, who having travelled all day seeing the countryside only through the tinted and grimy windscreen, gets out at last and stands looking about him on the road, Ned rejoiced to find that everything here, at any rate, was real.

He breathed in the wild currant leaves, hot in the sun, and the laurel, the acrid greenery of the shrubs – arbutus, syringa and lilac. He turned his eyes upwards at the topmost sunny, fluttering leaves of the poplars; and downwards at the fidgeting blades of grass. He enjoyed the smell of all this living greenery in the hot air; but, arrived at the gate, he savoured equally the cold and mouldy atmosphere given off by the wet moss on the gateposts, in the shadow of the yews.

Opposite the gate, lime and elm trees grew out of the hedgerow. And below, in the ditch, appeared the Japanese antics of that bamboo-like plant whose many heads spread abroad flatly in trays of white stars, and resembled a blowsy sort of ditch dwarf-pine. And these grotesques sprang out from a tangle of nettles of the darkly brilliant purple-flowering kind, out of a break of speckled grasses and convolvulus and a lot more country stuff.

Ned was excited by the multitudinous presence of all these things, and wanting to hit upon some striking and honouring thought, he began to reflect that these live organisms round him were in reality a great army of conquering desperadoes, lined up, having (as *he* had also), through thousands of years of bloody battle, reached, at the identical moment, this spot at the end of Flitchcombe drive to stand up facing each other at long last, green limbs and pink – victorious!

Ground into the tarmac, as he passed through the gate, the mosaic of a frog, spreadeagled decoratively flat where some motorist had squashed it, revealed one now of the vanquished, and he stepped over it.

He turned left, to the village.

He would walk to Softon Woods, there to submerge himself deep in vegetable system, and forget for an hour or so the cramping culture and the Chinese deformities of his own unsatisfactory race.

A spruce black dog sat bolt upright in the middle of the road fifty yards ahead, opposite the council houses. With paws neatly together, neck stretched primly up, and pricked ears all agog, it stared eagerly as he approached.

This dog was there always, in the middle of the road, sitting opposite the gate of the bungalow where it lived. Not till he got quite close – five or six yards – did it get to its feet and unobtrusively trot off down the little lane beside the bungalow. For it was invariably all eagerness like this at first and never failed to melt away exactly as the crisis approached.

There was usually in this section of the road between the school house and the chicken farm a certain obstinate cat. Fat and black, it habitually squatted amongst the dock leaves half-way up the steep bank-side, glaring round-eyed from between the fronds at the passers-by. And there, sure enough, Ned saw it now. Ned stopped and, bending over, flicked his fingers, calling out, 'Puss! Puss!' at which it stared obstinately back with no expression. When, tired of snapping his fingers at this unresponsive creature, Ned straightened up and walked on again, he had only gone three yards when up jumped the cat and rushed along the bank beside him with its belly held close to the ground and its ears flattened out, and, ignoring his reproachful exclamations, shot across the road in front of his feet, cutting him dead and disappearing through the hedgerow opposite.

This was just the kind of nonsense Ned was in the mood for.

At the bottom of the hill, outside the builder's yard, the builder's kitten was often playing in the ditch beside the roadway. Water ran there over the leaves and pebbles, and the kitten was often chewing beetles and things among wet grasses.

Today Ned spied the fat, elderly builder, with his scarlet neck, and wearing gaiters, breeches, and a tweed Norfolk jacket – spied this man in his yard with a big cap on his head, and his kitten lying out flatly along the top of it, eyes shut, fast asleep. The builder was often seen carrying the kitten round about on his head in that manner.

The village had its due share of cats, bantam hens, dogs,

goats, budgerigars, pigs, sparrows, rooks, and all the rest of it. Ned welcomed them all this afternoon. In the mystical mood that he had fallen into he hailed them one and all as envoys from some well-loved place to which he felt himself somehow returning; and he compared their spontaneous antics very favourably with these of his own race, who, he thought, were for ever pacing their dim corridors carrying their own heads under their arms, or else sitting motionless in circles swaddled in criss-cross grave bands, like the friends he had left behind at Flitchcombe Manor.

Just before reaching Major Crumple's house he turned off the main road and through an iron gate into a mustard field.

On the further side he came to a sloping bank, at the top of which waved sunlit turnip leaves against the sky.

Ned climbed the hill and up into the turnip field, for on the far side lay Softon Woods.

This part of the walk was a bore, the field stretched away for ever in a desert of dark-green turnip leaves which reached to his ankles and flapped against his shoes with a dry, scruffy sound, and it was far too hot in this plateau in the afternoon sun.

At long last he reached the further side, where another gate led him out on to a path of soft dust, running through long grasses. This was a pasture ground, and in the middle, without ceremony, stood up Softon Wood, basking in the sun, guarding its dark central avenue of beeches.

The avenue, planted in the early eighteenth century, ran straight through the woods to the great house – Softon Magna. The lodge at this end had long ago fallen into disuse – had in fact been bodily removed together with the gates, so that the avenue, in all its spacious and formal, archaic, architectural majesty, standing here in this weedy cows' field, was absurd.

Ned entered, stepped silently along over the fallen leaves. Half a mile ahead, at the far end, daylight showed.

Looking upward to where the leaves met overhead in a crowded roof, he seemed himself as far away from the ceiling up there as were the earwigs weaving in and out among the leaves beneath his feet. Apart from some celestial and echoing whistlings among the leafy rafters there was a midnight hush.

He walked on down the avenue, penetrating among the twilight and damp smells, sinking into its deep chlorophyll slumber as he had intended.

He paused for a moment where a monstrous form, a vegetable alligator, had fallen across the way, barring it, and before threading his way round couldn't resist putting out his hands to feel its smooth and muscular torso beneath the silver skin. But Ned rested only a minute or two by the log. Then he was off again, this time down a track leading off at right angles away from the avenue to the further edge of the wood.

The particular genius of his afternoon was impelling him all the time onwards to a further spot; a place to confront which a potent undertow had steadily been drawing him.

The wood ended without warning, as it had begun. Ned stepped out into the open upon springy turf.

This, in the sunlight, was common land, cropped close by rabbits and sheep, which fell away downhill in front of him, revealing Softon Valley below.

Ned was now on a rough track running curving along the crest, where a perfumed breeze, coming across a clover field close by, eddied lazily across the turf, warming and disturbing the heavy air. He had to pick his way between stray tufts of gorse and straggling thorn roots, stumbling over all sorts of hidden stunted odds and ends. Everything in the valley – the white thread of road down there, the green fields filled with willow trees, the farmsteads and the bridges, the barns and haystacks scattered round about, the shadowed hillsides on the farther side together with the glittering green verdure of those trees that stood oblique upon them and caught the full dazzle of the sun – all these glimmered together mazily, lying in siesta under a shimmering weight of heat.

He remembered the place in winter : a cold nothingness of atmosphere under a wan sky, a skeleton, with its frozen roads and trees standing up like rusted wires. Since then something other had come flooding in, 'liberating' the place, blowing up old conceptions, throwing open new routes and marshalling battalions (of the vegetable, chemical kind), establishing itself victoriously over all the land – in short, summer. And now everything was drowsy with ripeness; drenched in golden languor; burdened with the agony of its heats and thrilling all through.

And so it was with Ned.

Of a victim of desire it is often said that he is drunk – intoxicated. And certainly Ned had felt in himself his focus altered and his balance thrown out, had felt within him also old bridges – old conceptions – being blown up, routes being thrown open, and battalions marshalled; for in his system, too, there was preparation for an infiltrative act. He, too, was to liberate his chosen territory. And so the two worlds stood facing each other, animal and vegetable, on the crest of the hill.

In the valley rumbled a lorry, on a hidden road some-where, and after a few moments there was some kind of impact and the sound abruptly ceased. Afterwards a dog began yapping shrilly, so perhaps there had been an accident with another vehicle on the road, but it was so far away that the rumour floated only thinly up before the silence returned again.

It has been said that in falling in love there is much of

madness and of dream. Up here where was only turf, heat, and silence, dream was manifest and come into full summer power with a resonance of vibration, an inaudible undertone of potency, stupendous and immeasurable.

He walked along the crest to where the track dropped sharply down among some chestnut trees below. These bordered a small road, which curled away round a corner out of sight still running sharply downhill, its surface of chalk dust nobbled over with emerging flints.

Ned stepped down on to it and, thrown forward at each step on to his toes with the steepness and the pull of the valley below, went round the bend.

He knew well what lay below, and would come into sight any moment now, at the bottom of this familiar road. And sure enough, gathering momentum, with a squirling, eeling motion the road disgorged him abruptly at the bottom facing the well-known old place.

The road meanwhile ran on round the place, petering out, however, immediately behind it, amongst ruined barns and rotting farmyards.

Ned had stepped straight across the road and laid his hand upon the wrought-iron gate, rusted and curled, of the place itself, which stood ajar.

He entered.

The weed-choked ground round his feet was not a drive, had never been more than a wide sweep round towards the house.

Tall, tough, stringy plants flapped against his knees scattering their white fluffs and tangling round his ankles as he moved towards the house, and then walked along its ruined frontage.

Not a large place, it had, all the same, been in its lifetime elegant; a little manor house, a small farmhouse really, of the late eighteenth century, with a fine coping, spaciously designed, running under the eaves and giving an impression of leisure and elaboration.

Ned had been there before more than once and knew its history. Owned by a man who lived not so very far away and who wished to preserve the surrounding woods undisturbed for game, it had been left purposely without tenants for a great number of years. It was tumbling now after such long neglect, and wore a look of helplessness in face of catastrophe and general ruination.

Boards, nailed together, were fastened roughly over the front door, hiding the flanking pilasters and the carved fanlight. Planks were nailed over other windows, too, and all this wood was bleached silver with countless winters' rain. Those windows on the ground level left unboarded were hardly visible between the tangled climbers and creepers.

Most of the upstair windows gaped darkly without glass. Worst of all was the way the wall, from the front door to the end of the house, had sunk into the ground, so that the small eighteenth-century bricks careered perilously downwards, dragging the roof with them and causing it to ripple like an old shawl.

Ned walked round to the back, passing the overgrown scullery and kitchen windows, and, turning the corner of the house, found the back lawn, or what had once been such, bordered by trees and shrubs in rank disorder. The grass here was tall and growing in clumps and tussocks as in a field; a primeval forest of gigantic nettles, head-high, stood all around and filled up the shrubberies through which could be seen the old barns and cowsheds of the farm behind.

Ned waded through the rank docks and grasses and, passing along the back of the house, made for the long drawing-room at the end, whose window stood open, giving an easy entrance.

He found the sash thrown up from the bottom by about two feet, through which he clambered in.

The window-seat was scattered over with rusty nails and crumpled things, dried-up putty and fragments of plaster. Once inside he stood up and brushed the dust off his trousers. He was in a long room with panelled walls, and with panelled shutters in the deep embrasures, and broken plaster decorations on the ceiling.

Through the panes of the two windows, untidy with dusty spiders' webs and a host of dead flies, through the branches of a bay tree growing outside, showed fields of wheat-stubble and blue sky alight with sunshine.

This gave a queer light, and a tragic light, to the empty room. The faraway sunlight of the outside world echoed in this dead place dully, seeming to strike against the ceiling only, perhaps because the room was so sealed away by the screens of foliage at the windows. The floorboards, the bare walls and the room in general resounded harshly to Ned's tread, and seemed to be coarsely 'answering back' and rudely ignoring his humanity; not at all receiving him with the smug complacence it would have accorded while still itself alive.

Something extraordinary was on the wall facing the windows! It was in the centre of the elegant Adam fireplace – a ghostly, phosphorous, immense, and spectral *thing*, filling up the mouth of the fireplace. It was so terrible in its unearthliness and ghostly horror squatting there that Ned got a fright, and his heart began to race. The next instant he realized what it was, however, and remembered having seen it there before. It was the result of many many industrious spiders' weaving. The entire grate was filled and stuffed up with spidercloth: grey gauze as fine as puffing smoke and as dense – denser – and arranged in folds and pleats extraordinary; it looked like an ectoplasmic presence from another sphere.

Ned gaped for a few moments at this spiders' shroud cloaking the chimney, then through the half-open door he left the room and wandered through the rest of the house.

The broad stairway was oak, seamed and cracked. It re-acted alarmingly under his tread. The landing at the top stretched away revealing doors ajar and rooms opening out of each other.

Faded wallpapers hung out into these rooms in peeling streamers. Everywhere leaking ceilings had produced brown stains, crinkled at the edges like maps of the continent, and toadstools cancerously abounded. In one of the rooms he noticed, when looking out of the window, the shutters had rotted and fallen into the garden below. But elsewhere there did not appear to be any shutters, and all through the house the daylight glared insolently into the sightless, wide-open eyes of this once private body.

He did not linger upstairs. The aridity appalled him of this abandoned place so helplessly invaded by the bright public stare of the outside, so unguarded by polite curtainly evasion or any musliny reservation.

Ned thundered down the back stairs. He stood for a mo-ment on the stone flagging outside a closed door, chocolate and shining. These were the servants' quarters.

He opened the door and peeped in. A mound on the floor hindered the door from opening properly. He sidled in, some-how, squashing himself flat against the wall. Yes, it was the kitchen sure enough, but almost dark, for the nettles blocked up the windows entirely. The nettles were backed in their turn by a heavy creeper, so that it was not easy to see the rusty tins and bottles that stood about everywhere, and the two mammoth bundles of what appeared to be mattress stuff-ing, and the kitchen range gaping cavernously in the wall, with, to one side of it, a great boiler with twisted pipes and taps.

When he got accustomed to the green twilight, he saw that a large cupboard with shelves was standing wide open. Yet one could hardly call the place empty, for the strips of wall-paper hanging outwards from near the ceiling in jagged loops and arches and springing almost into the very centre of the room made of the place a kind of monstrous grotto.

A few brick steps led up to a small doorway. Ah! It was the kind of doorway which leads often to some attic under the eaves where old suitcases are piled or apples are stored. And up there was a very curious little room, if he remembered right.

He went up the steps and entered it. The room was small, low of ceiling, square, and deadly silent. And this seemed to have something to do with the window, which, unexpectedly, was too high up to see out of properly.

On the whitewashed wall were scratched in pencil, thick and black, or thin and barely visible, or in some cases in coloured chalk, pornographic drawings, rhymes, odd scraps and phrases and unprintable four-letter words. Village youths from the countryside round about had been here by the score, that was plain, and girls, too, without doubt, leaving behind them no uncertain mark.

In fact the dreams of a large part of the countryside seemed to be here portrayed. There were chains and naked females within them. There were whips. There were rhymes calculated to excite, and as counterpart there were – bold, large, and many times drawn upon the wall – pictures of excitement's consummation.

He recognized some of the jingles. For instance he had seen many times before, this one, scratched in blue chalk:

> Ashes to ashes,
> Dust to dust,
> If you don't — me
> Someone else must.

He spent a long time looking them over, missing nothing,

and thought: Here, in silence, hidden in this empty house at the bottom of a deserted combe, was inscribed in a universal language, stylish in its pure honesty and lack of cant, a chapter of conflagratory import, one might say of vital import, to everyone upon this earth alike. The wall, so marked by human hand, contained dynamite. To prove the fact, no printer would dare to publish a facsimile.

On Ned the effect was immediate. Ignited already, he felt the flames in him leap up responsively to the hot allusions on this wall.

He looked at all of them a second time; not with the surface laughter of a man remote in company, but with the natural eye, and with the eye of a man suffering from desire and alone in an empty place.

There was one in particular, written up sideways at an angle with thick black lead: A naked woman, with a fringe of darkly crooked pencil strokes, lay on her back, and beside was scrawled in capitals: 'If only she would lie down and let me — her.' Close beside it, large and formidable, was pictured the organ with which it should be done. Ned stared, fascinated. It so exactly voiced his own thought. Nothing that he had ever read, however fine or powerful, had brought home to him with such a stab the heart of the matter as these eleven words from the unknown village youth.

It so exactly expressed his own need, without a word to spare. He looked at the pencilled woman. He thought of Marina. He pictured Marina – exactly as he so wanted her. She was there always anyway, in his nerves and in his mind; now she materialized, the bouquet of her personality inundating him. As her image suffused him he felt he was trembling, melting away from place and time to meet her, so that he didn't any more clearly know anything beyond the urgency of her image and of their embraced desire. His happiness in her grew; their intimacy became each moment more palpable; and he felt growing in himself the presence of an ocean of erotic power unfathomably deep and himself borne forward on a groundswell of passion and of lust towards her – the one he wanted. And the pressure of this groundswell grew every moment more, the madness and the urgency with which he experienced in imagination her sex and tasted all that was erotically, ecstatically, coarsely, divinely *her* formed a mighty current in which he streamed journeying to her; it was her name 'Marina' that burst from him unimpeded as a lightning flash, when in the violence of his impetus to her he arrived – they met and fused.

And so was completed, in his imagination, that which is loneliness's opposite and the reverse of solitary selfhood – the sexual act.

Immediately he opened his eyes and saw, small, finite, unfurnished, and whitewashed, the little room, like a prison cell. It was all a ghastly lie; he was alone.

It had been a stupid delusion; he was there of course as usual just a separate entity, entombed in sterility by himself.

And where was *she*?

Now it was afternoon, not yet tea-time. Almost certainly she was – and had been in that moment which held for him divinity – simply shopping. With paper parcels. Down Oxford Street.

His awareness of the ludicrousness in the depths of his frustration scalded him with its bathos and its blasphemy.

He had come to, only to find that the cruel and heartless hum-drum held him in its pincered grip again; and through his defeat he felt his own raining tears.

He left the empty house; retraced his steps up the steep hillside along the chalk road.

When he regained the hill crest out in the open again, above Softon Valley, he paused, then sat down to rest a moment on the hot and springy turf, inhaling the sweet heaviness from the neighbouring clover field.

There below him again lay the valley, its willows and farmsteads and white chalk road, the flat fields of grain and hay intersected by dark hedges, rolling away to the shallow downland country with its dark patches of woodland and the pale-blue shoulders of the higher hills rising beyond.

He stared at all this sadly – it was a mirage, azure, sumptuous, velvety, impalpable, shining through leagues of air burning with sunlight, and he an exile, fallen, and barred outside.

There lay a summer dream fulfilled in a vegetable reality. But here sat a schoolmaster in solitude, merely thinking of another man's wife.

He sat there for some time, alone and holding on to his private dream, cut off, he and it, there having been, he felt, a calamitous failure of negotiation with their fleshy part. So that they were without material relationship – unable to find a foothold upon the world. And he asked himself: If that is not by definition madness, then what is?

17

NED'S walk across the summer fields, his visit to the empty house, the books he had come to reading in her absence (for, like a veritable schoolboy, he had come to searching the book-shelves for the thing of which he stood in need), at the indignity in which these things involved him, his soul had revolted. He felt that he could not assist at his own castration a day longer. He must finish and put an end.

But how? And, particularly, where? Thought was necessary. A discreet plan of campaign. Above all, speed – for there remained only a week before the holidays broke up and Marina (for the time being) would be lost to him.

For two days he pondered, and then, on the Saturday afternoon (and Marina had arrived back from London in the morning), his way became clear.

A children's party was proceeding in the schoolroom when the incident took place.

All the morning a mist had blanketed over the sky, hills and village alike, and even nearby trees were hidden in the dimness so that it looked as if the rest of the world had been sliced off like a piece of cake at the bottom of the garden and nothingness was revealed all round the lawns. Newspapers foretold local thunderstorms, and certainly it felt sultry enough. When Ned went out after breakfast with Co-Co to search in the summerhouse for a line and other properties for the children's games in the afternoon, the air was hot – scorching – and even without a jacket he broke into a per-spiration at each movement, and it was unpleasant.

In the darkness of the summerhouse Ned turned to Co-Co, who had opened the lid of the croquet box and crouched with his head buried in it.

'You won't find the line in there, I'm afraid. Gwen said it was in a black box with the shuttlecocks and battledores.'

'*Battledores!* What on earth are they?' said Co-Co con-temptuously. 'In any case, it's no earthly point looking out things for French and English, egg-and-spoon races, and all the rest of it, when it's going to pour with rain. Anybody could see that, I think.' He was annoyed at having to shift about the games boxes and struggle with rusty locks in the burning summerhouse.

'I think you're right, Co-Co. All the same, I suppose it might clear up.'

Ned found the line at last in a box of wooden flowerbed labels. And carrying the dartboard, some bows and arrows and an old brass whistle on a chain they passed along the little pear-tree avenue on their way back to the house.

They found Gwen in the kitchen, organizing sandwiches for tea. Ned and Co-Co put their things down on the dresser. At the same moment Marina burst into the kitchen, followed by Violet. Both were clasping armfuls of striped scarves and coloured handkerchiefs.

'Whatever is all that for?' demanded Co-Co.

'You have to scatter these things on the ground for French and English. Besides, there's the three-legged race. The ankles will have to be tied up with something.'

Gwen thanked them both profusely and expressed fear that such smart things might be damaged by the childlren.

'No, no, there's nothing to hurt here. But I'm rather afraid they won't be necessary ... it's going to pour.'

So it did.

By half-past three the orchard and half of the croquet lawn had been sliced off and thrown into outer space along with the rest of the world, and shortly after rain started to patter down. It wasn't bad for the first few minutes, but then the wall of mist arrived at the house and revealed itself as nothing but a shower-bath moving with stately gait across the land.

The first arrivals out of the wet, some six or seven children, were taken along to the schoolroom by Gwen to play the gramophone until tea. But meanwhile two of Gwen's own friends had arrived – Elsie and Lacy – and also she was expecting momently the earl, the ambassador and the Indian prince. She returned, therefore, downstairs to greet her own guests, and passing through the front hall – where more children were arriving with much banging of car doors from outside on the drive – she met Ned, and asked him if he would take her place in the schoolroom till the children's tea should be announced.

Ned paused in the hall, on his way up to the schoolroom, to help a small girl, not more than five years old, in short flounced skirts and with long tow-coloured hair cut in a fringe across her forehead like a doll, to remove her wet galoshes as she sat perched up on the oak chest. Beside her, her older brother obviously, a coarse-faced boy of perhaps nine, but looking clumsily overgrown, was standing nose against the barometer, absorbed in tapping it. There was no nurse with them, and Ned supposed they must have been dumped in the hall by the chauffeur. At any rate, he took charge of them, and taking the doll-like girl by the hand hurried them on up to the schoolroom.

In the long schoolroom they found the assembled children at a loss.

Four or five were grouped round the portable gramophone, which was on the floor. Jazz, of the suburban English kind, came swooping and hiccuping out of the machine in spasms, loud and savage as an attacking aeroplane:

'... *Lady in red!!*
Tra-la-la-lee, it is that Lady in Red!!
Quacketty bik quick-quack-quack backetty quick – Oh it's that Lady in Red!'

Two small boys in grey flannels stood opposite Josephine Barrow, a tall creature with blonde shoulder plaits. There was also a child in a white muslin frock, stolid and square as an old-fashioned pincushion, and with just as handsome a pink-silk face. A white-faced male sprite with dark hollows under his eyes was close by, whoever he was. They all stood there looking away from the gramophone, listless and bored.

Beside the water-tank, now draped with the flags of Italy and Japan, stood Violet. She stared silently at the party round the gramophone.

'... *it's that Lady in Red!*

… Lady in Red!

Quacketty bick quick-quack-quack backetty quick –
Wheee-ee-ee – it's that Lady in Red!'

Industrious rain was pelting down outside the windows.

Ned went over to the gramophone.

'Why don't we have a better record?'

He searched among the pile of records on the table under the window. 'Yodelling Song.' 'Whistling Rufus.' 'Umbrellas to Mend.'

'I'll find one!' cried Co-Co, behind him, who had just burst into the room; and rummaging with speed amongst the discs pulled out one with the title 'Ices' and put it on the machine.

The window in this wall looked down on to the heads of a mixed jungle of bushes and trees. Lilacs, magnolia, holly, laurel and fig, and more besides. As Ned stood there the rain increased momently, and soon it became a curtain of water hurtling down past the panes with a thunderous drubbing sound, on to the tops of these trees whose branches were at the same time wildly tossing in the storm wind.

The record 'Ices' began to play and some of the children had started to skip, three and four together, in the centre of the skipping rope in the middle of the room. The passage door opened and Marina came in.

She made her way past the skippers and, after pausing to watch them a few moments, gravitated in the direction of the gramophone where stood Ned.

She came to a halt opposite him, with the portable (now raised up on to a table) between them. In the dark rain-sodden air, loud with the confusion of water rushing and pounding down outside, and inside the tangle of tweedling ineptitudes that was 'Ices' and with the thump thump of the skipping rope and children's shouts beating through she perhaps found it hard to materialize, at any rate when Ned spoke to her she merely stared, a placid phantom, not taking him in.

Several times he spoke to her. She only looked at him, flickered her eyelids and absentmindedly moved her lips. He could not get her to enter into conversation or engage her interest.

He felt snubbed.

'Ices?' queried the portable.

He tried again.

'Do you think the ambassador and his party will really put in an appearance for tea?'

Marina stared at him blankly.

'... They haven't arrived yet, I don't think,' she murmured after a second.

Ned tried again.

'You must be careful that the prince, when he arrives, does not empty his cup of tea over your hair,' he advised her. 'It depends what part he comes from, of course, but I understand that in Siam, for instance, that is the form a compliment takes when dusky royalty wishes to signify his approval of a lady's charms.'

She did not look amused. He cast down his eyes in his humiliation. He put his hand down to the gramophone and began to fiddle with the speed regulator. It was the first time he had been alone with her since her return from London, and that she should have so far failed to respond to their remeeting left him confused and appalled.

They had fallen silent and the composition, 'Ices', rose up between them and fretted the atmosphere without hindrance. A shuffling discomposure of a piece it was, a debilitated entanglement of notes played upon pipes and clinking things mainly, carried forward endlessly in a sameness that was tangled and matted and totally without focus – no introduction, no afterglow, no beginning, no middle and, apparently, no end; and ever and again in the multiplex welter there rose up a little vocal question – *'Ices?'* – a gnat-like challenge with never a response.

Marina was speaking to him, at last, through all this:

'If you are thinking of coming to London next week, for a night or two before the term begins, we could offer you the spare room at the flat. It's not very comfortable, I'm afraid, but still ... But I'm sorry that Aron won't be there.' (Ned had raised his eyes to hers at the words 'spare room' and she had immediately turned hers away toward the window so that the news that she was sorry Aron would not be there was delivered to the rainwater swirling down the window-pane.) 'Aron has to return to Oaklands early, of course, it seems, on the 21st, the Tuesday itself, for a confabulation with the builder before the boys get back ... but, all the same, if the spare room were of any use to you ... if you had any chores I mean to do in London ... you don't have to go down to the school till the end of the week, I take it ...'

She didn't look at him and arranged her null expression carefully.

'Oh ... but how very kind of you. I – well I *have* many things I should do just at that time. Notably see my brother and sister-in-law whom I haven't yet seen since my return from America, but on the other hand ... And Violet? Won't I be taking up her place?'

'Violet sleeps in the dressing-room. Often. Any time. But I think as a matter of fact she may be going to stay a night or two with her grandmother then.'

'I see. I see ...' Ned felt a thrill of alarm and couldn't go on.

'Ices?'

Still the tweedling little tune skeined on and on, bob-tailed and lop-eared and fleeting, fanning out and shrinking in, yet always with a tousled sameness, wheels within impotent wheels. But Ned heard nothing more. It had vanished as far as he was concerned. Like a schooner in an arctic sea, which finds itself rushing forward through fog on to a floating mountain of ice, he held his breath with a sense of touching wood and crossing fingers against an imminent catastrophe that had steered thus without warning, glitteringly close.

'Let me know later, then, if your plans are not yet fixed,' Marina was saying. 'I only wanted to tell you that we *have* a spare room there, and you are welcome to it. It doesn't have to be yes or no now.'

'But of course I shall come!' he burst out then.

They looked quickly at each other in a lightning conscious glance. As quickly she switched away her gaze, but a curious silence followed.

Then Marina walked off, and out of the schoolroom door.

Ned drew a long breath.

Now that she had gone he was able to perceive the whole panorama of her behaviour in focus. He saw that she had come upstairs to the schoolroom only to make this one remark about the spare room at her London flat and to invite him to stay. She had said nothing to any of his vague conversational openings, had not even heard them, but not, as he had despairingly supposed, from boredom, but merely she was doing nothing, like a bad actress, waiting only for her cue, thinking only of how she would say her lines. And when she had said them – immediately she had gone away. He was relieved beyond measure at how it had turned out.

And now the record on the portable was positively – or almost positively – drawing to its close; which could be sensed by the more than average falling away and petering out amongst washy dregs ... 'Ices?' for the last time – faint and far away. Then the savage growl and bark of the needle as it tottered around the central spoke – everything over at last.

The schoolroom door opened. As Ned put out his arm and took the record off, Gwen ushered in more chattering children, with tall, spiky nurses sticking protectively up amongst the bunch.

The children's tea was ready in the dining-room, it seemed, and Gwen had come up to shepherd the whole lot of them down. 'The grown-ups are having tea in the octagonal room,' Gwen turned round and said, and Ned followed along after.

18

THE Oaklands term began on Friday, 24th September. But Aron, as new headmaster, was to go down early, on the 21st. Ned was to follow on later, in time only to greet the returning boys.

Tuesday the 21st arrived. The holidays were over and the four visitors leaving the house. Aron to go straight down to Oaklands. Marina and Violet to the London flat. Ned to London also, pressed by Marina to occupy the one spare room.

But first they were all going to the roller-skating competition at the Malton Pier Kursaal. After tea Marina, Violet and Ned were to catch the London train. Aron, too, would catch the train to Somerset from Malton, only half an hour later.

It was a grey day, warm and rather windy. Just after a quarter-past two the whole lot of them, Reamur as well, having packed their suitcases and themselves into Gwen's car (she at the wheel), started off for Malton.

'I think we shall just about make it,' murmured Gwen.

Marina said, 'Violet! Your jam!' Violet gave a scream and went pale. Gwen had made her some confiture marrons out of the chestnut tree in the yard to take back to school.

'Co-Co, run back and fetch it. It's on the hall table in a tin box,' said Gwen.

Co-Co shot out of the car, flew off and was back in a moment with the box, which he threw over the car seat on to Violet's lap.

'Careful, Co-Co!'

Gwen started up the hill again. 'I don't expect they will start the competition very punctually at three.'

'At three o'clock! Of course they will start the competition at three! It says so on all the notices,' said Co-Co, leaning forward from Ned's knees, where he sat behind, and breathing vehemently on to Gwen's neck as she accelerated up the drive. The lodge gates came into sight.

'Well, Co-Co, I think there will be so many people like us driving over after luncheon from their various homes round the countryside that they will probably hold things back till most of the seats are filled,' Gwen told him. 'It's a sort of regatta, or something of the kind, at Malton today, as far as I can make out. Elsie Anstruther was speaking of races in the old harbour. I think there are going to be some film stars there giving away prizes.'

'If it says it's going to *start* at three, of course it *will* start at three!' muttered Co-Co, with bitterness and despair in his voice. 'I shall lose my turn, that's all.'

They stopped in front of the iron gates. Violet tumbled off Marina's lap, where she sat in front beside Gwen, and ran to open them.

The car went slowly through and, turning to the left, waited on the roadway for Violet. Trees were tossing in the wind from the direction of Flitchcombe cliffs again, all the nettles in the ditch and the cow-parsley swinging.

'You needn't fuss, Co-Co. We shall arrive long before three o'clock,' said his father. He was leaning back in the corner, immediately behind Marina, the rugs tucked up round his long legs meticulously. His languid hands laid out on the rug like a dying man's, he rested his head back on the shelf, where there were umbrellas and briefcases.

Violet climbed back into the car and on to Marina's knee. Marina slammed the door and off they shot again.

They had not got far before Marina gave a scream. 'My clock! My travelling clock! I've left it!'

Gwen slowed down.

'Gwen will send it on to you,' said Aron firmly, and Gwen accelerated again.

Aron, in his pork-pie hat and voluminous cinnamon over-coat, was crushed on the back seat between Reamur and Ned, with Co-Co kicking at his shins as the car swayed. He noticed Co-Co's face, white and strained and with fevered eyes, and felt sorry for him. In order to cheer him up he talked of how the weather was obviously clearing, of how there would be sunshine for the regatta, and of how there would certainly be ices on the pier and special cakes, on ac-count of the competition, in the tea-room.

'Are you really sure, Co-Co,' asked Gwen, 'that you would not prefer to go to the Geisha Café for tea? You could have a poached egg there. It's on the way to the station from the pier, so we should have time.'

But Co-Co was determined to stick by the skating-rink at all costs. He seemed to think that there would be some fun going on the rink after the competition had finished. He had made friends with some of the other children who fre-quented the rink and wished to sport about with them.

'Who do you think will win the first prize, Co-Co?' Marina, turning her head round, asked him.

'Horrie.'

'Which is Horrie?'

'*You saw Horrie*, last week, when we all went in.'

'You mean the young man from the hairdresser's? The tall one with freckles?'

Co-Co did not answer. With tense face he stared out of the car window. They were passing the washerwoman's cottage with its waving flounce of thatch and its tiny windows like hedgehog eyes. The door was open and Mrs Dodden was standing, as it happened, on the threshold, her overall ruffling in the wind; and the small blue and pink flowers in the border under the windows bending, gibbering, sideways. But Co-Co saw none of this. His large, dark eyes were blind and smouldering.

Violet said, 'Yes, you remember, Mother! The young man who is working as an apprentice at that hairdresser's, Lorelei, on the Parade. That's the one they call Horrie. He's a marvellous skater and absolutely sure to get the first prize, anyway.'

'Oh, that young man!' exclaimed Gwen. 'I've had my hair shampooed by him. He's very good.'

Marina threw out her hands: 'Oh, *heavens*!'

'What?' asked Gwen.

'I do hope I haven't left the water running in Violet's bedroom basin. I was washing off inkstains from my hands after writing out the labels, and Aron called me away ... Violet, *did* I?'

'I don't know, Mummy. I didn't go back in again there after I'd tied the labels on in the hall.'

'Oh Gwen!'

Gwen had first to brake and looked anxious.

'Nonsense,' said Reamur firmly. 'Drive on. Of course she hasn't. Anyway, her tank will merely empty. What does it matter? The boiler isn't on. Or is it?'

'No, it isn't,' said Gwen, and put her foot on the accelerator again. 'I don't *think*,' she added doubtfully and slowed down again.

'And what about your skating partner, Co-Co? She's very good, isn't she? Perhaps *she'll* get a prize,' said Aron, to distract attention. He didn't want to turn back.

Co-Co hung on the window-sash dumbly. He hadn't heard.

Gwen, however, accelerated again, to everyone's relief.

They passed the tall village school with its yellow stone motto. Then Mrs Hornet's chicken farm, and Ned caught sight of her taking a whack with a bucket at a cluster of ducklings, and sending them flying as the car sped by. As they passed the builder's yard, the stout builder in his norfolk jacket and gaiters was talking to Major Crumple. The kitten was on his head again, lying out flat.

They passed under the boughs of the leaning arbutus tree, followed the wall round the major's house and, as the creosoted box that was the village hall appeared at the top of the bank on their right, Reamur asked Ned if it was really so necessary for him to go to London? And tried, as he was thrown sideways against his window – for this was a hairpin bend in the road – to persuade Ned to change his mind and come back to Flitchcombe again with him and Gwen, after the skating, that night.

'You don't have to visit this Gabbitas and Thring – is that the name of the place? – in person, I'm quite positive,' he expostulated mildly. 'There won't be a row of maths and history masters sitting ready at the counter to be interviewed by you. You will have to make an appointment surely? And, in any case, you will have oceans of time to collect your staff. Could you not go up for the day from Oaklands?'

Ned was looking his last at the Flitchcombe village green on their left. The village shop slid past Reamur's profile.

With both windows and door shut and nobody about, it looked like early closing day. But Ned knew it was Friday afternoon, and this was simply the Flitchcombe look. On the far side of the green, on the road leading up to the Tortoise Head cliff, the black hearth-rug dog lay sleeping, as usual, stretched across the white chalk road. Ned twisted his shoulders and looked from the back window at the sleeping village, its church and rectory, and the group of flint cottages scattered untidily about, facing at odd angles amongst the tall blackberry hedges that bordered the village road. Then the car had swung almost full circle and they were running down-hill into the valley of Softon.

'It isn't only because of Gabbitas and Thring that I'm going up,' murmured Ned. He prevented himself from looking across at Marina's back as he spoke. She knew why he was going. He felt that everybody in the car was reading their thoughts and could see their guilty plans inside their heads.

'You see,' he went on, 'I haven't seen my brother and sister-in-law since I've been back from America, and they want to hear about everything, you know. It's an awful nuisance, but I don't see quite how I can get out of it ...'

This was a complete lie. So that when Marina gave a shriek as if she was publicly protesting at it, Ned started violently, his nerves were so strung up.

'I've left Violet's party frock behind! In the bathroom!' she wailed. She had put out a hand unconsciously on to Gwen's wrist on the steering-wheel, and Gwen slowed down thinking she meant to stop her.

'Shall we go back?' she asked.

'How *awful*!' said Marina.

Gwen brought the car to a standstill on the hill, doubtfully. 'I'm afraid it's going to make us late for the competition,' she said.

'No, no, Gwen – I didn't mean to stop and go back for it. Of course not!' said Marina. 'I only couldn't help exclaiming. It's too idiotic! Really, I can't *think* what's the matter with me!'

They began to pass along the chalk road running along the bottom of Softon Valley, passing, on the left, willows and farm buildings, and on the right, the steep, rough, grassy hill, along the crest of turf and gorse roots where Ned had walked upon a former occasion.

Once through the valley they shot out towards the coast-line, crossing the bleak and flat plain there upon a good main road, passing and meeting many familiar tradesmen's vans upon it.

Reamur, Aron and Ned said little in the back of the car on this last half of the journey. Co-Co had barely spoken the entire way, silent and straining towards the window, seated on his father's knee. Gwen and Marina, however, chattered unceasingly, about plans and clothes. Gwen also gave them all a description of a local institution which she referred to as the 'Art Bus', explaining how a white chara-banc took members of the County Cultural Society on expeditions every month to see, or listen to, things of artistic note. 'But why,' she had demanded, speaking of the feeding times between artistic experiences (affairs of sandwiches and Thermos flasks inside the white Art Bus), 'why do the powers that be – in other words Major Goddard – invariably arrange for this ceremony to take place drawn up beside the road with never a pub in sight?'

So that the whole car drive had passed, at least officially, upon a chain of trivialities.

Soon they came to ugly suburbs. They passed the great granite mountain of a grammar school, passed the railway station and, leaving the town of Malton on their left, made for the municipal car-park – a bare and straggling arena of gravel and cement, ringed by petrol pumps, where a number of excursion buses stood.

Once out of the car, they crossed the bit of common land, its moulting grass untidy with a dandruff of sand, and stepped up on to the esplanade, which they reached at that spot where the main bus timetables and the cinema notices stood.

In the blinding dazzlement of the glare here beside the breaking of the Atlantic, there was a dis-orientating change of scale. Here the ironwork benches, shelters and petrol pumps, and the buses, the villas, too, were dwarfed, holding no more significance than might a few scattered pins untidying the halls of some *grand couturier*.

The Flitchcombe party, silenced by their sudden immersion in vacancies and emptinesses echoing with the complaints of waters and of birds, turned to their left, facing Malton, and walked along the esplanade towards the pier.

19

THE party reached the pier four minutes late for the competition.

Co-Co's silence still held as they hurried through the turnpikes into the shadowy, pillared vestibule. Here, at this end of the pier, shadowed over by cloakroom buildings, power stations, and other service huts and covered over with an iron roof, the only brilliant lights were those between the floorboards, which revealed tossing seas below.

There was a roaring, confusion of noise – a great wall of sounds it was that hit them. A shuffling, veritable army – thumping of footsteps over boards, and a diffused murmuration of waves, and conversation and laughter chopped up by mechanical musics and fun-fair machinery.

As they stepped out of the vestibule the sea-glare hit them, and everyone clutched their headgear under the onslaught of wind. As they advanced along the pier they heard the waves retching and regurgitating violently as they battled with the stairways and pillars beneath; particularly at the landing-stages the waters rioted together, slapping the iron struts and belching and gobbling and roistering with the spectral, Rabelaisian jollity of their kind.

Co-Co led the way. They followed along outside the windows of the central halls. These, of course, ran down the middle, pullulating interiorly with revellers thick as ants inside an ants' nest, and led them down to the Kursaal door. The party endeavoured to peer through these windows as they rushed along, and made out two long halls filled with the fun-fair machinery, and then an antechamber, darkened, empty, and stacked with concert chairs. Into the door of this dark antechamber Co-Co plunged. They all rushed down the aisle between the chairs, and through the door at the far end they found the skating-rink.

The seats round the rink were already crowded, and the competition already begun, yet the party managed to find their places with the aid of a female gnome attached by her neck to a big tray of lemonades, whilst Gwen went off with Co-Co to the retiring room behind the stage, at the far end of the hall.

A gold loudspeaker beside the concert piano immediately below the stage was draped with flags and had potted fuchsias standing on it. On the stage itself sat the judges, eight in all (members of Malton borough council), framed in beaten-brass vases of maidenhair and sweet pea. Pedestalled

vases stood along the walls as well, filled with potted fuchsias and more sweet peas; in between their fronds passed
and repassed the strollers outside against a background of
heaving seas. The main thing was the thunderous racket of
the roller skaters, of the trampling crowds outside, of the
roar of voices and screams of children from the amusement
halls, of the washing-up machinery in the cafeteria next
door, of mechanical pianos and radio songs, and through
all the deep crashing uneasiness of the waves.

The skating itself was no doubt a fine sight, but Ned
could pay no attention to it. It was a short affair, in any case,
and everything over in half an hour. He did notice Co-Co
sailing by with his partner Josephine Barrow, a fat girl-
friend in a knitted cap, but when, at the end, they had been
together tied third, and presented with chocolates on the
stage, and draped and buckled into red satin sashes with
white heather, and generally acclaimed, he had formed no
opinion as to whether the merits of their competitors had
been accurately gauged.

He had been thinking all the while of the approaching
night. Of how he and Marina would spend that night. His
stock of anxieties had passed in their familiar review; com-
parisons with past occasions floated through his mind,
mechanical plans, and the remembering of this precept or
that; but mostly like somebody just about to sneeze, he did
not clearly think at all, but was swept forward dimly, made
anxious by the realization that some initial step would
certainly have to be taken, at some moment by him, before
the rest could follow.

He heard everybody clapping. Then the winners' names
announced. First prize to the young hairdresser already
referred to in the car, Horrie, aged seventeen. Second prize
to Jacqueline, tall and dark, aged eighteen. Third prize,
Maggie of the knitted cap and Co-Co tied. There they all

stood hovering awkwardly amongst the fuchsia vases on the stage. Everyone in the Flitchcombe party was clapping and laughing, Violet loudest of all, only Aron looked pale and glum. Or was it Ned's imagination?

Now the audience was on its feet looking for coats and bags and dispersing through the various doors.

The Flitchcombe party rescued Co-Co from the stage and took him through into the tea-room beyond, and still in his red be-heathered sash. His cheeks were burning, but he still spoke not a word.

In spite of the crowd they found seats at a table by themselves. They sat there, close up against the great horseshoe of glass panes that formed the far end of the tea-room, looking at the sea and at the boats on the horizon. When the waitress came she complimented Co-Co, looking at his red sash, and praised his skill upon the skating-rink, which she had watched from the tea-room door.

The tea and cakes seemed long indeed in coming, and when they finally arrived there was a general discomfort owing to the need to catch the train. Everyone looked at their wristwatches perpetually, whilst Violet told them all about life at her grandmother's house, where Marina had, it seemed, arranged that she should go and stay a couple of nights somewhat unexpectedly.

'And then you see there are all these hours of reading aloud of useful books,' said Violet. 'I mean, useful books about sheep's wool, and how the sheep are sheared, and how it is carted away, and how it is spun, and afterwards carded, and all the rest of it. Of course they are in the form of story books, and, you see, children are supposed to derive pleasure from them and yet education at the same time. And then there are the ones about cotton spinning, and then tin mining, and every *kind* of useful thing. And when that stops, then there's all the enforced tree climbing.'

'Enforced tree climbing! Surely your grandmother doesn't force you up into the trees?'

'That's *exactly* what she *does* do. And it's a most fearful, terrible strain. One simply longs, and longs, and pines, to be safely on the ground again.'

'Oh, nonsense, Violet! I never heard of such a thing. Of course your grandmother doesn't force you to do any such thing.' Marina's voice sounded very near to laughter or to tears and her cheeks were burning too. Aron, beside her, was not eating, and looked, Ned thought, tired and ill. Ned gazed at him reflectively across the table. He was certainly very yellow. He kept looking down at his pipe.

'But what I don't want, Mother, please, is to be left alone with Denis at the matinée.'

'Why ever not?'

'Oh, I don't know. He's so *slimy*. I can't bear him.'

'Oh well, Margaret will be there – you can devote your attention to her . . .'

And so the tea went on.

Ned, who had been watching Aron's face during the meal, now became convinced of his friend's melancholy. All through tea he had sat motionless, his egg and tomato sandwich untasted (a favourite fare), his elbows on either side of his empty plate, his hands idly resting upon his patent pipe cleaner. He neither talked nor cleaned his pipe. In fact this usually so buoyant man, always to be seen cutting full speed ahead no matter what the wind or weather, now seemed becalmed; deserted by the divine afflatus; discomforted.

Ned argued that Aron merely had that particular yellow pallor that accompanied his liver attacks. But he knew that this was no bilious attack. His friend was simply aware of things.

This was Ned's first glimpse of the impact upon Aron of

– well, of what exactly? What precisely was there for Aron to become aware of all of a sudden? Ned paused. Surely – why surely nothing less, he felt bound to admit it (and was appalled at the notion) – nothing less than the projected theft of his wife.

At that Ned felt not guilt, but a wave of sympathy for Aron. It was intolerable that he should be plotting to leave his friend here alone, helpless, whilst he stole off with his happiness and feasted upon it in private, out of range.

In that flash of time Ned realized certainly and with finality that what he was doing was unthinkable. What – serve out this delightful fellow in that way? It couldn't be done!

Yet – if this misery were to be stopped it must be stopped *now*. During the next minutes.

Already Gwen's gloved hands were grasping the table-edge as she leant forward to move back her chair and leave the tea-room. All was set in train for the departure to London. Marina, having seized the bill from Gwen, rose, declaring this was to be her treat. She started to fumble in her bag for her money. In less than half an hour, Ned knew, she and he would both find themselves in the moving railway carriage.

'I say, but it's high time to be off ...' Reamur was looking at his watch.

'Heavens, yes,' said Gwen. 'We have the bags to collect, and the car to get.' She rose to her feet, and there followed a general scraping-back of chairs.

Ned put his hand on Gwen's wrist.

'Gwen! ... I wonder if it is too late to change my mind? Take advantage of your kind offer ... and come back again to Flitchcombe with you tonight, after all? I don't feel I can face my brother and sister-in-law!'

'Why! Of *course!* We shall be only too glad! It does seem

absurd for you to go all that way to bore yourself with relatives.'

'Ah, that's more like it! I'm very glad,' said Reamur.

Ned did not dare look at Marina.

He and she had been arguing about the paying of this bill a few minutes before, for each one was determined on this occasion to play host, and the bill was on Marina's plate. Unable to look at her face, he stared down at the table and saw her hand stretch down and take possession of it now, still standing there. Next, grasping her bag, she walked away to the counter where the cash-desk stood. Protesting still, mechanically, about the bill, he unhappily followed her, quite confused as to what he should do next.

The mahogany counter ran along the panes of glass, and the cash-desk stood at the end. On the counter was a copper coffee-urn, and one for tea beside it. The rest of the counter space held tall glass bells under which stood rock cakes, sandwiches and rolls. The fat old lady behind there stood with one glass bell raised in her creased, white hand, watching a customer choose. Through the glass bell the sea glinted, seeming to bear all the stale rock cakes and thick sandwiches upon its heaving bosom.

Marina was standing against the coffee-urn. She wore her black London coat and skirt. A shaft of sun, entering the big windows, slanted behind her, lighting her shoulders and her carroty hair, but leaving her face in the shade and colourless.

As Ned approached she put the bill with some silver on it upon the shining wood of the desk. The girl inside had the money drawer open and searched about for change.

As Ned came beside Marina she raised her bent head from her purse and looked into his eyes with her own grey and gleaming ones, and, for the first time in their acquaintance, her feelings were baldly displayed.

Ned could hardly believe what he saw.

He had expected reproach, indignation, frank outrage, perhaps a sense of loss. But there was nothing so passive in Marina's eyes as a mere 'awareness', or any such acceptance of her situation. They were simply alight with uncontainable pain. She seemed to be shrieking to be released. He was looking at an animal caught in a trap crying out to be saved.

It was a shock.

He was unprepared for the revelation and had no idea that her feeling would be of that kind. He was appalled at having to witness her piteous signalling for mercy. Above everything he was surprised.

He turned his head from her and, half muttering he didn't know what, moved swiftly off to the others.

'We're so late!' said Gwen as he rejoined them. 'We must hope to find a taxi miraculously waiting our arrival out on the promenade, or they are going to miss their trains.' And raising her voice, 'Marina! darling ... this way! Come on!' And, making towards Marina, she grasped her and flurried her away towards the door of the rink, the others following in her wake.

They passed through the rink, which was empty now, except for two attendants carting away the chairs. Then through a further door again into the darkened antechamber beyond, with all the concert chairs. From there out again to the daylight of the pier to make their way through the milling crowds as best they could, towards the turnstile gates.

Violet and Co-Co ran to the opposite side of the pier and scrambled along by the railings there, peering over the edge at the fisherman's lines dangling into the sea, squealing, then racing on ahead. Aron went to keep an eye on them, his loose overcoat bellying in the wind, his green hat crushed under his arm.

Marina and Gwen walked ahead of Ned and Reamur with the crowds milling in between, so that it was hard to keep them in view; Gwen in her purple tweed, Marina in her black coat and skirt with a green cap on the back of her head round which her red hair sprayed and whipped about in the breeze. Ned noticed that she clutched her large green vanity-bag awkwardly to her side, in a cramped, awkward gesture that he had never seen before.

As they dodged the shuffling holiday-makers down the pier, Ned did not take his eyes off that figure in the black costume.

As she walked he absorbed her every line and motion greedily for his thought was that he was watching her walk out of his life. He said to himself: When she reaches the turnstiles – that will be the end.

Meanwhile he had vouchsafed to him only infrequent glimpses of her back and green cap between the holiday-making crowds.

The two women approached the turnstiles at last.

Ned's mind was strangely blank.

He knew only that he had committed an unnatural act of violence, had sliced himself in two and thrown half away. And that now – like those guillotined heads, doubtless, that are reputed by onlookers to have grimaced and changed their expression for at least several minutes after having rolled into the guillotine basket – he felt himself just enough alive to grasp some sort of catastrophic loss; but numb yet as to what that loss actually meant to him in the fullness of the event.

Yet though too dazed to work it out – whatever the vital thing that had been lopped off, he would know all about it pretty soon, when the wounds began to throb.

Gwen and Marina had disappeared into the shadows beneath the iron roof where stood the turnstiles and the luggage cloakroom. On approaching closer Ned could make out Marina bending her head low over her bag, her red hair falling down over her eyes, searching for her luggage ticket.

Now Reamur walked ahead under the iron roof, and stood in the dark vestibule also. At the same moment Aron and the two children cut in front of Ned's feet in a hurry, and went to join the party at the luggage-office door.

Ned halted. He stood outside, looking at the people all round, at the little decorated pier kiosks, at the seagulls, at the post-card stalls, at the grey sea and sky. He disliked this feeling nothing in particular whilst yet his brain sema- phored in the background that he was in fact enmeshed in a movement that was going to drag him off in directions he couldn't guess at yet. He reflected, with some bitterness, how it is always so: when the main movements of life are ushered in, the brain is invariably too far away to be able to reach out and touch them and steer the course.

Meanwhile the others were busy, not noticing him. So he was able to watch Marina as she searched everywhere for her suitcase ticket – through her pockets, her gloves, and again in her green bag. At last she found it. Ned could see only her ear and temple from behind her where he stood, but her hand, holding out the pink ticket to the luggage- man, was shaking in such a violent and obvious tremor that the pink ticket shivered ludicrously.

'Why, what's the matter?' asked Aron. 'You're shaking with cold! Haven't you brought an overcoat?'

Marina did not reply. She stood mutely waiting to receive her suitcase.

The time had evidently come to say good-bye. But was Ned really to take Marina by the hand, look into her face, and produce the conventional phrases of leavetaking? ... Now? After what had happened?

Impossible.

If he went to her now to take his leave, it would be a complete stranger to both of them who would be shaking her hand, staring at her face, pronouncing senseless words; and it would be horrible.

In this way it dawned on him that what he had lopped off – cut away from him – was the person that Marina had known all through the last weeks at Flitchcombe so well: his own natural, warm-blooded, instinctive self. *That* was what had been cut away. And that was the image that Marina carried round with her. And that had been the being whose radiance he had felt by reflection, whose warmth had made him whole.

But that being was inseparable from *her*. So that in fact they stood there together, Marina and that image, both by the luggage-room door, both bidding him good-bye.

Meanwhile his diminished self that was left over, his new self – the traitor, the Judas, the cold-blooded beast that she assuredly now saw him as – hung back ashamed. It could not enter the shadowed vestibule with all the others, must stand instead outside in the glare, an unpopular stranger (but one with whom he must go forward now alone).

And in becoming conscious of this black magic to himself (really the story of 'Beauty and the Beast', only put into reverse) he shivered bodily and put his fingers up to draw his overcoat collar close. For it was as if a hand had stretched out and uncovered him, leaving him unprotected, standing in the cut of the cheerless autumn wind.

He sidled up to Reamur.

'Could we not say good-bye to the others here, instead of going to the railway station?' he murmured. 'We could stay here ...' He tailed off uncertainly as Reamur turned and looked at him in some surprise.

He wanted, now, to throw some of his intolerable burden into Reamur's arms; though he did not see quite how it could be done. There was so much to express – and yet all so inexpressible.

They stood there facing each other, no words between them.

Reamur then seemed to find some message in his face that alarmed him. 'I'll get rid of the others first, then ...' He turned back towards the group round the luggage hatch.

Ned then went inside, stood by the pier railings with his back to all his friends.

Far below him, on the pebble-covered beach, a black fluffy dog was racing in and out of the water, barking without cease. Ned obtained a few moments' relief by watching this dog. Certainly it behaved rather surprisingly. Nose down, it sniffed again and again at the water to find out what kind of an animal it could be. But at each breaking wave it fled as if pursued by sharks, and scrabbled up the pebbly bank, at the top of which it would wheel round abruptly and, barking bravely would descend again but cautiously, dislodging showers of pebbles at every step. Ned watched him many times picking his way coyly across the intervening beach towards the ocean, where, head down, he began sniffing again at the foaming water as it swirled sideways on the stones, barking loudly, and again rushing away pursued by the ferment of boiling foam, to where, at the top of the bank, the whole thing started over again.

When Ned at last looked round at the others in the dark vestibule, the luggage was being piled upon the turnstile table, and a taximan was taking the bags away, one by one, as they were passed over.

So they had found a taxi! And would be in time for the train. And as he watched, he saw Aron turn away from the turnstile to take his wife by the arm and say loudly, 'But you're still shivering! Look here! Put on my overcoat ...'

Ned did not wait further but walked quickly away, quite out of range down the pier.

He stopped beside a kiosk of sweets and cigarettes in the end. Putting out his hands he grasped the tops of the curly white ironwork railings here, and stood, determined to wait there until Reamur should come to fetch him.

In front of him he saw only gulls swooping, many of them quite close, and waves breaking far out in the sea; in his ears the roar of the elements, and intermingled with them the clatteration of the pier.

Looking back at the beach he saw the black dog had stopped playing with the sea and was scampering along sideways over the pebbles worrying something white.

Ned started to envisage his future relations with Marina. When she saw him again she would dislike him. He couldn't get much further than that.

Feeling a touch on his shoulder he turned, to find Reamur.

'Gwen will call for us with the car in about an hour's time. She has some errands to do in the town before the shops shut. She will meet us in the tea-room here again at half-past six.'

So they both turned again and started off together down the pier.

As they went, Ned kept stopping and putting pennies into the various games-machines, somewhat in a spirit of a dentist's patient who wriggles his toes, taps his feet and clutches the arms of the chair to distract himself from the drill.

20

WHEN they reached the rounded end of the pier they mounted some steps to a small upper deck, then sat down on a bench running round a corner, where a lifeboat gave some protection from the wind, and from where they could see houses along the seafront, the town roofs behind, and beyond again, the green downs rolling away on every side.

It was nearly half-past four, a great glare, the sea imperceptibly roughening, clouds overhead – many ceilings one above the other – scudding, tortoiseshell and mother-of-pearl. Every now and then the sun broke through and laid a finger of illumination along the houses on the parade.

Ned was stunned. He still saw Marina's face and the look in her eyes.

'But *was* it my fault?'

The words had broken out aloud from him.

'What is it? What has happened?'

He saw Reamur looking at him anxiously from across the corner of their bench, the collar of his grey tweed overcoat turned up against the wind. His usually pallid, gas-lit face now stung and all alight with perturbation.

'There has been a most fearful collision downstairs in the tea-room. A quarter of an hour ago. In front of the coffee-urn.'

What was he saying? How absurd! Reamur would imagine teacups clashing and spilling their contents in mid-air.

But in Reamur's face he read that he had instead more accurately translated it.

'I must think it out, try to discover what has happened.' Ned told him. 'Whatever it was ... good God ... it started three or four or five weeks ago ...'

Ned started going back in his mind over the history of his summer holiday at Flitchcombe.

'Do you remember, Reamur, how, in one of the first weeks of the holiday, we held a conversation, early one morning, me lying in bed, you in your London overcoat waiting for the taxi to take you to your train. I remember how I bragged to you that morning that I was an integrated man! Boasted to you that life had become for me a kind of pie – that I could digest, use for nourishment and even hand round in slices to other people – do you remember, I wonder?' Ned blushed and put his fingers over his eyes. 'I must have been mad! I really thought, I remember, that I had become an integrated man! I'm afraid I spoke all too soon ...'

'You at any rate had an integrated *opinion* of yourself that morning, I remember, certainly!' said Reamur, with a smile.

Ned shut his eyes in shame.

'You wouldn't believe how happy I was at that time,' he said after a moment. 'I remember how grey the weather was. And how quiet the Flitchcombe rooms and passages – before the others had come.'

'Yes. I remember.'

Ned kept silence. He couldn't explain to Reamur how the place was ringing out in his imagination all the time with voices and figures, with stir and bustle, the whole place humming like a singing-top with his own future life. His future life there with Aron. It was a glittering construction that he had fitted inside the walls of Flitchcombe like a Chinese box – with not a quarter of an inch to spare.

He leant back, thinking regretfully, with bitterness, of the serenity of his grey afternoon walks, which he had so much enjoyed, of his peace and of his joy in his work, all of which seemed to belong to another man, in some other life.

'It was my fantasy in the matter of the school, you know,'

he confessed to Reamur, 'that Aron and I were two journey-men-craftsmen, working together on a particularly engaging architectural construction, the pleasure of it being that it was going to take so long.'

'I can well understand that.'

'But then suddenly this erotic element cut in –' Ned drew in his breath sharply and flung his hands out along the top of the seat. 'And following its own sweet laws, vomited all over our precious scheme; utterly sweeping away all the precious architecture of that new life.' He stopped, quite dismayed at the bleak truth of what he had just said.

'Is it Marina?' enquired Reamur tentatively. Ned nodded.

Reamur appeared much perturbed.

'And so you were going to – to be with Marina – in the flat – the next few days?'

'Till the very last minute, in the tea-room, she was expecting me to go.' Ned paused. 'I double-crossed her rather unexpectedly, I'm afraid ...' His voice, husky at all times, was barely audible and trailed away.

'But the problem goes on!' he suddenly cried out. 'What on earth am I to do, Reamur? When Aron and I and Marina are working together at the school, as we shall shortly be, meeting daily – hourly, I should say – why, it's going to be frightful! Everything will start again. I shall have to remake the decision I made in the tea-room – daily – hourly! There's no question of holding out against her there indefinitely. Not that she'll want me in any case, of course – now.'

The head of an elderly man appeared rising up the steps to this upper deck. When he had arrived he turned out to be a mammoth sort of walrus, with bloodshot eyes and uncomfortably mottled skin; however, after looking around, he turned and clambered down again.

'But what is Marina's side of it?' said Reamur.

Immediately Ned saw her long look of agony in front of the coffee-urn. He groaned.

'You mean, what has she been feeling all along? Why, it's impossible to explain it all to you in a minute, you'll think it too odd, but, do you know, down there in the tea-room was the first time the veils had ever properly come away ... the barriers had come down. Suddenly I saw this terrible thing...'

'What terrible thing?'

But Ned would not go on with that.

'You see we had been able to communicate so little. We were never alone. Or if we were we preserved the decencies. I had picked up a few signals from her. A few straws in the wind ... ah well, let's be frank, Reamur! The fact is we understood each other perfectly.'

He stopped again. He felt it indelicate to confess that he himself had thought of the whole matter (he only now fully realized it) in terms only of pleasurable excitements and lusts; and only five minutes ago had he perceived, beside the coffee-urn, that he was dealing, not with merely an exciting animal, as he had thought, but with a deeply wounded human being.

But Reamur was pressing him.

'What, at any rate, is really the nature of your own feelings for the girl? Are you – are you much in love with her?'

'Why, Reamur, how can I explain ... No ... No! No! No! I counted myself in love with Octavia, as you know. Well, but how does one decide that? Is it because she produced some sort of illumination which remains with me still? But Marina, you know ... has illuminated nothing. When we part I am sure she will drop out of my life as if she had never been. It must have been solely the desire for the female in her that stirred me. Yes, that. And, rightly or wrongly, I refused to credit that with the name of love.'

'And yet it seems that she has turned you completely inside out. Forgive me, but you're not the same man that you were when you came to us these holidays. It was noticeable.'

Ned groaned.

'Ah, but that's the point – the very point I want to make!' he cried. 'That is the very thing which is crushing me. True love one doesn't resent, it provides a kind of meaning, a sense of value, a justification of its own. It caters, you see, among all the other things, for the individual – for the human soul. Pure lust, on the other hand, is a mad, blind process, makes no sense to the wretched individual at all. It is designed for the benefit of the race, presumably. I don't know anything about that! All I know is that when the meal has been taken it provides no nourishment to the individual, the mind, the heart, the soul, at all. *That* is my grievance, that all this bother – that I didn't ask for – this ruination of my cherished works, this tidal-wave that all through the summer holiday has inundated my carefully constructed world – yet makes utter nonsense at the finish. I can't forgive *that*. No – I can't swallow it.'

Reamur was looking musingly along the coastline. Beyond Malton Bay two or three promontories ran out into the sea, and uprearing behind them, grey in the distance, could be descried the Tortoise Head, running out from Flitchcombe village.

'But imagine! – how can I possibly continue with my plan to share the school with Aron?' asked Ned. 'Surely I shall have to throw the whole scheme up! Look out for work somewhere else ... Oh, heavens, what a disaster.' And added, after a few moments' reflection, 'And what makes it bitter is that my throwing the affair up won't make any difference in the long run! If Marina is that kind of wife to him – not the monogamous kind – in that case, if she is not to be made unhappy by me, she will be made so by some other man. In some other place. And that man will make her unhappy too. Or she him. It's the general law. It is, let us admit it, in the nature of things – each to depend upon somebody else for happiness and to be disappointed ... However, that's all rubbish! *I'm* not going to take part in any of it. I must throw the whole school scheme up. I owe it to Aron. I shall write him a letter tonight.'

'Don't do that,' said Reamur. 'Your feelings may well blow over in a couple of months – weeks, or even days! Desire is completely treacherous. And that, mercifully perhaps, cuts every way. One moment one is whirled through five continents, and the next second one is dropped suddenly to the ground. *Finis!* You're free again.'

'Oh, I know you're right. It's impossible to calculate what may happen. No human being can guess, curse it. Nevertheless the whole thing is like an enormous bone stuck in my throat. Something has got to be done, and be done quick.'

For some time then he remained without moving, exhausted by his problem. He could think of no solution; it was all a misery.

All of a sudden Reamur gave a cry. He had been looking over the rail of this upper deck on to the crowds pullulating below. Amongst the scarves streaming out seawards and the flowered skirts fluttering and cavorting in the wind, he had caught sight of a handkerchief waving on the end of a strange lady's arm which was evidently signalling up at him. Then he had recognized her: a certain Mrs Thatcham, a country neighbour, and not a congenial one, who lived not far from the town and with whose daughter Dolly he and Gwen had been friendly before she had married and gone to live abroad. Now the mother showed signs of mounting the little stairway to their retreat.

'Sapristi! I must head this good lady off at all costs!' he

said, rising. 'I'd better speak to her a moment down there: then I can leave her and return again in peace.'

Holding his coat collar together in the wind he went off down the steps.

Ned was left alone by the boat. He laid his arm out along the rail that ran around the corner bench there, and resting his chin upon it, with shoulders hunched, stared out across the sea.

His mind kept returning to, searching for some key in that early-morning scene when he had told Reamur that he was a happy man.

Why, then, if he had been so happy, had he rushed with such frenzy after another man's wife, for all the world like a starving mouse rushing into a mousetrap after cheese? Where was the serenity in that?

Looking back from his present vantage point, he began to feel that it must have been merely the blessed lull in the complex struggle of things that had made him happy at that time. His youth had been a disturbed one, both with women and in his work; and this new, so satisfactory solution, of working with Aron had given him an illusory sense of power over life. He had added up his case – scatterbrain that he'd been – without reckoning in the demands of sex. And what a blessed lull that had made to be sure!

A horrid noise had been hovering on the margin of these thoughts for some while, and it now broke through. A small boy had been blowing blasts on a toy trumpet repeatedly, below him on the pier. Now howls and cries echoed out as well. He looked down and saw a knot of people closing in upon the infant in his red jockey cap, one of whom, an elderly man, had put out a firm wrist and spirited the trumpet away. The thing was ending in tears – but only for the little boy.

Further along, two of the pier fishermen, who had been

lounging all afternoon near by their rods, which were tied to the rails below, had abdicated from the sea he noticed, and were winding in their lines.

It was turning, he saw, into a deadish September evening. Overhead all the clouds were drawing more closely together – several continents of them – floating upon different levels in the air.

At the same time a finger of gold sunlight appeared along the promenade. The little houses on the front were illuminated silver and gold and red and grey and seemed to stand forward a little out of their proper place, so clearly were all the details of their windows and fretted balconies suddenly shown up.

The light moved slowly along, away from the town and, fanning out, softened and spread itself over the downs inland so that the green hill-folds gleamed through a kind of sunny mother-of-pearl.

A whistle sounded from those downlands now, the faint whistle of a train, echoing among the hills before it reached Ned through the uneven winds of the sea. A long white scarf of green smoke caught his eye against the green hill and under it a toy train made its way along parallel to the shore.

The London train? Ned looked at his wrist-watch. It was five minutes to five. Apparently only forty minutes had elapsed since he had left the others getting into their taxi at the end of the pier. Assuredly this *was* the London train.

He strained his eyes to watch it creep along. The windows – could he see them? Which carriage, which end of the train was Marina in? For sitting in that creeping snake she assuredly must be.

He tried with all his might to see her there – the size of a fly, of course, inside that three-inch travelling worm.

His eyes nearly dropped out of his head trying to pierce the distant haze. He urgently craved to keep physical contact with his experience. Here was a magical fact: she was corporeally *there*. He had a mystical feeling that he wanted at all costs to form part of the same landscape with her, as indeed he, after a fashion, did.

The train moved out of sight into the hills. He began to picture his own return now to Flitchcombe without her. How was he going to reorientate himself, so that he could endure the long minutes, hours and days until he was in her presence again? For he realized that she possessed him in a definite manner still. He was still existing within a framework of her movements, her gestures, her recollected glances and tones of voice; he still had with him his old 'familiar' – that biting, crooning parasite that had inhabited all these weeks his blood and his nerves – was still a mere convenient habitation for the Arabian bird. No sacrificial gesture such as the one he had just made in the tea-room had altered that.

Was it then any use sitting and thinking about the matter further? There had been so much talk as to what he was to do! Had he in fact any choice in the matter?

And he began reflecting upon all the varying forces, the primal instincts, and the contrary warring impulses of civilization, all the pressures and the propulsions which seemed to set upon a man and tear him bit by bit to rags; all the desires and the counter-desires, the pressures of heredity, and of environment; of all the blades with which a man is cut in half. And a picture formed in his imagination of a multitude of varying jets playing upon him from different angles and keeping him upheld in position by virtue of their very multiplicity, just as a celluloid ball may be upheld, dancing, in the centre of a fountain's spray.

This was very different to the pleasant image of the stationary waterfall, to which he had likened an integrated man only a few weeks back.

Glancing round he saw that Reamur had returned, unheard and unseen as usual, and was standing opposite him, leaning against the stair-rail.

Not so much like a man as a lantern slide, he remained motionless, with one long white finger raised and seeming to support on the tip of its nail the lifeboat up aloft – a trick of the light and of his queer position, no doubt.

Ned felt heavy with caged emotions. He turned his wind-reddened face away from Reamur. Since seeing the train he no longer had the heart to talk with him.

'Mrs Thatcham has been shooed away,' murmured Reamur softly at last.

He had noticed the change in his friend's face.

Saying nothing further he took his place beside Ned on the bench once more. They sat in silence listening to the sounds of the pier. At length Ned turned round to Reamur.

'You mustn't think I'm taking this as a tragedy, but I do feel you know that it is all an exasperating nuisance. After so many trying years in the past, everything had just been so beautifully settled – and now this booby-trap falls suddenly on to one's head! Damned nuisance. Even one's worst enemy could hardly have wished it on one.'

Reamur leant languidly back against the wooden slats and gazed benevolently at his friend from the depths of his dreamy, green eyes.

'So little freedom for one's movements – so little elbow-room!' cried out Ned, shoving with his hands deep into his overcoat pockets.

'What makes this world so dreary is that for the individual there is no direction, almost no direction he can move. I was just thinking, while you were away, that one is as surely the mere plaything of the combined pressures and propulsions of the universe as a ping-pong ball supported on the jets of some great fountain. How nice!'

Reamur meditated upon this for a few minutes while he looked down at his toes. Suddenly he looked up.

'I wonder if you are being quite fair, either to yourself or to the Cosmos?'

Ned raised his eyebrows glumly.

'Fair to the Cosmos? *I* didn't create the situation in which I find myself! One simply finds oneself placed, helpless, amongst all these gigantic forces. One hasn't *chosen* to be elbowed about all over the place by destiny. Surely I am allowed to feel aggrieved.'

Reamur hesitated. 'You say you feel aggrieved. But have you forgotten that you are simply a part of all the forces you mention? All these pressures – these tendencies – they have moulded you! You are conditioned by them now. And so you see ... Who are you? What are you apart from them? Do you, in fact, exist at all apart from them?'

Ned looked askance.

'Yet you sit down, postulate a position separate from the world for yourself, invent an artificial battle between you and all these tendencies – which you have apparently decided to call a "hostile destiny" – and so on and so forth, but all of which assumptions, my dear fellow, are quite unwarrantable.'

Ned closed his eyes wearily.

Reamur laughed.

Ned muttered, frowning.

'What did you say?'

'I said, what then is the correct picture of things?'

Reamur hesitated again.

'It's extremely hard to express. Well ... you might put it like this, and say, that existence is largely frost-bitten. Can only be felt in certain parts – in fact in that part we call the "individual". The rest remains numb. And the individual has got into the habit of referring to that part he cannot directly feel – as Fate, Destiny, and so forth, blaming it as if it were something outside himself.'

Ned kept his eyes shut and remained mute.

'Yet,' continued Reamur, 'there is a perpetual attempt on the part of man to chase away that numbness and become aware of those tissues which are lost in him, and which are yet somehow his. He wants to cure that frost-bite, make sense of, and to make living, all the parts.'

'But how can he do that? How? How?'

'Step by step, inch by inch, by ever progressing observation and calculation, he endeavours to eat away this numbness. As I say – gradually to extend himself and rightly come alive. Sitting down and blaming odd fragments of the continuum does not help him in this task. Aggrievement rather wastes his time than otherwise.'

'I can't quite understand what it is you're trying to say to me, Reamur. What really is your point?'

'I am trying to cheer you by pointing out that instead of being so up *against* the forces of the universe you are much more *of* them, and *with* them, than you think.'

'Oh dear, this is very complicated. Are you trying to persuade me that I am so much one with my destiny that I positively wanted all these painful things to happen? Are you telling me that I am to rejoice in my fate?'

Reamur sat looking in silence at his friend. Then he raised his long conjuror's finger and pointed past Ned's head in the direction of the crowds treading the pier-boards below.

'Look at the holiday-makers down there.'

Ned turned his head and leaning sideways did so.

'We human fish,' Reamur continued, 'we creatures that at one time inhabited the waters below and floundered in liquid chaoses, now – as you can see – come waddling and thundering triumphantly at long last over the cut-and-dried boards of Malton urban council's sociable construction.'

'You mean the pier?'

'The pier,' assented Reamur. 'A great change that! We hardly recognize ourselves!'

'We *don't* recognize ourselves.'

'No. Yet we learn that all life came originally from the sea. In as many more years from now man may have changed his nature as much again, perhaps. I hope he may. Surely he needs to change: But still, at the present moment' – Reamur pointed his finger to the crowds again – 'there is Man. And don't you see, Ned, that though our physical eyes announce, with their old-world naïveté, that on this pier there are a number of separate beings, it would be more essentially true to say that down there, galumphing about over the pier, is simply a great mass of fusible material. A material comprising many forces, many pressures, many tendencies – a most ambiguous tissue. And what I want to point out is: that it was in your capacity, in your role of "fusible material" that you surrendered your "individual" happiness into Aron's hands just now in the tea-room. You may laugh.' (Ned hadn't laughed.) 'But that, I do assure you, is a thing to be very much relieved about. For what happened in the tea-room, in one small corner of the pier, was a kind of pledge; it testified to the solid reality of the sociable construction as a whole, to that thing which saves us from the fishy maw of chaos. Look there along it now . . .'

Once again he pointed his finger in the direction of the tarred floorboards and the curling white-painted ironwork of the crowded pier. Then turning to see how Ned was taking it he caught sight of such a doleful look, a look so near to tears, that he broke off abruptly.

'All right, poor Ned, I'll have mercy on you. We won't pursue the argument. I'm just a windbag – please forgive me.'

Ned merely sat silent, looking despondent.

'I know you're trying to comfort me, Reamur,' he said at length, 'I know you want to point out to me the larger view and the larger satisfaction. But to tell you the truth I think it is the very largeness of the view which appals me. All these vistas ... are oppressive as a jungle! I feel the forests of the night are boundless. It's crushing. One feels helpless. Hopeless. Oh, let's throw up the sponge.'

Ned turned sideways on the bench; leaning his elbow on top of the back he put his fingers across his eyes.

'I'm afraid, Reamur, that without bell, book and candle, I can't be rescued. I need Marina, and that's the only reality to me. I am in a place, with her image, where you can't reach me with all of this. And in so far as you might succeed in making real to me the labyrinthine maze outside you only terrify me.'

A thunderous flapping had begun amongst the canvases on top of the lifeboat. The wind was rising. Through the thudding sound from the boat floated up puffs of a song that issued from a loudspeaker immediately beneath: 'Jeepers ... Creepers ... where d'ya get those peepers? ... eyes? ... Where d'ya get those eye ... s ...?'

At this moment Ned thought he heard his name called.

He looked down over the railing and saw Gwen in her purple, with round her neck a convulsively whipping scarf. Beside her stood Co-Co, his hair on end, licking something pink on a stick. Gwen waved and shouted up at him, but he could not hear what through all the racket. However he stood up, preparing to descend the little stairway, and waved his hand back at her in a gesture of affability. And though each of them, then, shouted out something to the other, whatever it was, the commotion of the winds, the crowds, and the waters, smothered it.